DANGEROUS
WITHOUT YOU

Visit us at www.boldstrokesbooks.com

DANGEROUS WITHOUT YOU

by

Lexus Grey

2021

DANGEROUS WITHOUT YOU

ISBN 13: 978-1-63555-947-7

This Trade Paperback Original Is Published By
Bold Strokes Books, Inc.
P.O. Box 249
Valley Falls, NY 12185

First Edition: September 2021

CREDITS
Editors: Jenny Harmon and Cindy Cresap
Production Design: Stacia Seaman
Cover Design by Tammy Seidick

Acknowledgments

Shoutout to my editor, Jenny, who helped me tremendously with adapting to BSB style and told me the rules of POV, which thenceforth ruined my enjoyment of any published book that does not follow the rules of POV!!!!! LOL. But seriously, thank you for all of your time and effort and expertise, Jenny. You made the process streamlined and easy for me!

To all the fan fiction writers out there
who do this for free and the readers who comment.
Thank you for the encouragement during my humble beginnings.

Chapter One

Tick. Tick. Tick.

Every minute dragged on forever, and each time the clock ticked, the sound was magnified, like you see on those shows where the entire class is waiting for the bell to ring, and the clock goes in slow motion. Like *Dazed and Confused* or something, except not as exciting when the bell did actually ring.

Remington Stone was leaned back in her desk, one foot propped up on the support bar between the two front legs. Boredom threatening to choke her, she shifted in her seat, the buckles on her jacket jingling. That jacket was her baby, and she never went anywhere without it, even in the summer. Her daddy'd given it to her before he—well, he'd given it to her.

She flicked her pencil back and forth in the air; never put it to paper. She refused to do homework in detention, just to piss off the proctor, but she always got it done before it was due. Homework was for home, she thought, and there was no way in hell she was going to let anyone see her doing it, anyway.

Finally, the last tick echoed in her ear and the bell rang, signaling freedom. She tossed the school-provided pencil back onto the proctor's desk, watching it skitter across and plink to the floor, then stood and threw her backpack over her shoulder, crumpling the empty piece of paper and tossing it into the trash on her way out.

"We recycle, Miss Stone!" came the irritated proctor's voice from inside the emptying classroom.

Remington snorted, ignoring the balding, spectacled man, adjusting her backpack as she walked.

Noise off to the right caught her attention, and she wondered for a brief second what it would be like to be a cheerleader, then laughed and fished her keys from her pocket, depressing the button to unlock the doors and deactivate the alarm. As she slid into the driver's seat of her sparkling clean black Mustang, she quickly checked her reflection in the rearview to make sure she was presentable and headed to BJ's, the burger joint she worked at after school to pay for the car. She was going to be late, and she'd damn well better not get fired.

❖

"You're such a dork."

"Shut up." Aspen laughed and shoved Denna's face away from hers, then flopped down onto the grass and started picking at the blades. "How many more minutes?"

Denna checked her phone and then slipped it back into her spankies. "Two."

"Sweet. What are we doing after?"

Denna eyed her friend, jealous of the way her long dark hair curled perfectly, without gel or spray or anything. "You mean you don't know? Somehow the Queen Bee didn't get that information from her faithful drones?"

"Just tell me," Aspen said with a groan.

"Riker and Bryce want us to meet them on the corner. They said they've got booze."

"When do they not have booze?" Raleigh asked as she walked by, on her way off the field.

"Shut up, Ral, you know you're invited too," Denna said with a grin, reaching out to grab Raleigh by her skirt and yank her backward.

Raleigh fell on her ass with a squeak and scowled. "If you just got grass stains on my skirt…"

"Don't you know, club soda gets out anything." Aspen snickered. "Anything."

"You would know," Raleigh said, standing up and brushing herself off. "How many inappropriate stains have you scrubbed out this week?"

Denna's hand flew to her mouth, but it was no use trying to cover her laughter. "Raleigh!"

Aspen sat up and sighed. "Not enough."

"Slipping, are we?" Denna asked.

"I haven't been propositioned at all today," Aspen mock-pouted. "Is it my hair?"

"Yeah, right. I'd kill for your hair." Denna rolled her eyes. "Maybe it's just that you've gone through the entire student body."

"Hardly," Raleigh said. "Just the males."

"Not all of them," Aspen said, ripping a blade of grass in two. "Riker still hasn't put out. He only lets me jerk him off or give him head."

"That's disgusting," Raleigh said, looking at Aspen. "You're disgusting."

"You love me, Ral," Aspen said, holding her hands out, and Denna grabbed one hand while Raleigh grabbed the other to help pull her up.

"I tolerate you. There's a difference."

❖

Remington was just getting ready to close up when a group of drunk idiots from her high school poured through the door. "Shit," she muttered under her breath. Now she'd have to stay late. BJ always said, "never turn down a customer unless the door is already locked." Stupid fuckin' BJ. He never worked closing shift, so of course he'd say that.

She stood, unimpressed, as they huddled around the counter, staring at the menu taped to it instead of looking up at the giant, lighted menu on the wall behind her. A few of the girls started giggling, and one with long, dark hair, Aspen Wellington, glanced up at her. Aspen had never spoken to her before, but Remington knew who she was. Rem knew who everyone was, she just didn't like any of them.

"Does BJ stand for blow job?" Aspen's words were slurred as she asked the stupid question.

Remington refused to answer or meet the girl's glassy eyes. She made it a rule not to speak to anyone she went to school with unless absolutely necessary. Answering that question was not, in any way, necessary.

"She asked you a question, bitch." That was Bryce Tanner, who wasn't normally so bold, and he pointed a fumbling finger at her.

Jaw clenched, she quickly surveyed her options. Kick the shit out of all five of them, threaten them, or say something witty.

She chose to threaten them. "You're all underage, right? Hang on a second, I've got the cops on speed dial." She reached toward the phone on the counter beside the register.

Riker seemed not quite as drunk, and held up his hands, shaking his head. "Whoa! We were just leaving."

Remington didn't move, just stood there casually holding the receiver.

Aspen's eyes narrowed, but before she had a chance to say something else stupid, Riker was ushering them all out the door, none too subtly. That suited Remington fine.

As soon as the door shut behind them, she was out from behind the counter to lock it. She shut off the outside lights, then the blaring neon Open sign, and went about closing up. It was eleven o'clock before she finished counting the till and making the deposit into the safe, clipping together the day's receipts and putting them on BJ's desk, washing the grills and utensils and sweeping the floor. At least a janitorial service took care of mopping, and cleaning the restrooms. As it was, she would barely have time for homework and a shower before bed.

"M'home!" she called, dropping the mail on the entry table and heading up the stairs to her room. Mama probably wasn't home yet either; she had to work two jobs to afford the mortgage on the house.

Bed looked so, so inviting, but she refused to even touch her sheets until the day's grease and grime had been washed away. She stripped and took a quick, hot shower, pulled on a clean tank top and pair of panties, and slid into bed. Homework would have to wait until the morning.

Aspen was pouting, sprawled on Denna's bed. Riker hadn't even let her give him a hand job before he left. She wasn't *that* drunk, not drunk enough for consent to be an issue. Was she? Hmm, maybe she was. "Why is Raleigh on the couch?" she mumbled, waving her hand slowly in front of her face.

Denna set down her hairbrush and divided her hair into three parts, beginning a tight braid. "Because you're on her side of the bed."

"She doesn't live here," Aspen said. "And hey, there's room. Lots of room. It's a big bed."

Denna looked a little too smug, finishing the braid and winding a rubber band around the end. "She pretends not to like you much."

"Why?"

"Because you fuck everything that moves? And she's afraid you'll go after me?"

Even drunk, that offended Aspen, and she frowned. "I wouldn't do that. And if I did, you wouldn't. She should trust you at least."

Denna shrugged. "I don't really care, and I'm tired. Good night." She climbed under the covers, reaching over to shut off the bedside lamp.

"You realize I can hear you," Raleigh said from the couch, which happened to be about ten feet from Denna's bed.

"Yes, dear," Denna said. "Good night."

A few minutes passed, and then Aspen spoke up again. "I don't fuck everything that moves."

"You're right, it doesn't even have to be moving," Raleigh said.

"I'm fucking tired!" Denna shouted. "Shut up and let me sleep!"

Another few minutes. "What do you mean by that?" Aspen asked, frustration seeping in alongside her confusion. Why was Raleigh talking in circles? Was it just because of the booze that she didn't understand, or was she really as dumb as she felt right now?

"For fuck's sake!" Denna screamed, rolling over and shoving Aspen hard, out of the bed. "Shut up or get the fuck out of my room!"

"Ow." Aspen somehow found her way to her hands and knees and crawled over to Raleigh. "Can I sleep on the couch with you?" she whispered. She wasn't sure why she didn't want Denna to hear the question.

"Not even if a portal to another dimension opens up and sucks every other piece of furniture out of this house."

"What if it sucks every—"

"No, Aspen," Raleigh said. "That answer was a no."

"You can have the bed."

"Do you honestly think I am going to disturb her after that? You're the idiot who got herself thrown out of bed. Now suffer, and leave me in peace."

Aspen sighed and laid her head on the couch cushion by Raleigh's waist. "It must be nice to have someone to love."

She could feel the tension as Raleigh removed herself from the couch and was pleased with herself at the small victory.

"Enjoy the couch. I hope the fruits of your manipulation serve you well."

"I got your side of the bed back for you, honey," she heard Denna say.

"I'm surrounded by subterfuge." The deadpan quality to Raleigh's voice made her snicker.

"Love you too," Denna said, and there was the sound of a blown kiss.

Chapter Two

Y ou threatened to call the cops on Bryce Tanner?"
Remington's head snapped up and she narrowed her eyes.
The skinny little girl who wrote for the school's newspaper backed
away, obviously wishing she hadn't asked the question. Remington
scarcely had time to wonder how the incident had gotten around so fast
before Bryce, who had been standing in the doorway, spoke up.

"I was being a drunken asshole. She was just defending herself."

Remington whirled on him, hands clutching the edge of her desk
until her knuckles hurt. The drunken asshole part was right, but it wasn't
self-defense, and she resented the implication. She knew everyone was
staring at her, waiting for her to say something, and she felt backed
into a corner. She grabbed her backpack and stood up, glaring at Bryce
as she strode to the door and forcefully pushed past him, making her
retreat.

Denna watched Remington leave and looked at the clock. Why
wasn't Aspen here yet?

"Why doesn't she ever talk?" the newspaper girl asked, sliding
into her seat. "*Can* she talk?"

"I heard her say something freshman year," Denna said. "I don't
remember what it was." She knew that Raleigh and Remington used
to be friends, but they weren't still in touch very much by the time she
started dating Ral. She had never asked what happened because there
were certain things Raleigh didn't like to talk about, and her childhood
was one of them.

"God, she's hot," Bryce said, jolting Denna from her thoughts. He
shook his head as he sank down into a chair.

"Dude, she almost called the cops on you," Connor, Bryce's best friend as far as Denna knew, reminded him.

"What's not hot about that?" Bryce asked. "I like assertive women."

"I don't think she's even into guys," Connor said, folding his arms over his chest.

"Like I'd have a shot even if she was. That doesn't mean I don't think she's hot."

Denna looked at him for a second, then turned to her notebook and got out her homework.

❖

The din of the cafeteria buzzed around her, but Aspen sat pouting down at her lunch. Somehow, she wasn't hungry. She was angry. Memories of Friday night had been hazy at first, but over the weekend they'd filtered back to her, and she was angry. Denna manipulating her out of bed, that was fine. Raleigh refusing to let her share the couch? Fine. Even Denna confessing to her that Raleigh pretended not to like her very much was fine. They were her friends. They could treat her like that. What was not fine? Remington Stone threatening her. Outsiders did NOT get to treat her and her friends like that. Who did the little bitch think she was? Sure, she was all hot and rebelly and always in detention, but that didn't give her the right to call the cops on Aspen fucking Wellington, head cheerleader and teacher's pet, whose family practically owned this town.

"Don't," Raleigh said as Aspen started to stand up.

"What?"

"As much as I dislike you, I feel I should warn you against what you are about to do."

"Why?"

"Because while you may think you are above reproach, and that may be true as far as the school board is concerned, that girl's father is in prison, and she is quite the daddy's girl."

"Meaning?"

"Meaning she wouldn't just make an idle threat, she'd follow through."

Aspen sighed and sank back down, shoving her tray away from

her in disgust. As angry as she was, she didn't feel like risking another round on the losing end of an intimidation showdown. "You really think she'd do something here? In the middle of a crowded cafeteria?"

Raleigh's smile was less than friendly. "Please, do find out."

Aspen kicked her under the table, and Raleigh scowled. "I will," she said determinedly, getting to her feet.

Remington sat at a table with a group of guys that never tried to talk to her, but always sat around her. She liked it that way. She speared an apple with the little plastic butter knife that came with her lasagna and brought it to her mouth, taking a crisp, juicy bite just as she caught sight of Aspen headed her way. Ugh. The cheerleading uniform made her want to, well, heh. Maybe not so much gag as put her hand up the skirt. She raised an eyebrow as Aspen stopped at her table, not having expected that, and chewed the apple more loudly and obnoxiously than was necessary.

Aspen folded her arms across her chest. "Remington, right?"

Remington did not give her a response.

"Well, Remington, normally I wouldn't be caught dead speaking to you, but what I really want to know is what the fuck do you think gives you the right to threaten me?"

Rem made sure her facial expression didn't change. She slowly extended her free hand, fingertips slipping beneath the hem of the cheerleading skirt and crawling upward until her hand was slapped away. As soon as Aspen touched her, she was on her feet, fist clenched tightly in a polyester uniform collar.

Remington stood, breathing heavily, unmoving, until Aspen spoke, sweat dripping down the side of her face. All eyes were on them. "Release me, immediately," she whispered.

Remington tightened her grip and pressed a fingernail against the corded muscles in Aspen's throat.

Aspen's eyes went a little wide and Remington could feel how fast she was breathing where her wrist touched Aspen's chest. "Please let me go."

Well, that was much better. *Please*, that Remington could work with. She removed her hand and gave Aspen a hard shove away from her, delighting in the stumble she caused and the way Aspen almost fell. Satisfied that she'd gotten her point across, Rem rolled her eyes and sat back down.

Aspen didn't walk away, though. "You're an asshole, you know that?" she said.

Remington lunged at her and Aspen jumped, muttering something Rem couldn't make out as she finally walked away.

Aspen rubbed her throat absently as she sat back down, a tiny smear of blood coming away on one fingertip. She gasped, a little alarmed that she was bleeding even though it was barely any, and pulled out her compact to survey the damage.

"It's barely noticeable," Raleigh said, finishing her own apple and laying the core back on her tray. "And I believe I warned you." Pause. "Yes, that is my way of saying I told you so."

"She's fucking unhinged," Aspen said, sounding a little too breathy instead of the angry confidence she was going for. That irritated her even more and she snapped her compact shut after fluffing powder over the faint wound. "Speaking of, where's Denna?"

"Eye doctor."

"I hope she doesn't need glasses. She'll have to wear contacts for cheering." She pictured Denna cheering with glasses on, the horror of the glasses falling off and getting smashed, and the ensuing chaos that would erupt.

"Your shallowness is astounding."

"Hey, Mama," Rem called out as she shut the door behind her.

"I have to go back to work now; can you fix yourself some dinner? Sorry about the timing, baby."

Rem nodded, giving her mother a quick hug. "I'll make macaroni and cheese. I'll save you some."

Mama kissed her forehead. "I wish I could stay home with you and just talk, or watch a movie, or play a game, but I can't afford to lose my job. Either of them. I know you know that but—well, anyway, I love you."

"It's okay, Mama, I get it. And I love you too," Remington said, and when she was alone, she slipped out of her school clothes and into a pair of more comfortable sweatpants and an old, faded T-shirt.

By the time she finished cooking she was starving again and ate half the box right out of the pot, not bothering to dirty a bowl. She packed up the rest into a Tupperware container and put it in the fridge, then stuck a piece of tape on the lid and wrote the date before moving to wash the dishes.

As she sprawled on the floor doing her homework, her thoughts drifted to Aspen. Haughty, self-righteous Aspen, and how good it'd felt to scare her a little. She imagined Aspen struggling, begging her not to hurt her, apologizing for even approaching her in the first place, and with a shiver, she got up and closed her bedroom door, then climbed into bed and shut off the light, dipping a hand beneath the waistband of her sweatpants.

❖

"Do you think I should press charges?" Aspen examined her throat in the mirror.

"No."

"Why not? She assaulted me."

Raleigh tried to be patient, but Aspen really pushed it sometimes. "I would hardly classify it as assault." And Aspen had gone over to Remington's table, so what did she expect? The lack of common sense was entirely grating.

"I haven't gotten laid in days," Aspen said. "I need something to focus on so I don't lose my mind."

Raleigh pulled a pipe from her back pocket and tossed it on the ground at Aspen's feet, followed by a small baggie. "Smoke some of that and be silent." She went back to reading until Denna's bedroom door opened and closed, and she looked up, pressing her lips together to keep from smiling. Denna had glasses.

Aspen had picked up the pipe and chosen the biggest bud, tearing off a piece that would fit in the pipe and packing it in, and was looking for a lighter when Denna showed up. "Oh God," she said, rolling her eyes. "I hope you got contacts, too."

Raleigh bristled, setting her book aside and swiftly crossing the distance to Denna, kissing her and nuzzling her neck. "I think they look sexy."

Denna was probably shocked that she had just used the word *sexy*, because the look on her face was somewhere between stunned and amused. She could always tell when Denna was trying to hide surprise because her eyes narrowed the slightest bit and crinkled around the outer corners.

Denna slid her hands around and cupped Raleigh's ass, giving it a squeeze. "Thanks, honey. It's good to know the only opinion that *matters* is positive."

Aspen found a lighter and flicked it, placing the pipe to her lips and sucking a long, slow breath, holding it in before exhaling through her nose. "I meant because they'll fall off during cheers, you assholes." She held the pipe out, but when Raleigh and then Denna refused it, she shrugged and took another hit.

"You missed it," Raleigh said to Denna after a few minutes of comfortable silence. "Your best friend got into a little scuffle with Remington Stone during lunch."

"Uh!" Denna said, her mouth falling open. "What?"

"She grabbed our dear Aspen here by the collar."

"Why do I hear sarcasm when you call me that?" Aspen asked, finishing off the bowl and climbing onto Denna's bed, sprawling out across it.

"Are you fucking kidding me? She manhandled my best friend and I missed it? Fuck!"

"Have I mentioned what good friends you are?"

Raleigh felt suddenly mischievous, biting her bottom lip as she looked up at Denna. "Is there anything I can do to assuage your frustration?"

Denna froze for a split second, and then, "Aspen, get out."

"Too tired. Raleigh just gave me weed."

"Suit yourself," Denna said with a one-shouldered shrug, locking the door. "But you do have to move over."

Aspen pouted and rolled to the other side of the bed, and as she heard kissing noises and felt the weight of her friends on the mattress behind her, she wondered for a brief, fleeting moment what it would be like to have a relationship like theirs. Of course, that just wasn't for her.

She had never really tried it, partly because she couldn't imagine just being with one person and partly because no one had ever shown any interest in more than sex. Maybe that was her fault; maybe that's what she projected. She couldn't really blame the guys she slept with, because it wasn't like she called them the next day either.

She thought about whether she would even like getting flowers or something and decided she wouldn't. Flowers died, anyway, and what did it mean to give someone flowers that were just gonna die?

No. She was better off alone.

Within a few minutes, Denna's ridiculous mushy noises got too much for her, and she rolled onto her back, smacking her friend in the arm, which she should have known would be a huge mistake, because Denna's blindly-flailing fist repaid her right under her eye, and she shrieked, deciding to leave after all.

CHAPTER THREE

Denna gave a snort of laughter as soon as she saw Aspen in the hallway before homeroom.

"You realize you could have given me a black eye or something, right?" Aspen asked, shoving Denna lightly as she fell into step beside her.

"You realize you interrupted me during sex, right?" Denna replied, matching the shove with one of her own.

Aspen just frowned, pulling a water bottle out of her backpack and offering it to Denna. "Thirsty?"

"Mm," Denna said, accepting the bottle and taking a sip. She stopped and spit the foul liquid into the nearest trash can with a disgusted shudder. "Aspen!" she hissed, thrusting the bottle back at her cackling friend. "Not before noon." How Aspen could drink at all hours of the day was beyond her. She enjoyed a good falling-down-drunk time as much as the next person, but not in the morning and not at school. Jesus.

"Payback's a bitch. Raleigh's going to smell that on you and refuse to kiss you."

Denna snorted again. "Hardly. You know I keep a toothbrush in my purse." There was this one time she had eaten tomatoes for lunch and Raleigh swore she could smell them on her breath, so after that, a toothbrush had become a permanent fixture in her purse.

Aspen grumbled as she walked into the classroom and found a seat. She had never really noticed before, but Remington was in their homeroom. Now she noticed. The bitch was on her radar, and the hair on the back of her neck stood on end as she slid into the desk and did her best not to throw a glare behind her.

When Connor came in a few minutes before the bell, he sat in the desk beside Aspen and teasingly chucked her in the arm.

Aspen hated that. Like so much. She hated being treated like one of the guys, so she made a show of turning her head away. Except that was the direction she was trying not to look in the first place, and she caught Remington looking back, chewing on the eraser of a pencil. And her nipples were clearly hard under her tacky white tank top. Aspen swallowed, her throat suddenly dry, and forced her gaze away, intending to tell Connor to fuck off, when the thud of boots on linoleum echoed through the room, and she knew Remington had just stood up. She didn't want to look again but she had to.

"Hi," Rem said slowly, taking a step toward Connor, leaving her chewed pencil on her desk. Aspen didn't know which of them she was talking to.

The closer Remington got, the harder it was for Aspen to breathe.

"What the hell?" Connor asked, standing to face Remington. "What are you doing?"

Yes, Aspen wanted to say, *what are you doing?*

Remington hooked her thumbs in her pockets and came to a stop just behind and to the right of Aspen.

Aspen snapped her head to face forward because she couldn't look at that fucking smug expression. She felt Remington lean down and put her nose to the top of Aspen's head, breathing in the scent of her shampoo, and then the faint touch was gone.

Aspen held her breath, all sorts of prickly senses standing up all over her body, and thank God she was saved from further torture when the bell rang and the teacher came scurrying into the room, apologizing for almost being late.

As Remington retreated back to her desk, Denna leaned over toward Aspen. "What the hell was that?"

Aspen only then realized how hard she was gripping her math book, and slowly flexed her fingers, her jaw working for several seconds before she could even find an answer. "I have no fucking idea," she said honestly. It was the first time she'd heard Remington's voice, at least while sober, and the low, smoky timbre gave her the chills. She had the random thought that it should be illegal to sound so...stimulating. Especially when only saying the word hi.

❖

After lunch she found a note in her locker.

Dear Aspen,
So sorry about the misunderstanding in homeroom. Is Connor still spinning in circles trying to figure me out?
All my undying love and affection,
X—Remington

Face burning, Aspen quickly crumpled the note in her fist and shoved it down into the bottom of her backpack, glancing around to make sure no one was looking at her before she shoved her head in her locker, forehead resting against the cool metal, to catch her breath. She wasn't even going to dignify the note with a response. She did wonder how Remington knew which was her locker, though. Maybe she should find out.

❖

Remington looked up as she heard footsteps approaching in homeroom the next morning. As Aspen made to set something on her desk, she shot one hand out and grabbed the slender wrist, using her other hand to pry a note from Aspen's grip. She delighted in the soft gasp and the way Aspen snatched her arm back, and the way her skirt raised to show her spankies as she spun around to walk away.

Rem didn't bother being discreet about opening the note. She smoothed it out on her desk and snickered as she read it.

Dear Remington,
How did you know which locker was mine? You better not have followed me after class.
Love and kisses,
X—Aspen

She waited until she knew Aspen was watching from her peripheral vision, then pressed the note to her lips, giving the paper a kiss, then folded it and tucked it into the top of her pants.

She turned the tiniest bit to catch Aspen watching, and the embarrassed surprise on Aspen's face as she turned away was very satisfying. She could see the rigid posture and unblinking eyes staring at the teacher, and she knew Aspen was trying to concentrate on anything *else*. That was going to be difficult for Aspen because the teacher wasn't saying anything.

❖

"What's that?" Denna asked, and when Aspen reacted like she'd caught her making out with the principal, she knew she had to have the note. "Raleigh, hold her down."

"No."

Denna growled at Raleigh and launched herself at Aspen, toppling her over in the grass, emerging victorious with the note in hand. "Dear Aspen," she read.

"Stop it!" Aspen shrieked, grabbing for the note, but Denna sat on her head.

"I followed your scent," she continued reading aloud. "You're the only girl I know that uses Bliss Lemon Sage shampoo."

She stopped reading and moved herself down to sit on Aspen's chest so she could lean over and smell her hair. "How the fuck could she tell exactly what shampoo you use? You just smell like lemons." She looked at Raleigh. "Smell her hair. Can you tell what shampoo she uses?"

"How long have you known me?" Raleigh asked.

"What?"

"Twelve years. And have I ever once given you any indication that I would be willing to smell Aspen's hair for you?"

"Let me go!" Aspen yelled, and with a mighty struggle managed to get Denna off her and reclaim the note. She crumpled it and put it in her mouth.

Denna did not like to give up easily. "Are you really going to keep that in your mouth for the whole practice?" she asked, then shook her head. "Never mind. You're used to having foreign objects in your mouth."

Raleigh, ever the picture of composure, laughed.

Aspen glared at her and Raleigh and picked up her backpack, then strode off the field toward the parking lot. Denna watched her until she disappeared between two rows of cars, and then sighed. "Raleigh, I hate losing."

Raleigh looked at her. "I am aware."

❖

Finally alone, safe, and locked in her bedroom, Aspen smoothed the note out on her desk and reread it.

Dear Aspen,

I followed your scent. You're the only girl I know that uses Bliss Lemon Sage shampoo.

Kidding. I threatened Bryce Tanner into putting the note in your locker for me.

Why is Connor so protective of you? I know he's not your boyfriend. I'm deadly curious. If you don't tell me, I promise I'll make your day tomorrow very uncomfortable.

And I always keep my promises.

Love and butterflies,

X—Remington

Palms flat on her desk, eyes glued to the scrawling penmanship, Aspen chewed her lower lip in worry. No one had ever treated her so flippantly before, and she didn't know how to respond. She was intrigued, obviously, but she was also unnerved, and then the fact that she was intrigued and unnerved made her angry. The low pulsing in her belly at Remington's promise also made her angry. And sort of jittery, like she didn't want to hold still. But mostly angry.

She pulled her water bottle from her backpack and took a long swig of the nasty tasting but potent liquor, then slumped in her chair and pouted. Should she tell? Or not.

A half hour later, she was drunk and still hadn't decided whether to tell or not. It wasn't even an exciting explanation. He was protective because they lost their virginities to each other.

She clutched her pen, poised above a blank sheet of notebook paper, and her mind wandered as she started to write.

> Dearest lovelyRemington,
>   Who do you think you are? I love bliss shampoo it's good for my curls. have you usedit?

Her pen slid across the page, and she blinked at the line now marring her beautiful letter and scribbled it out, then continued.

> whered you get your sexy leather jacket, and why dontyouw ear a bra? I could see your

When she came to, she groaned, lifting her head and wiping drool from her cheek, giving another groan when she realized she'd passed out at her desk and now had a headache. She glanced at the time and groaned *again*. She sounded like some kind of one-man ogre band. And it was quarter past one in the morning.

The real horror began when she turned on her desk lamp and looked at the letter she'd been writing. "Oh God." She covered her eyes, hoping that would make it go away. Sexy leather jacket? Why don't you wear a bra? For fuck's sake. Even if Remington's jacket was sexy and she always noticed that Remington wasn't wearing a bra, which meant she must look at Remington's chest a lot, but— No, no, no. She could not *say* those things! She tore the note into pieces and threw it in the trash, then scribbled a quick new one to take its place.

> Dear Remington,
>   I don't owe you an explanation for anything. Fuck off.
>   Love,
>   X—Aspen

Chapter Four

Aspen slapped a note down on Remington's desk with a scowl and went to her usual seat at the front of the room.

Rem watched her go and then read the note, carefully tucked it into her underwear, and moved desks, taking the empty one to Aspen's right.

"What are you doing?" Aspen asked, turning wide eyes on her. "Did you not read the note?"

Remington's response was to scoot her desk closer, so that if Aspen wanted to get out she'd have to climb over the other side. She didn't look at her or speak to her, just sat in her personal space to make her uncomfortable. She had promised, after all.

"Miss Stone?" the teacher asked as he took his place at the front of the class, eyeing her and the misplaced desk.

Remington waited for a few long seconds, biting the inside of her cheek, staring the teacher down, and then moved the desk back where it belonged.

Aspen breathed a sigh of relief, and when the bell to end homeroom rang, she was out of class in a flash, determined to put as much distance between her and Remington as possible.

"Why are you walking so fast?" Denna asked, taking longer strides to keep up.

Aspen didn't stop until she reached her locker, and was about to explain her haste to Denna when she felt a sharp smack on the ass and spun, awestruck, to see Remington continue walking down the hall, giving a fingery little wave over her shoulder without turning her head.

Even Denna was stunned into silence, jaw dropped, staring after Remington along with her.

Finally, Aspen turned back to her locker, not quite wishing that Remington hadn't done that. She reached a hand absently under her skirt to rub the sting out.

A few seconds later, Denna doubled over with laughter.

"Can you believe she...?" Aspen asked, letting the rest of the question trail off, still idly rubbing her ass. When she noticed she was still doing that, she stopped. She took out her frustration on her English Lit book, trying to shove it into her backpack. She struggled to get it in all the way and one corner was refusing to cooperate and she stared at the ceiling and growled and stomped her foot and shoved the book harder and—*for fuck's sake, pull yourself together!*

"I can't," Denna heaved, distracting her from her frustration. "I really can't. I actually saw it happen, and I just—Let me see." She pulled up Aspen's skirt and yanked aside her spankies and underwear. "Ooh, it's all red."

"Denna!" Aspen shrieked, drawing the attention of several passing students as she jumped and batted Denna's hands away, mortified. "It is?" She tried to look but couldn't see, and shut her locker, heading for the closest bathroom.

"Aahahahah, you liked it," Denna cackled, following Aspen into the bathroom.

"I did not," Aspen said, narrowing her eyes, pulling up her skirt in front of the mirror and moving her spankies and underwear out of the way so she could see the red mark. "Ow," she said quietly, running a fingertip over it.

"Maybe Raleigh would let me do that to her."

"Maybe you're suicidal." Aspen didn't know much about Raleigh's family life, she just knew bits and pieces and that it was never good. She couldn't imagine Raleigh letting Denna spank her in any kind of way.

"Good point." Pause. "Although once upon a time I would have said someone would be suicidal to do something like that to you, and yet here you are, staring at your ass in the mirror instead of running to Mommy and Daddy."

"Shut up," Aspen said, not really focused on Denna's words, giving her ass another little rub before fixing her clothes and hoisting her backpack over her shoulder. She checked her face and hair in the mirror, finding them flawless, and went out of her way to bump into Denna on the way out the door.

❖

"Angel?!"

"Hey, Daddy," Remington said with a beaming smile, laughing as her dad snagged her into a fierce hug. "I miss you."

"I miss you too, Angel. You takin' care of your mom for me?"

"Best I can. I have a job now, you know. To pay for my car. Anything left over goes to Mom to help with the mortgage." She paused, biting her lip, and then continued. "Except for the little bit I've been saving to pay for an appeal."

"Remington Stone." Daddy held her at arm's length. "You know damn well I'm guilty. Don't you dare waste your money on an appeal. You give that money to your mother or use it to buy yourself somethin' nice, you hear me?"

"But, Daddy, I—"

"No buts. I didn't raise you to shirk responsibility, and I sure as hell ain't gonna do it myself. I did the crime, I'm doin' the time, like the saying goes."

"Mama needs you," Remington said softly.

"And she'll have me when my time is up, but for now she's got you, punkin, and nobody could ask for better'n that."

"I'm not twelve," she said, rolling her eyes and shrugging his hands off her shoulders.

"I know you're not twelve!" He laughed. "Anything interesting going on at school?"

"A girl tried to talk to me."

"Oh Lord," her dad said, putting a hand to his heart. "Anything but that!"

"Daddy!" Remington scowled, exasperated. "You know I like to keep to myself. And this girl is a rich, snobby brat who thinks she owns everyone and everything."

"There are many ways to show rich, snobby brats that they don't own you, punkin."

"I know." She grinned.

"What did you do?" He looked suspicious now.

"I might've smacked her on the ass in the hallway. Maybe."

"Remington!" He shook his head and ruffled her hair. "You are your daddy's girl, aren'tcha?"

"Born and raised," Remington said with a grin, smoothing out her mussed-up hair. "I gotta go. Are you doing okay in here?"

"I don't need you wastin' your hard-earned money on an appeal, if that's what you mean."

"That's what I mean," Remington said, wrapping her arms around him and hugging him tight. "Love you, Daddy."

"Love you too, punkin. Be good now."

"I will." She kissed his cheek and stood at the door of the visitation room until she was buzzed out, then made the long walk back to her car and climbed in, resting her forehead on the steering wheel before starting up the engine. At least she'd made one confession. Too bad she hadn't had the nerve to tell him just how much Aspen was getting under her skin.

❖

"I saw Daddy today."

Mama paused with a bite of broccoli halfway to her mouth. "Oh yes? How's he doing?"

"He's good." Pause. "Why don't you go see him?"

"You know the answer to that."

"They let you have conjugal visits, you know."

"Remington," Mama said, and Rem thought she looked tired. "I just can't. I can't look at him and know he won't be coming home with me."

"So you're going to go the next five years without seeing your husband, at all? Because you can't stand the thought of him not being at *home*?"

"Remington Stone," Mama said, voice low and wavering.

The rest of dinner was silent. And tense. The only sounds came from the clink of silverware on plates. When she'd finished, Remington folded her napkin on the table and looked at her mother. "May I be excused?"

"Yes," Mama replied. "Is your homework done?"

"I was planning to do it when I finish the dishes."

Mama nodded, and Rem cleared her place, rinsing her plate, fork, and knife in the sink before loading them into the dishwasher. She put the leftovers in the fridge and washed the pots, and as she turned around to head upstairs, she found herself enveloped in her mother's arms.

"I'm sorry, baby. It just upsets me so much to think about."

"It's okay, Mama," Remington said softly, hugging her back, and when she realized her mother was crying, her heart broke. "Mama, please don't cry. I'm sorry I brought it up."

Mama sniffled and clung to her for another minute before pulling back. "Do you want to watch a movie? While you do your homework?"

Remington smiled and nodded, grateful for the suggestion, glad Mama wasn't upset with her. "Sure. You pick?"

Halfway through the movie, Rem looked up from her homework and blurted out, "Hey Mama, can I tell you something?"

"Anything, baby, you know that."

"There's a girl at school I can't get out of my head."

One eyebrow slowly lifted, and Remington shrank into the arm of the couch under the scrutiny. "Oh? Is this the part where I realize I won't be having grandchildren?"

Remington relaxed instantly, grinning. "Mama, seriously."

Her mother got serious. "Are you actually interested in this girl?"

"No, no, I can't stand her."

"Is this like the girl you couldn't stand in ninth grade?"

"No, I was lying about that because I was afraid to tell you I liked girls."

"With good reason. You had no assurances that your father and I could be so forward thinking."

"We're missing the point here, but thank you for not making me feel bad about being scared to tell you."

"All right. What's so bad about this girl?"

Remington made a face. "She's rich."

"Well, let's kill her."

"Mama! She's rich, and completely arrogant, and—"

"Is she a Wellington?"

"How did you know?!"

"Her parents practically own the town. It was just a lucky guess. But knowing that, I'd say it's safe to assume that she gets her sense of entitlement from her parents. They're the same way."

"How do you practically own a town?" Remington asked, the entire concept baffling to her.

"Oh, you know. Donate money to the mayor, donate money to the police, buy your way onto every board and committee in existence."

Rem kicked her foot against the coffee table. "Why can't people with money use it for something else?"

"Like helping your overworked mother pay the mortgage?"

Deflated, Remington accepted the fact that she was pouting. "Yes."

"Because that's not the way the world works. And honestly, honey, I wouldn't have it any other way. We are who we are in this family because we've had to work hard for what we have. If someone tried to hand me my life on a silver platter, I'd refuse. At least I'd like to think I would. No guarantees, though a trip to Disney World does sound pretty amazing."

Remington laughed. She loved it when her mother made jokes. "So you think I should cut her some slack?"

"I think you should cut your whole high school some slack, honey. When was the last time you spoke two words to any of those kids?"

Remington had to actually think about that. "Two days ago."

"And before that?"

Remington just shook her head.

"That's what I thought. You're missing out on a huge part of being young."

"It's too late." She shook her head again. "If I started talking it up now, someone would call in a priest to perform an exorcism."

"Remington!"

"Hey, how did Daddy get you to give him a chance?" She changed the subject.

Mama stood up, pointing at her. "Good night, Rem."

"The movie's not over!"

Mama kissed her on the forehead and grinned, heading toward the master bedroom. "I'd tell you most things, honey, but I'm not going to tell you that. Good night."

"Good night. Love you."

"Love you too."

She'd get her dad to tell her.

CHAPTER FIVE

Aspen hated her parents' social gatherings. She was expected to put on a fancy dress and act like a politician's wife among the most boring, inconsequential people she'd ever met. Any excuse to miss one on her part was met with a threat to take her credit cards.

"Absolutely not," Raleigh said, flipping the page in her physics book.

"Please?" Aspen whined. "Denna can't come."

"No," Raleigh said. "You'll drink yourself into a stupor and abandon me to the socialites while you jerk some politician's son off in the bathroom."

"I won't do that, I promise," Aspen said beseechingly. "I'll smoke you out first."

"I have my own psychotropics, thank you."

"Come on, isn't there anything I can do to make it worth your while?"

Raleigh regarded her intently, as if deciding whether or not to entrust a sacred task to her. "There is one thing."

"Anything," Aspen said, trying not to sound too eager but probably failing.

"The next time you're giving head to that Neanderthal Stefan Drumm, bite him."

Aspen scoffed, ending up laughing for lack of a more appropriate reaction. "What?"

Raleigh's eyes narrowed. "Have fun at the party, Aspen."

"All right!" Aspen shrieked in a rush. Anything was better than enduring her parents' party alone. "I'll do it."

Now Raleigh looked suspicious. "How do I know you'll actually do it?"

"Because if I don't, you'll never trust me to bribe you into a party again, and I might need to do that sometime."

"If you so much as look at any of the blue-blooded aristocrat youth in a way that suggests you might be considering a trip to the bathroom, I will leave."

"Fuck off." Aspen groaned. "I won't, I swear."

❖

Aspen kept her promise, but she did drink herself partway into a stupor. Not sloshing drunk, but tipsy enough to make the evening go by faster. Raleigh stood at her side like a member of the Secret Service and had nothing to drink. Dilated pupils told of her herbal indulgence, though Aspen did note that being mildly high did nothing to Raleigh's vigilance.

It was too bad Raleigh hated high society, because she'd have fit in perfectly. She wore fancy dresses rarely, but very well. And her posture and countenance were both above reproach. Aspen noticed her straighten even more as a well-dressed young man approached them. "I'm not taking him to the bathroom," she leaned over and said into Raleigh's ear.

Raleigh's face remained impassive.

"Good evening, ladies," the man said, giving a cordial bow.

"Good evening," Aspen replied, trying not to laugh as she attempted a sloppy curtsy.

Raleigh's hand shot out and grabbed her arm before she could topple over into the punch bowl. Oops. "What do you want?" Aspen was glad she didn't get *that* tone of voice from Raleigh anymore now that they'd been friends for a while. She secretly called that one the Murdery Voice.

The man folded his hands in front of his expensive-looking belt. "I would like a dance with Lady Wellington."

Aspen snorted in amusement. Lady Wellington? Sure, if this was a Jane Austen book.

Raleigh's eyes narrowed. "And who are you?" Murdery Voice.

"You may call me Lord Hadley," he said, looking rather self-important if Aspen did say so herself.

"May I?" Raleigh asked. Ooh, that was the You're Intolerably Stupid Voice. "As you can see, Aspen is in no condition to dance."

Hadley smiled, though it didn't reach his eyes. "It is no concern of yours," he said, taking Aspen's arm and beginning to pull her onto the dance floor.

"Hey," Aspen said, a little too loudly, stumbling along after him, catching the attention of several other guests, and most notably, her father.

"It's all right, Aspen," Hadley said close to her ear as they reached the dance floor. He attempted to slide an arm around her, to move them into a comfortable dancing position, but she threw her hands in the air, knocking him away from her.

"Get your hands off me!" she shouted, tripping over her dress and managing to fall somewhat gracefully to the ground.

Raleigh moved to intervene but wasn't quite as quick as Aspen's father.

Aspen had never seen him so angry. He hauled her up off the floor by one arm and backhanded her swiftly across the face, his ring cutting across her cheek. "You are a disgrace to this family!" he shouted, releasing her and watching with bulging eyes as she fell to the floor again without the support. "Get out of my sight!"

As soon as her father walked away, Raleigh was at her side, helping her up and out of the banquet hall.

Aspen's head was spinning, a throbbing pain in her cheek, a warm wet sensation dripping down the side of her face. "Raleigh, what? I don't understand." She whimpered, confused and hurt and overwhelmingly sad.

Raleigh led her up another flight of stairs and down the main corridor of the west wing, to her bedroom and private bath. She watched Ral lock the doors behind them and then Raleigh was easing her onto a plush velvet chaise, carefully pushing her hair away from her face. "You're drunk," Raleigh explained, "and you publicly fended off an advance from an influential guest."

"But he's never done that before," Aspen said, bringing her fingertips to her face, fluttering them across the wound with a flinch.

"I'll clean you up," Raleigh said. "Let me just text Denna." She got out her phone on her way to the bathroom.

Aspen just tried to relax, playing the scene over in her head, trying to pinpoint the exact moment her father had lost his mind. He had never, ever done such a thing to her before. He rarely even acknowledged her at all, let alone showed enough of an interest to be angry with her. To hit her. What was it about that Hadley person that made him fly off the deep end?

Her head hurt and her face hurt and she was exhausted, and she fell asleep.

Raleigh put some cold water onto a folded-up paper towel, her hands shaking as she shut off the tap. She stopped at the bathroom door when she saw Aspen asleep in the chair. What was she going to do about this? Aspen said it hadn't happened before, but what if she was covering? Maybe she was embarrassed, or thought it was her fault, or any of the hundred things Raleigh had thought when she was ten years old and someone she was supposed to trust was abusing her and her little brother Danny. People were supposed to be able to trust their families. Their fathers, their older brothers. And what were you supposed to do when you couldn't trust those people? You were supposed to ask for help. But she hadn't, so why should she think Aspen would?

Everything nasty and terrible she had ever said to Aspen took on a whole new meaning for her in that moment and she choked back a sob, refusing to fall apart. No. This wasn't her trauma, this was her chance to help Aspen like she hadn't helped herself. Or…or Danny. But what could she do?

Remington had been the one to finally save her and Danny. Maybe Remington could save Aspen too.

❖

Raleigh got to school early the next morning so she could catch Remington in the parking lot before homeroom. When she saw the flashy Mustang, she got out of her car and waited for Remington to do the same. When she caught Remington's eye, she held it for a few seconds so Remington would know she wanted to talk, before she got back in the car.

Remington nodded and made her way over. She pulled the door

open when Raleigh unlocked it for her and slid into the passenger's seat. "Raleigh," she drawled, putting one foot up on the dashboard.

"Aspen's father hit her last night." Her stomach lurched as she said the words.

The only thing that betrayed any reaction was a twitch of Remington's eye. "And?"

"And?" Raleigh asked, widening her eyes, burning with righteous fury. "I tell you a friend of mine is being abused, and that is your response?" This was a bad idea. She should not have done this. She didn't know what she had expected, but casual acceptance of something they had a shared history of fighting against was not it.

Remington gritted her teeth and Raleigh could see the tension tightening her jaw. "There is nothing I can do about it."

"What happened to you?" Raleigh asked, and she felt like she was suddenly mourning an era. She should have known better than to count on Remington to fight her battles anymore. That closeness between them had been gone for a long time. Which, she knew, was because of her, even if it wasn't her fault. She had been young, and ashamed, and confused, and when Remington had tried to talk to her about everything, she had exploded and ended the friendship. Now that they were older, they both understood that it was nobody's fault, but they had never been close again. "Please, Remington." She couldn't keep from asking one last time. She didn't even know exactly what she was asking for.

"You don't understand!" Remington suddenly shouted, spinning to face her. "I. CAN'T."

Raleigh narrowed her eyes. "The Remington I knew would never say that." She turned to look out the window. "The Remington I knew stormed into my bedroom and screamed and threw things until I wasn't being hurt anymore." She was angry and disappointed, no matter how hard she tried not to be. Why couldn't things be as simple anymore? Black and white? A is happening, so B is the answer. The air started trying to suffocate her. She had to get out of the car. Without waiting for a response from Remington, she got out and walked away.

Remington sat staring out the front windshield as Raleigh walked away, her heart racing. What the fuck was she supposed to do? She had promised her mother a million times that she'd stay out of jail. And it wasn't her problem. She didn't even like Aspen. She actually had a strong dislike for her, even though—no, maybe it wasn't a *strong* dislike anymore. But regardless, Aspen didn't deserve to get knocked around by her father. Nobody deserved that. She'd just have to figure something out.

With a kick to Raleigh's dashboard, Rem finally got out of the car and ended up being five minutes late to homeroom. Not that the teacher cared. It was homeroom. She clenched her jaw as she walked by Aspen and saw the poorly covered, bruised welt on her face.

Connor was late, too, coming in after her, and the teacher wasn't even there, which was odd given that there wasn't a sub. But again, it was homeroom. It was a ten-minute class that served no purpose other than providing ten minutes to organize yourself for the day.

As soon as Connor saw Aspen, he dropped his books and bent over to examine her, shooting a glare at Remington. "Did Remington do that?"

Why did he automatically assume it was her? She didn't go around punching girls. She might not talk to anyone she went to school with, but she wasn't just randomly assaulting anyone, either. Fuck, he was annoying.

"No." Aspen laughed, overly casual about the whole thing in Remington's opinion, and waved a hand around dismissively. "I ran into the corner of one of the kitchen cabinets."

Connor laughed too, shaking his head. Remington knew she was lying, but Connor had no way to know. "Dumbass," he muttered, and Aspen stuck her tongue out at him.

Remington was outraged at the fact Aspen was covering for her asshole of a father, and got to her feet, hands curled into fists at her sides. She strode toward the door, stopping to give Aspen a disapproving look, then continued on her way out.

"What?" Aspen called after her. "Are you pissed that you're leaving before me, so you can't stare at my ass?"

The room went quiet. Rem's eye twitched but she kept walking. She wasn't going to let Aspen bait her into action a second time.

❖

Aspen found a note in her locker, unaddressed and unsigned, but it was in Remington's scrawling handwriting.

You are a liar. I know what happened to your face.

Remington's notes made her embarrassed, and this one was no exception. But how the hell would Remington know she'd lied to Connor? How the hell would Remington know what had really happened?

Before she had time to think any further, a stinging smack landed on the seat of her skirt and she spun around, her embarrassment intensifying, a gasp on her lips. This time she didn't let Remington walk away. She followed, despite the heat blooming on her cheeks. "Who the hell do you think you are?" she asked, matching Remington's quick strides. "Why do you think you have the right to do that to me?"

Remington stopped walking and leaned against a row of lockers. God, why did she have to look so nonchalant? She looked nonchalant while Aspen felt like exploding.

"Hello? Can you answer the fucking question?"

Remington examined her fingernails, made a sucking noise with one side of her mouth and then looked Aspen straight in the eye. "Does he hit you a lot?"

"What? No!" Aspen said, irritated at the ridiculousness of the situation. "Never before. I seriously don't see why you care, or how you even know what happened in the first place."

Remington regarded her for a few seconds and then pushed off the lockers to stand up straight. "You're lying. Nobody's father hits them just once."

"I'm not fucking lying!" Aspen shrieked, wondering how in the hell she'd ended up explaining herself to Remington fucking Stone. "Why would I lie?"

"You lied to Connor."

"Because I didn't want to admit in front of the entire class that my father hit me," Aspen said, in a little bit of disbelief at Remington's audacity. As if this girl had the right to question what she did or did not choose to share with the entire student body. "You of all people should understand not wanting the whole world to know your business."

"What's that supposed to mean?" Remington asked, and Aspen was glad to have put her on the defensive for once.

"It means you don't even say hello to anyone, let alone air your family's dirty laundry. Why are you riding me?"

The defensive expression faded into a grin and suddenly Aspen couldn't look away from Remington's lips. "If I was riding you, I'd have my spurs on."

Aspen quickly looked at the ground, fumbling to find words. No girl had ever spoken to her that way before, and the implication sent a rush of liquid heat into her belly. She ended up opening and closing her mouth without speaking.

Remington shifted her weight, flicking an imaginary piece of lint from Aspen's shoulder. "Can I see?"

"See what?" Aspen managed to ask without breathing. Her voice sounded weird.

Remington's expression took on a decidedly wicked edge, and it reminded Aspen of this one cocky superhero she had seen in a bunch of movies. What the hell was her name again? Ugh. She couldn't remember. But Remington was totally channeling her with that annoying smugness. And then Remington was reaching for the hem of Aspen's skirt. "See if I left a mark, of course."

Aspen smacked her hand away. "No you cannot!"

"How old are you?"

"What? I'm eighteen. Why?"

"Just making sure that if you press charges, I won't be in trouble for assaulting a minor. Or get a lewd and lascivious behavior charge when I finally do put those spurs on."

"Oh please," Aspen said, crossing her arms over her chest. "I'd be too humiliated to recount the incident. And you can't press charges against someone for flirting, can you? If you can, maybe I will." She looked at the lockers behind Remington, avoiding eye contact. "No, I won't. I wouldn't even know what to say."

Remington grinned. "Someone less perceptive would miss the implied consent you just gave me."

"Are you a lawyer now?" Aspen asked, not sure why she couldn't just deny Remington's statement.

Rem leaned closer, running her tongue along her teeth. "Does it sting, Aspen?"

Aspen's breath caught, a shocked, soundless sigh escaping her open mouth. "What?" she asked. What were they talking about again? Her face, or…?

Remington's fingers crawled under her skirt again, and Aspen was too distracted to slap her hand away this time. She slid her palm across Aspen's hip to lightly squeeze the cheek she'd smacked. "This."

For someone so used to this kind of thing, Aspen was completely out of her element. It was like just because Remington was a girl, she had lost her game. It shouldn't be that different, should it? She should be able to flirt back without sounding like an idiot or falling all over herself. But she couldn't think of what to say, how to make Remington squirm, because honestly, she was unable to think of anything other than the hand squeezing through her spankies. Remington had asked a question, right? Whether the smack stung? She shouldn't even answer. She should slap Remington across the face and walk away. "A little," she said. *Fuck.*

She should not have said that, because Remington slipped a hand beneath the elastic of her spankies and underwear, letting out a little groan that almost killed her.

And then Remington was leaning closer, wild blue eyes trained on her lips. Jesus Christ, Remington Stone was going to kiss her. She couldn't let that happen, could she? No. She could not. She pulled in a shuddering breath, her eyes drifting closed, and halfheartedly attempted to push herself away with hands on Remington's shoulders. "Stop," she said, and wow, because she didn't even sound like herself. She sounded like some—ugh, she didn't even know. But it was pathetic.

Remington slid her hand out of Aspen's panties.

Aspen's eyes flew open. Remington had even put a foot of distance between them. "Why'd you stop?" She couldn't read the expression on Remington's face. Something between regretful and amused. Was Remington regretting that she said stop or regretting trying to kiss her?

Remington gave a subtle tilt of her head that did nothing to help Aspen read her. "You said stop."

"Yes, but I—"

"Don't say stop if you don't mean it," Remington said, winking as she spun and walked away.

That wink definitely felt like spurs.

When Aspen could notice things around her again, she noticed Denna beside her, staring at her.

"What the hell. Did I just see?"

Aspen scowled, though it was ineffectual since she was still winded and flushed. "She smacked my ass again."

"That is not what I just saw," Denna said.

"Then she tried to kiss me."

"Uh-huh. *That's* what I saw."

After a moment of silence, Aspen asked, "Well?"

"Well, what?"

"Well, do you have anything useful to say?"

"Huh! Fuck you."

Aspen laughed, shaking her head. "But do you?" she asked again, serious this time. "Have any advice, I mean."

"Advice on what? How not to have eye sex with Remington Stone in the hallway?"

"Yes, please, that's exactly what I need. Please help me figure out how not to have eye sex with Remington Stone in the hallway, because I'm lost without you."

Denna snickered. "Almost time for P.E."

"No, I'm skipping. My head throbs every time I lean over."

"So how come I never knew about this before?" Denna asked, slightly changing subjects.

"Because there was nothing to know!" Aspen shouted. "Why does everyone keep assuming it's happened before?"

"It hasn't?"

"No! I would've told you! I fucking hate you sometimes, but you're my best friend. I wouldn't keep something like that from you."

Denna nodded, backing off the interrogation a little. "Raleigh just figured that if he would do that in a roomful of people, she didn't even want to guess at what he'd be willing to do in private." She paused. "I fucking hate you sometimes too, but yeah, you're my best friend. Raleigh and I were both just concerned."

"We're hardly in the same room together. When would he have time to abuse me?"

"I believe you; I'm sorry," Denna said, holding up her hands.

"Would you get Ral to believe it, please? And how the hell did Remington know what happened to my face?"

Denna shrugged. "I don't know. Maybe Raleigh told her? I don't know why she would, but I know they used to be close."

"Raleigh and Remington?" Aspen asked. "I think I knew that. I just can't picture how they would have ever become friends."

"They were neighbors until tenth grade."

"Mystery solved. Why didn't I know they were neighbors?"

"You never asked?"

"But why would Ral go out of her way to tell Remington something private about me?"

Denna started to shrug, but then dropped her shoulders and Aspen watched her lips pull into a tight line. "Raleigh thinks your father habitually abuses you. Remington's father was a cop known for handling domestic violence cases. He was off duty and ended up killing a man, trying to defend the man's wife, remember? That's what he got sent up for."

Aspen put two and two together and thought she was going to be sick. Right there in the hallway, just all over the linoleum. "Shit."

"Indeed." Denna nodded. "We need to talk to our bitches."

❖

Raleigh looked up and smiled when Denna joined her in the lunch line. "Hey, gorgeous."

"Honey, why did you tell Remington about Aspen's dad?"

Nothing like getting straight to the point. Raleigh narrowed her eyes a little as she thought back to her conversation with Remington. "I asked her to help. She told me no."

"What were you asking her to do?"

"I don't know. I'm not the one good at protecting others, she is."

"You protect me," Denna said, grabbing a plate and a tray. "But, baby, it is unfair of you to ask Remington to get involved. I wish you would have told me what you were doing, because I could have told you that this isn't an ongoing issue. It hasn't happened before. Unless it happens again, there is nothing that needs doing except being there for our friend, if she *wants* to talk about it."

Raleigh's concern dampened, but not by much. "Are you certain of that?"

"Certain enough to believe Aspen when she tells me, yes."

Her thoughts drifted to her own situation again, how she had never told anyone what was going on with her older brother. She had only been a child, but not once had she ever considered asking someone for help. So again, she couldn't be sure that Aspen would ask for help, either. But if Denna believed it was a one-time thing, she could at least try to put her own experience aside and not let that color her thoughts of Aspen's current situation. Finally, she cast her eyes away from Denna. "It was awful, Denna," she said, low enough not to be overheard by the others in line. "All those people staring and none of them doing a thing. Like it was perfectly acceptable for a man to strike his child." Her stomach churned just thinking about it and she might not be able to eat lunch now. The food suddenly looked less appetizing than usual.

Denna moved closer and laid a hand on her back. "I'm sorry you had to see it, baby. I should've been there instead."

"She was bleeding and—" She stopped talking and shook her head, trying to force the memory out. "No. Let's just eat."

Denna looked like she wanted to push, but Raleigh knew she wouldn't. It was something that had taken them a little bit of time to get right, but it was now mutually understood that she would talk when she was ready, and Denna never pushed. Raleigh appreciated her so much for that; she knew she should probably say it more.

She cleared her throat as they left the lunch line, heading for a table. "Thanks. For not pushing."

Denna grinned at her and her stomach flipped for an entirely different reason. "Remember the last time I tried to get you to talk about something you weren't ready to talk about? Yeah, I'm not looking to repeat that experience."

Denna was referring to the biggest fight of their relationship, and Raleigh knew she was trying to keep the mood light, but that incident made her ashamed of herself. She had screamed at Denna to leave her alone and get out of her house, and Denna had been crying, not realizing what she had done, and Raleigh had just pushed her away. They hadn't talked for two days, and it was the most lonely she'd ever felt. Denna had been the one to patch things up, showing up at her house with Apology Taco Bell. "I—"

"Wait, Ral," Denna interrupted and she stopped talking. "Whatever you're doing in your head right now, stop it. I was just teasing. We're good, baby, I promise."

"But—"

"Don't make me kiss you in the middle of the cafeteria."

Raleigh let out a little stuttering laugh and sat down at their usual table. "I do not recommend that course of action." She was starting to feel less agonized.

"Then don't feel bad over something that happened years ago that I was only bringing up to make you give me a dirty look."

She could feel herself starting to grin and pressed her lips together to prevent it. She attempted the dirty look in question and felt successful when Denna scowled.

Crisis averted, she started to eat.

Chapter Six

After school, Remington was surprised to find a note in her locker.

Dear Remington,
    You have no right to pry into my life like this. Back off.
    All my love,
    X—Aspen
P.S. Denna says I should try not to have eye sex with you in the hallway.

❖

The next morning before homeroom, Aspen had a return note.

Dear Aspen,
    I don't know what you heard, but the only prying I'm interested in is… Well, I'll let you figure that one out.
    Missing you,
    X—Remington
P.S. Well said. Next time we should use the bathroom. Or your bedroom.

True to tradition, Aspen felt her face get hot when she read the last part. She stuffed the note in her pocket and got a piece of paper from her binder, scribbled a quick reply, and slapped it on Remington's desk before the bell rang, then she slipped into her own seat, keeping Remington in her peripheral vision.

Dear Remington,
 Maybe I'll even let you see the mark.
 Breathlessly yours,
 X—Aspen

Remington laughed out loud and tucked the note in her jacket pocket.

❖

On the way to her car after detention, Remington spied Aspen sitting alone on the bleachers, directing the rest of the cheerleaders on some moves. A sudden and vivid memory of Aspen getting a pencil stuck in her ear in second grade assaulted her and she stared at her boots until she could stop grinning. She hadn't thought about that incident in like ten years. For some reason it made her want to go talk to the brat.

It was totally out of her way, but she walked the fifty or so yards anyway and climbed the front railing, dropped into the bleacher box, and slid along the smooth metal bench until she was seated next to Aspen. "Yesterday's mark is long gone. You must have been referring to the next one."

Aspen laughed and told her squad to take five. "There's a party this Friday night at Riker's," she said without looking at Remington.

Remington played it cool, though the casual comment made her heart race. "And?"

Aspen shrugged. "Do you drink?"

"No."

"You don't?"

"No."

"I thought it was a rule of senior year."

"I'm not big on social rules."

"I have to get back to practice. But you should come."

"I should come?" It came out mocking.

Aspen looked confused. "What? Was that improper grammar?"

"I don't go to parties without a hot girl on my arm. I'm a loner on any given day, but going stag to parties isn't my thing."

"But I just asked you to go with me."

"No, you didn't. You said I should come. There's a difference."

"Semantics!" Aspen said, throwing up her hands.

"I'm not going unless it's a date," Remington said. Challenge issued.

"Fine, don't go."

"I won't." Rem shrugged and went to hop the railing, but Aspen jumped to her feet and blocked the way.

"If I let you pick me up and drive me home, is that good enough?"

Challenge succeeded. "Put the details in my locker."

"'Kay," Aspen said, and her attempt at being casual was glaringly obvious.

Rem could feel eyes on her as she vaulted the railing like it wasn't a five-foot drop to the ground.

❖

When Friday came around, Remington found directions to Aspen's house in her locker and a request to pick her up at eight. There was also Aspen's cell phone number, and she programmed that into her phone. As she disarmed the alarm on her car and slid into the driver's seat, she sent a text to Aspen.

Rem: *what should I wear*

A few minutes later, her phone buzzed and she glanced at the screen as soon as she was stopped at a red light.

Aspen: *not much*

It buzzed again.

Aspen: *just kidding. wear whatever you want*

She snorted and sent a response.

Rem: *what are you wearing*

She waited until she was home to check Aspen's reply. She opened the text—

Aspen: *right now? nothing*

—and dropped her phone.

It was a good fuckin' thing she was at home, and not somewhere people could see her. Dropping your phone? Amateur.

Rem: *to the party smartass*

Buzz.

Aspen: *what do you want me to wear*

Jesus. She took a few breaths before answering that one.

Rem: *short skirt. a thong. knee high socks. fancy shoes. you pick the top*

Buzz.

Aspen: *see you at 8*

Remington had already tossed down the phone and started stripping for a shower before she realized she was smiling. She quickly frowned and grabbed a towel, turned on the hot water, and climbed under the spray.

❖

Aspen's chest was heaving, her heart thumping against her ribcage as she set the phone down. What was she thinking, flirting with Remington like that, so shamelessly, when she'd never even kissed a girl in her life? Just the thought of it made her nervous and twisty, and more excited than she'd been in a long time.

She showered and shaved, making sure she used her Bliss shampoo, then spent nearly an hour blow drying and styling her hair as close to perfection as was possible to achieve. She pulled some of it on top of her head in a messy bunch, wrapping a band around it to hold it in place, then letting her curls fall haphazardly everywhere.

She scoured her closet for the items Remington wanted her in and came up with a lot of black. A short black pleated skirt, black knee highs, and a pair of shiny black heeled Mary Janes. At least her thong was red. Red, soft, satin. She got into all that and went through about twenty shirts before she picked a shimmery purple blouse with bell sleeves. She slid it on and buttoned it up and freaked out when she saw it was seven forty-five. "Fuck! Fuck! Fuck!" She scrambled around gathering her makeup from its various locations in her bedroom and bathroom and brushed her teeth before starting with foundation.

She was staring into the mirror above the sink at her perfect smoky eyes and perfect subtle red lipliner when the doorbell rang. "Kelly!" she shrieked, popping her head out of her bedroom and calling down the wide marble corridor to the latest in a long line of housekeepers. "Can you get that and tell her I'm almost ready? *Please*?!"

She heard displeased mumbling, which meant Kelly would do it, and she hurried back to her vanity to finish her lipstick. A few seconds later, she ran a gloss over her lips and pouted them to make sure she hadn't missed any spots. Finally, she grabbed a purse that would go well with her shirt and emptied her credit cards, ID, keys, and some cash from her schoolbag into it. "Coming!" she yelled, turning toward her bedroom door, intending to calm herself just before descending into view on the staircase, but Remington was leaning in the doorway, the look on her face leaving nothing to the imagination.

Aspen wasn't quite so suave. She froze, jaw dropping. Remington was dressed as usual in her jacket and thin white tank top, so obviously without a bra, but in place of the jeans she always wore to school was a pair of jet-black, skintight leather pants. Her thumbs were hooked in the front pockets and her lips were painted a glossy bubblegum pink.

"You look," Remington said, her eyes raking over Aspen's body, "delicious."

Aspen was at a loss and shook her head to clear it. "Thanks?" she said, almost a question. "So, are you ready? Let's go."

"There's one thing I want to do first," Remington said, stalking toward Aspen, who felt suddenly like a sleek predator's prey. When she reached Aspen she circled around behind her, moving close and giving her a swift, firm smack on the ass.

Aspen gasped, knowing she should have expected it but somehow having not. Her belly tingled, chin dropping to her chest so her hair would hide her face. "Fuck."

"Now we can go," Remington said with a nod, striding toward the door, leaving Aspen to collect herself and follow.

Trailing a few seconds behind, Aspen gawked a little as they reached Remington's Mustang and slid inside when the double beep told her she could without tripping the alarm. "Nice car," she said, buckling her seat belt. She lifted her hand to run it along the dashboard.

Remington drove a little too fast on the way to Riker's, with Aspen remembering to shout out directions at the last second before every turn. She could hear music blaring before she even got out of the car, and she grinned. The place was already packed with people, most of whom she knew in some capacity or another. She started up the walk and stopped, turning to wait for Remington to lock her car and catch up. She liked the way Remington didn't walk so much as swagger.

When they were almost to the door, Remington grabbed Aspen's elbow and held her back a minute. "If I cross any lines, you have to tell me. Because I don't—I'm not used to parties, and I'm not used to straight girls. So, you know, if I make you uncomfortable, just push me into an empty room and tell me off, okay?"

Aspen wasn't really sure what to say to that, but she could certainly speak up for herself if lines were crossed, so she nodded. "Okay."

"Okay." Rem raised her hand to knock, but Aspen just opened the door and walked in, expecting her to follow. There were so many people it was hard to move without touching someone.

The first place Aspen went was the drinks table. "Do you want a soda or something?" she asked because she remembered that Remington didn't drink. She grabbed a beer for herself and twisted off the cap. "I can get you one from the kitchen."

Remington leaned against the wall behind the table and gave a slight nod. "Sure."

Aspen disappeared into the kitchen. She rooted around in the fridge until she found a Sprite and carried it back to Remington. "You don't want me to drink this, do you?" she asked, indicating her bottle while she held out the soda. She didn't know what it was exactly that gave her that impression, because Remington didn't seem annoyed, but there was just *something*. It lingered in the air.

"Thanks," Remington said, taking the soda and popping it open. She looked at Aspen for a few seconds before she answered. "Honestly? I wouldn't mind if you had a few, but I wouldn't want to deal with you drunk, if it was up to me."

"Because you're afraid I'm an obnoxious drunk?" Aspen asked.

Remington chuckled and leaned closer. "No. Because I won't make out with you if you're drunk." She pulled back and watched Aspen and took a drink of her soda.

Aspen nearly choked on her own breath, so she tipped back her beer and took a long swallow. She didn't see Riker or Denna and Raleigh anywhere. Oh well. They'd show up eventually. She grabbed Remington's wrist and dragged her into the living room, squeezing onto the crowded sofa and pulling Rem down next to her.

There were strobe lights going off everywhere and Remington squinted a little as she settled in beside Aspen.

❖

Aspen stopped at two beers for Remington's sake. She'd found Riker at some point and dragged him to the living room, rejoining Remington on the couch while he danced with some girl she didn't know. She was just about to relax when Remington put a hand on her knee and squeezed.

"Let's dance."

"Really? You'll dance with me?" she asked, surprised that Remington was willing.

"I'm bored." Remington rolled her shoulders like she'd been sitting in the same position for three days. "Dancing is better than sitting here while you go off in search of things and wander back when you feel like it."

"Aww, you don't like being my eye candy?" Aspen asked with a mock pout, then a snicker as she stood and pulled Remington with her, moving a few feet away from the couch before starting to move her hips.

"Oh, Aspen," Remington said, shaking her head. "It's such a bad idea to tease me. I hold grudges and you will never see revenge coming." Her hands went to Aspen's waist and she stepped slowly closer, bringing their hips together, one leg sliding between Aspen's.

Aspen didn't say anything because what in the hell could she say to that? She just pressed even closer, continuing the teasing as she started to grind. She ran her hands down Remington's arms, rolling her hips to the beat, never quite allowing herself to make contact with Rem's thigh. Her pulse pounded in her ears, heart racing faster with every move Remington made.

Remington slid down Aspen's body, hands pushing at the hem of her shimmery blouse on the way back up. She dropped the blouse, but her hands continued to feather over the soft material, around to Aspen's back, and up into her hair with a squeeze. "Don't tease me." She grinned.

Aspen slid her fingers into Remington's belt loops and tugged, finally settling fully onto the muscled thigh between her legs with a soft groan. "Who said anything about teasing?"

Remington's hands tightened in her hair, pulling their faces together, their lips an inch apart. Aspen could feel warm breath on her skin, see right into dilated pupils that jumped every time a strobe flickered, and she thought she might be about to get her first real kiss from a girl, but she wasn't. Remington dropped down again, slinking her way back up, and Aspen groaned. She wanted that kiss. But if Remington wasn't going to give it to her, she was at least going to keep dancing. She spun around and pressed her ass snugly against the front of those tight leather pants.

Remington gave a quiet, breathy moan, almost too soft for Aspen to hear it, and wrapped her arms around Aspen's waist, resting her palms flat on Aspen's belly, under the blouse.

Remington's hands felt so good on her bare skin. She ached for Rem to go lower, to slip a hand into the thong she was wearing and take her. Remington ground her hips against Aspen's ass, and the leather chafed where her skirt rode up.

Aspen's thoughts turned positively indecent, and she spun again, burying her face in Remington's neck and taking a deep breath in, reveling in the scent of her glistening skin. "Kiss me," she said, close to Remington's ear.

She heard Remington's breath catch at the request. Rem gripped a handful of her hair at the base of her skull and tugged her head back, Rem's wild blue eyes searching her face for guidance. But Remington was hesitating. Maybe Rem didn't think she was serious.

She sensed the need to repeat it and swallowed, her throat suddenly dry. "Kiss me," she asked again, louder, leaving no possible doubt.

Remington's jaw clenched as she slowly pulled Aspen's face to hers, not stopping this time, thank God, their mouths connecting, Aspen's already open and begging to accept her tongue.

Remington didn't disappoint. She pushed her tongue firmly into Aspen's mouth, swallowing Aspen's moan, tightening her fist in Aspen's hair.

This wasn't just kissing. This was transcendental. Aspen had never enjoyed kissing someone so much before. She tangled her tongue with Remington's, then sucked on Rem's lower lip until she drew out a moan of her own. Hearing that from Remington, the most badass chick she'd ever known, was exhilarating. She wanted to hear it again. She raised a knee between Remington's legs and kissed her harder, shivering in excitement at the sound she received in reward.

Remington broke the kiss, panting, and shook her head. "Aspen, don't."

"What?" Aspen asked, winded and confused. "Why—"

"It's hard enough to keep my hands out of your skirt without you egging me on."

"You can go in my skirt," Aspen said, as if that should have been obvious. "If you're worried about propriety, just rub me through my panties."

"Jesus Christ," Remington said, flexing her fingers against Aspen's scalp. "You'd let me do that, right here, surrounded by dozens of people?"

"You want to," Aspen said. "Why shouldn't I let you?"

"Because you would be letting me disrespect you." Remington's eyebrows were starting to draw down, and Aspen could feel the concern in the look to go with the concern in the statement.

She didn't know how to deal with concern, and she didn't know how to respond to that, so she leaned forward and breathed into Remington's ear. "I'm wet for you."

"Aspen," Remington said. "You're so beautiful. I want to kiss you, but I don't want to have sex in the middle of a roomful of people."

Aspen hadn't been sure if girls were going to be her thing, but as soon as she'd seen Remington standing in her bedroom doorway, all doubts had fled and she'd been ready for this. "So kiss me then."

Suddenly, there were someone else's arms around her neck and she jumped, turning her head. Denna.

"*Hi*." Denna grinned, and Raleigh was behind her with a disapproving look.

Instinctively, Aspen knew this was payback for interrupting Denna and Raleigh's make-out session, because there was no way Denna hadn't realized that she and Remington were about to kiss. "*Bitch*," she said with a groan, trying to pry Denna's arms from around her neck, with no success. And Remington took a step back.

Raleigh finally intervened on Aspen's behalf, pulling Denna backward. "Please excuse us," she said by way of apology, taking Denna by the ear to lead her away. "We'll see you later." Denna cackled and waved, then scrunched up her face when Raleigh tugged on her ear.

Aspen turned back to Remington, waiting for her kiss.

"What?" Remington said. "You don't really think I'm going to continue now, do you?"

"What?" Aspen asked, panic rising. "Why not?" Why did Remington suddenly not want to kiss her? Was she pushing too hard?

Did she do something she hadn't realized? Her heart thudded against her rib cage as she waited for an answer, and the feeling of being invested in someone else's opinion of her was terrifying. But there was nothing she could do about it, because she knew without a doubt that if Remington Stone did not want to kiss her ever again, she wouldn't just be disappointed, she would be devastated.

"When I get interrupted, I start back at zero," Remington said, and Aspen couldn't tell if she was teasing.

"Come on," Aspen said, rolling her eyes, resorting to humor to distract herself from her *feelings*. "Don't make me go masturbate in Riker's bedroom." No one had ever *not* kissed her when she wanted to be kissed, and she was desperate and confused and nervous at the same time.

"Go ahead." Remington shrugged. She let go of Aspen's waist.

Aspen had not expected to have her bluff called, but maybe if she could just get Remington excited again, the problem would fix itself. She grabbed Remington's wrist and dragged her down the hallway, ushered her into Riker's bedroom and locked the door behind them. "Stand here," she said, her voice clipped with the urgency of her nerves, and she positioned Rem at the foot of the bed, then climbed onto it.

"You want me to watch?" Remington asked, gaping slightly, hands on her hips.

Aspen didn't answer, just shimmied out of her panties and flung them at Remington's face.

Remington caught the panties and tucked them into her left jacket pocket. "You know I'm not actually going to let you lie there and do that in front of me, right?"

Aspen held out her arms, a grin finally emerging. "I know."

Remington took her hands from her hips and slid her arms crossed over her chest instead. Aspen didn't think she looked mad, but she wasn't coming closer, either.

"Come here. Please?"

Remington rolled her eyes but finally climbed onto the bed. She propped herself up on one elbow and looked down at Aspen. "What?"

Aspen laid a hand on the elbow that was propping Remington up. "I just...I didn't want you to walk away."

"I didn't."

"I know, but it seemed like you were going to and it made me nervous."

Rem looked a little surprised. "Nervous? What for?"

"Because you stopped kissing me. I thought—"

Remington kissed her. Just quick, but their lips touched. "Don't think so much. I still want to kiss you, a lot."

"I still want to kiss you, a lot."

Remington kissed her again, letting it linger this time. "Feel better?" Rem asked when she pulled back, her voice a little scratchy.

"Yes."

Remington pulled Aspen's panties from her pocket, dangling them over the edge of the bed.

Aspen laughed. "You can keep those."

"Oh no," Remington said, picking up one of Aspen's ankles and sliding her underwear over one fancy shoe. "You're not going without underwear. You're lucky I even let you drag me in here." She repeated the process with the other foot.

Aspen didn't struggle; she let Remington slide her panties up her legs and fit them into place over her hips, then she reached down herself to adjust them until she was comfortable. Or at least as comfortable as she could be with the *feelings* flitting all through and around her. Did Remington like her? Was she going to get to see Remington again outside of school? Was this just fun to Rem or did it mean something? Her stomach was a disaster.

She took a few more relaxing breaths before getting off the bed, and as they were leaving the room, she jumped in surprise at the solid, stinging smack to her ass. "What was that for?"

Remington pressed herself flush against Aspen's back, hands squeezing her waist. "For turning me on," she said, dipping her head down to suck an earlobe into her mouth.

"Oh." Aspen purred, tilting her head to offer more access. "I'll have to do it more often, then."

Remington flicked Aspen's ear with her tongue. "You like it when I smack your ass, Aspen?"

"Mm-hmm. It hurts so good."

Remington started walking them forward, their steps awkward due to being pressed together. "I need to get home soon. Are you almost ready to go?"

"Do I get to spend the night at your place?"

Remington chortled. "No."

"I can't believe you're not dying to fuck me."

"Who said I wasn't?" Remington said, giving her waist a squeeze. "I just have some self-control. Should we find your friends and say good night?"

"No, they're used to me disappearing."

"I'll bet."

"Shut up."

Chapter Seven

Hey, honey, good morning," her mother said as Remington emerged from her bedroom, rubbing sleep from her eyes. "Or good afternoon, actually. You want pancakes?"

Remington nodded and slid onto the couch beside her mother, curling up with a sleepy yawn, her eyes closing again.

Mama laughed and put an arm around her, giving her a squeeze. "You sure you're awake? Your hair is *something*."

Rem shook her head, making a little noise as she readjusted her position, burying her face in the back of the couch.

"Okay." Mama laughed again, kissing the top of her head. "You just sit there and wake up while I make your pancakes."

Remington whined and burrowed farther into the couch as Mama got up. She stayed like that until the smell of pancakes was too tempting to resist, then forced herself to sit up and stretch, rubbing her eyes again to clear her vision, and wandered into the kitchen.

A few minutes later, she was mostly awake. Awake enough to put butter and syrup on her pancakes, anyway, and sit at the table to eat them. "Are you having any?" she asked.

"Nope. All for you," Mama replied, flipping the last two onto a plate on the counter and shutting off the stove. She put butter on them for Remington and set the plate on the table, then poured herself another cup of coffee and sat down. "So, how was the party?"

Remington's eyes snapped to her mother's, her brows instantly furrowed. "I ended up kissing that girl I told you I couldn't stand," she said, feeling grumpy about it.

Remington could tell that Mama was trying not to laugh. "I

could've told you that was going to happen. Didn't you go to the party with her?"

"Yes," Remington grumbled. "But—"

"I saw you leave the house in leather pants, Remington."

Remington groaned. "Maybe I just wanted to look good in case there was someone else at the party!"

"I'm sure that's it, dear."

"Oh, Mama," Remington said, dropping her fork and burying her face in her hands. "What am I going to do?"

Mama sighed. "All right. Do you really want to hear the story?"

Rem perked up immediately, her half-eaten breakfast forgotten for the moment. "Yes."

"I can't believe I'm caving." Mama ran her hands over her face and took a slow breath. "Your father and I hated each other at the beginning of high school. And when I say hated, I mean hated. He was on the football team and I was in the math club. He made fun of me at every opportunity, and I used my position as a teacher's assistant to make his grades even worse than they already were."

"Math club?" Remington was horrified.

"Yes, please do hang on to that insignificant detail," her mother said. "Do you want me to continue?"

"Yes, yes," Remington laughed, listening intently. "Keep going. Please."

"Well, about halfway through his junior year, your daddy got injured and couldn't play football anymore. So with a football scholarship out of the question, he had to rely on his grades to get into college."

"So he asked you to tutor him?"

"Not hardly! But I got stuck doing it anyway. And I'm sure you can guess the formula from there. The more time we spent together, the more I realized that his way of making himself feel good was to pick on others. That boy was so insecure, Remington. You know he was reading at a seventh-grade level in eleventh grade? He begged me not to tell anyone and I said I wouldn't, as long as he quit trying to humiliate me. He knew I had the heavier bat, and he stopped making fun of me, and once he couldn't say anything mean, he actually started finding nice things to say, especially when I brought up his reading level two grades."

Remington was paying rapt attention, barely daring to breathe. She wanted to hear the rest.

"Then one day when we were huddled over a ninth-grade literature assignment, he kissed me, and apologized for being an ignorant you-know-what, and said he'd liked me since he first met me."

"It's like a fairy tale," Remington said with a grin, thinking for a minute. "But I think Daddy's problem was easier to solve than Aspen's."

"Oh?"

"It was easy to get him to stop being an ignorant you-know-what because you had blackmail material, right? All he had to do was stop saying rude things? Well, Aspen, she—" She sighed, pushing her last pancake around on the plate with her fork. "She sleeps around, Mama. I don't know how to fix that."

Mama was quiet for a minute. "Maybe it's not your job to try to fix it," she finally said. "She probably does that because she doesn't know how else to connect with people, but without knowing her I couldn't say for sure, I can only guess."

"Her parents don't pay her much attention. She has a couple of friends she doesn't sleep with, but that's about it as far as I know."

"Do you really like her, honey?"

"I hate that I do."

"Well, don't beat yourself up. We can't decide who we like when it comes to things like this. Believe me, I wasn't happy about liking your daddy at first, either."

"So what do I do?"

"Nothing. Just be yourself, baby. Don't try to fix her."

"That's kind of a relief," Remington said, admitting it to herself as well. "I really didn't want to try. I mean, I like her the way she is. I just don't want to do more than like her if she's not going to do more than just like me, you know, casually."

"I know. And I'd say try to protect yourself, but that only ever causes a great big mess. Go with your instincts, and if you like her the way she is, that's just fine."

"Thanks, Mama. How'd you get so smart?"

"Years and years of practice. Now eat up before it gets cold."

❖

Aspen burst into Denna's bedroom with a bag full of Taco Bell and dropped it on the floor so she could pounce on Denna and hit her repeatedly in the face with a pillow. "I'll kill you," she said as Denna fended off the attack.

"Is this about last night?" Denna squeaked as the pillow made contact again, and shoved Aspen away from her. Aspen landed on Raleigh, who grunted in distaste.

"Get. Off. Of. Me," Raleigh said through clenched teeth.

Aspen rolled away and jumped to the floor, collecting her bag of food and then flopping down on the end of the bed. "Yes, it's about last night, you complete and total asshole," she said, tossing Denna a taco and Raleigh a Mexican pizza.

"Mmm, lunch in bed." Denna scooted up to sit with her back against the headboard. "Ral, Mexican pizza," she said, wiggling.

"As lovely as that sounds, my focus is centered on not wetting the bed, after having a person thrown on my abdomen while I need to use the bathroom." Raleigh rolled over and climbed out of bed, then shuffled into Denna's bathroom and slammed the door.

"In my defense, I *was* drunk, and you've interrupted me during sex more times than I can count," Denna said, tearing into her taco.

"There is no defense for what you did. She *stopped kissing me*, Denna. And it gave me a complex. I thought she was never going to kiss me again."

"Maybe you shouldn't have been kissing in the middle of a crowded room then, if she's so skittish."

Aspen snatched the taco back and Denna shrieked, mouth dropped open in horror.

"That's mine!"

"Maybe you shouldn't have been eating it in a room with me so close to you when you're making fun of me, if you're so hungry."

"Give me my fucking taco!"

"No."

"You can't give me a taco and take it back, you stupid-ass bitch!"

"Well, you can't—"

Raleigh came out of the bathroom and Aspen hurriedly gave Denna back her taco.

Denna smirked and shoved almost half of it into her mouth, then chewed noisily.

Raleigh froze halfway to the bed and stared at Denna. "That is revolting. Please stop."

Denna gave one more chew in Aspen's direction and then stopped.

Raleigh slid into bed and picked up the pizza. "Did you remember to ask for no tomatoes?"

"And no meat, yes." Aspen rolled her eyes.

Raleigh opened the box and scowled. "There's a tomato!"

"Not my fault! I said no tomatoes. Just take it off."

"I'll still be able to taste it."

"So you're not going to eat it?"

"Of course I'm going to eat it, I'm merely expressing my displeasure."

Aspen was about to reply when her phone buzzed. She stretched across the foot of the bed on her stomach and propped herself up on her elbows, opened the text, and grinned.

Rem: *what are you doing?*

"You're grinning like an idiot. That must be from *Remington*," Denna said, wagging her eyebrows.

"Shut up." She reached one arm out to shove at Denna's legs.

Aspen: *eating taco bell with d and r. you?*

A few minutes later she had a reply.

Rem: *whatd you get? im about to shower*

Aspen was inexplicably giddy as she answered.

Aspen: *bean burrito. no onions i hate them. what are you doing after shower*

"You do realize you're bouncing, and making it difficult to eat without missing my mouth?" Raleigh said.

Aspen frowned and stopped bouncing. "I should keep doing it just to see the perfect one with a messy face," she said, almost starting to bounce again as her phone buzzed.

Rem: *me too. i might go for a drive.*

She bit the inside of her cheek, debating, and then sent what she wanted to send.

Aspen: *are you naked yet*
Rem: *im in underwear*
Aspen: *what kind*
Rem: *pink boyshorts*
Aspen: *pink!!!*

Rem: *not anymore*

Aspen ran her thumb back and forth across the keys, imagining Remington naked.

"Aspen!" Denna shouted, catching her attention and making her jump. "Are you sexting?"

"Not really," Aspen said. "Kind of."

Aspen: *wish i could see*

She sucked in a breath and looked sideways at Denna. "Now I am."

"If you're gonna masturbate, use the couch, and cover yourself with a blanket."

"Fuck you." Aspen stuck her tongue out and turned back to her phone. She sent another text before Remington had a chance to respond.

Aspen: *tell me what youd do*

Rem: *maybe later. i have to get in the shower. ttyl*

Aspen groaned, throwing her phone across the room, making sure it hit the couch and not the wall. "I'm gonna go masturbate now," she told Denna, slinking off the bed.

"How does a text message get you so worked up?" Denna asked, rolling her eyes.

Aspen scowled. "Haven't you ever read an erotic novel?"

"No. Why would I when I have Raleigh?"

Raleigh's expression was wicked. "I have."

Aspen looked at her in shock along with Denna. "You have?" Denna asked, eyebrows shooting up.

"Many times," Raleigh said, wicked expression still in place. "The written word can be very stimulating." She glanced over to Aspen. "What were you discussing with your new lady?"

"She's not my—" Aspen shook her head. "It was just starting to get hot. Then she said she had to go shower, and left," she relayed bitterly.

"Ew. Sorry," Denna said, but her laugh ruined the sentiment.

Aspen had calmed down somewhat, and didn't really feel like getting off anymore, but she still sent Remington a petulant message.

Aspen: *i hate you*

About ten minutes later, her phone buzzed.

Rem: *no you dont. and its good for you not to get everything you want*

Aspen: *youre right i dont but youre wrong about getting what i want. after your drive do you wanna go somewhere with me*

It was another five minutes before Aspen got an answer.

Rem: *like where?*

Aspen: *idk. anywhere*

Rem: *like a date?*

Aspen: *no like going somewhere*

Rem: *youre right. that wouldnt be a date at all*

Aspen: *shut up tease. where you wanna go*

Rem: *how about the drive in*

Aspen: *whats playing*

Rem: *does it matter? i know what youre gonna be looking at*

Aspen: *just come pick me up at dennas*

She sent Denna's address and directions along with her message, and it was a few minutes with no response, so she asked when Remington was going to pick her up.

Rem: *fifteen minutes*

Aspen: *thought you were going for a drive*

Rem: *i said i might. decided not to*

Aspen: *because you want to see me*

Rem: *maybe. maybe not. see you in 15*

She put her phone away, then bounced up from the couch and approached her cuddling friends. "I'm going to the drive-in with Remington. See you guys later. I'll be back sometime to get my car."

"I like your car. Leave the keys so we can joyride." Of course that was Denna.

"Um, no."

"Fine, don't. I'll just hotwire it."

"Fuck off." Aspen laughed, flipping her off as she slipped out the door and shut it behind her. She waved to Denna's father as she crossed the living room to the front door. "Bye, Mr. Ashford."

"See you later, Aspen," he said, giving her a smile and a quick wave before turning back to the television, and then she was out the door.

Chapter Eight

Remington pulled up to the curb roughly fifteen minutes later and reached across to open the passenger door when Aspen got close. "Hey."

"Fuck you," Aspen said with a laugh, sliding into the seat.

Remington snorted and put the car in gear, then pulled out into the street. "Fine, thanks, how are you?"

"Oh, I've been better. You realize it's twice now that you've left me all worked up?"

"Maybe it's because I don't want to be treated like a guy you're gonna fuck and forget," Remington said, tilting her head to the side.

That seemed to take the wind out of Aspen's sails because she stared ahead for a long time, not saying anything. Finally, she asked, "Do you really think I treat you like that?"

Remington waited until she was stopped at a red light, then turned and leaned over the seat, giving Aspen a firm, deep kiss. "No." She sat back down and drove when the light turned green. "I think you have a voracious sexual appetite, but I don't think you're using me. I think you just don't know how else to connect with people because you've never really had someone that liked you for you. Which I do, by the way. Like you." Shit, she hoped that wasn't too much to say, but she wanted Aspen to know she was paying attention. She couldn't look sideways because she had to keep her eyes on the road, but there was no forthcoming yelling, so that was good. Aspen was quiet for a few seconds longer than a normal conversation pause, though.

"Good. Because you know that if I wanted a guy, I could have one, right? Easily?"

Rem thought Aspen's voice sounded choked up and she wanted to look, but she didn't want to crash the car. "Yes, I do know that."

"And I like you too."

The rush in Aspen's voice made Remington grin.

Another few seconds of silence, and then, "You tasted really fucking good just then."

Thank God Aspen changed the subject. Rem licked her lips. "You tasted like a bean burrito."

Aspen snorfled. "I'll eat some fruity candy at the theater."

"Oh, you think I'm going to kiss you again."

"That or I'm going to kiss you."

Remington snickered, eyes still on the road. "I like bean burritos."

"Not sexy." Aspen made a gagging noise. "I'm eating fruity candy."

Aspen ate an entire box of Sour Patch Kids and was now working on a bag of popcorn, which she was sharing with Remington. The movie was about halfway through, and funnily enough, she had been able to mostly watch the screen. It was a good movie actually, with a lot of plot twists. Every so often she glanced at Remington, and every time found Rem watching the movie intently. She squirmed and turned back to the screen, marveling a little at how Remington's self-control seemed to be helping her control herself too, because she didn't want to risk trying to kiss Rem while she was so wrapped up in the movie.

Almost as if she could read Aspen's thoughts, Remington leaned over and kissed her.

Aspen mewled softly, not having expected it but more than willing to accept it, and clutched the popcorn bag tighter as Remington's tongue slipped into her mouth.

The next fifteen minutes were spent just kissing.

Aspen had never kissed someone for so long in her life. It was amazing. She could still feel the warmth of Remington's mouth when they pulled apart. "Wow," she whispered, fluttering her fingertips over her tingling lips. "Marry me?"

Remington laughed and leaned over to kiss her again, just a quick peck this time. "If that was impressive enough for a proposal, you must've been kissing the wrong people."

Aspen couldn't help laughing with her. "Well, I suppose boys don't put as much into kissing and foreplay. I didn't realize what I'd been missing."

Rem's laugh cut off abruptly. "All boys?" she asked, staring at Aspen. "I'm the first girl you've...?"

Aspen stared, something strange swirling in her chest, Remington's reaction making her shy. She bit her lip and nodded.

"Well, fuck me," Remington said, her blank expression unchanged.

"I've been trying," Aspen said, putting a tinge of a whine into her voice.

Just like that, Remington laughed again, and she reached out, shoving Aspen's face.

"Hey," Aspen said, not really upset, and then chewed one of her fingernails, blurting out without ceremony, "I'm nervous about reciprocating. I asked Denna to teach me some things and she kicked me so hard under the table I thought my leg was broken."

Remington stared at her until she wanted to sink through the seat. Finally, when Aspen didn't think she was going to answer at all, and was maybe going to get out of the car and leave her there by herself, Rem responded. "Try the internet."

"Oh my God."

"That's really not what I meant to say." She was looking at Aspen differently now, less panicked and more in control. "When it happens, if you even feel comfortable trying to reciprocate, just follow your instincts, and if you need it, I'll guide you."

Butterflies fluttered in her stomach at Remington's answer, a silly, sheepish grin on her face as she nodded. "And now you will forget that Aspen Wellington ever questioned her ability to perform sexually, in any situation, with any gender, at any time." She snapped her fingers in front of Remington's face.

Remington's expression shifted to that of a zombie. "Yes, Master," she said in a monotonous drone, then snorted with laughter and got out of her seat, throwing one leg over Aspen and settling down astride her lap.

Aspen groaned at the feel of Remington's weight on her thighs, her hands immediately going to Rem's hips with a squeeze. "Oh," she managed to say before Remington kissed her.

Remington's forearms rested on her shoulders, fingers idly twirling strands of her hair as she parted her lips eagerly for Remington's tongue. She swallowed everything Rem had to offer and wanted more. She tried to communicate that with fingertips dug into Remington's waist.

She couldn't keep her hands still when Remington's lips dropped to her throat, leaving a trail of open-mouthed kisses. The cool air of the car's interior bathed her sensitized skin, contrasting with the wet heat of Remington's lips and tongue. She moved her hands up and down Remington's sides, feathering light touches, but when Rem bit down on the space between her neck and shoulder, the light touches vanished, and she gripped Remington's thighs like a vise.

Remington groaned and, encouraged, Aspen started to slide her thumbs back and forth over the crease of Rem's thighs, almost brushing her sex through her jeans.

Aspen noticed that when she moved her thumbs like that, Remington kissed her harder. She experimentally moved her thumbs closer together, rubbing up the seam of the jeans, in awe when Remington jerked at her touch. "It didn't hurt, did it?"

"No, it didn't hurt," Remington replied through clenched teeth.

"Good." Aspen splayed her hands over Remington's back, under her clothes. She scraped her fingernails lightly up either side of Remington's spine and Remington shivered, rolling her shoulders back.

She brushed the hair out of Aspen's eyes. "We should probably—" She stopped talking when she looked at Aspen's face. Aspen hoped she didn't look as desperate as she felt. "Don't look at me like that." Pause. "Stop it." Pause. "Stop!"

"It's our second date already."

"I thought the party wasn't a date."

"Well, if you had no problem making out in a bed before we even had a first date, I don't see why you're suddenly having a problem messing around during an actual date."

"I'm not having a problem," Remington said, climbing off Aspen and back into her own seat. "Or at least I *wasn't*."

Aspen cast her eyes to her lap. "I'm sorry. That was a really stupid thing to say, I didn't mean…" She shook her head. "I just really want you. I'm not trying to be impatient, I swear." When Remington didn't answer, Aspen looked up to find her staring out the front windshield but couldn't read the look on her face. "I'm sorry," she said again. "Do you want to take me home?" Her lower lip quivered, but she swore she wouldn't cry. Even though she'd probably just screwed up her chance of getting to know Remington better by behaving like an ass.

Remington was prepared to snap at whatever Aspen had to say, but she heard the tears in Aspen's voice and all anger fled her chest without looking back. Which wasn't really fair, because Aspen had been the one to be rude, but the thought of making those tears fall made Remington twitchy. She did not want to see Aspen cry, especially not over her. Probably too many people had dismissed Aspen at the first sign of trouble, and Remington wanted her to know that wasn't the case here. But she wasn't about to get sappy, either, so she settled for middle ground. "The movie's not over."

Aspen was staring at her lap. "I'm not sure what that means."

"It means I don't want to take you home, but I'm still a little offended," Remington said, eyes turned to the screen.

"I don't know why I even care, but I do," Aspen said after a few minutes of silence. "The thought of pissing you off enough to not get a third date kind of makes me sick."

"You'll get a third date. Now shut up, this is just getting good," Remington shushed her, though she really had no interest in the movie whatsoever. She just wanted Aspen to stop talking because the more Aspen revealed, the harder it was for her to stay upset. And she liked holding on to her resentments.

"You're not even really watching!" Aspen said. "Your eyes aren't moving with the action."

Remington turned to her with a long-suffering sigh. "All right, Detective Benson, you caught me."

"Ooh, speaking of handcuffs—"

"No."

"You don't even know what I was going to say."

"No."

"I could have been going to say that I saw a pair in a store window for all you know!"

"You didn't."

"That's not the point."

"It is the point, because I did know what you were going to say.

And you're not putting any handcuffs on me." Remington didn't trust anybody to restrain her like that, not even a really gorgeous girl who was begging her for a third date.

Aspen smiled, her nose crinkling up as she let out a tiny laugh. That was incredibly cute. "No, I was going to say you could use them on *me* sometime. Jeez."

"Oh." Rem's heart raced. "Maybe." She tried not to get carried away picturing Aspen handcuffed to her bed. "Why are we talking about this?"

"For the future, if we get that far," Aspen said, her words all rushed together. "I'm not trying to manipulate you into going faster."

"Don't misunderstand," Remington said. "I want to. I just—I was brought up a certain way, and it's hard to get past that." What she wouldn't give right now to have been brought up in Europe.

Aspen nodded. "I can understand that. I'm just—I'm just not used to being told no." She laughed a little, though there really shouldn't have been anything funny about it.

"I'm not telling you no," Remington said. "I'm just telling you not tonight."

"So you do think I'm a hot piece of ass, right?"

Remington fought the instinct to comment on the self-deprecating nature of that question and smiled at Aspen instead. "Something like that."

"So what do you want to do for our next date?" Aspen asked after a few seconds.

"This one's not over yet!"

"I know, but as soon as you drop me off, it's all I'll be able to think about. You kind of invade my mind, like all the time, and it kind of drives me crazy."

Remington glanced at her sideways. "I think about you sometimes too," she said. "Mostly the way you quivered that day in the cafeteria."

"Um."

Rem cringed. Realizing her heartfelt confession wasn't exactly well received, she hastened to add something else. "And how pretty you are." When Aspen still wasn't impressed, she scrunched up her face and asked, "Does that make me fucked up? Fantasizing about how scared you were when I had you by the collar?" And yet, she just kept talking. "Because I haven't done that in a while, actually. Not since I started to actually like you."

"Please, do keep talking," Aspen said.

Remington's cheeks grew uncharacteristically warm. "Well, I'm new at this talking to peers about feelings thing. I also fantasize about—" She didn't get the rest of her sentence out because Aspen had leaned over the gearshift and kissed her, hard.

"I was kidding, Remington. You had me hooked at fucked up."

"You don't want to know what else I fantasize about?" Remington asked, her voice gone low and smoky after that kiss.

Aspen got up onto her knees and leaned closer, her lips to Remington's ear. "All right. Tell me."

Remington shivered, warm breath on her ear momentarily distracting her, but she licked her lips and continued. "I've thought about you begging me for things," she said.

"And do you give them to me?" Aspen gently nibbled at the shell of her ear.

Remington sucked in a breath, closing her eyes. "I don't know. I never get that far before I come."

Aspen made a strangled sound, losing her balance and falling forward across Remington, into the door. "Holy sh—fuck, woman," she croaked, bracing with her hands and pushing off the door, back to her knees.

Remington watched the entire thing happen, too intent on watching to think to help. When Aspen was back upright, Rem tilted her head to the side, looking over at her. "What?"

"Nothing," Aspen said, rubbing her shoulder, which had taken the brunt of the impact. "So, me begging gets you off?"

Remington nodded, the movement in slow motion. "In my head, anyway."

"We could see. What do you want me to beg for?"

Remington glowered at her. "You can start with a ride home."

Aspen bit her lip in a way that reminded Rem of a damsel in distress from an old black-and-white movie. She leaned forward again, one hand on the storage compartment between the seats and the other resting lightly on Remington's inner thigh. "Please, Remington, can I have a ride home? I'm sorry I made you angry, but please don't make me walk. It's dark outside, and cold, and it could be dangerous." She slid her hand higher. "Please, I'll do anything you want, just don't make me walk home."

Remington was suddenly breathing fast, her entire focus narrowed to the words pouring from Aspen's lips and the hand teasing her thigh. That *word*, please, in that desperate tone, even if it was only mocking. Her throat was almost too dry to swallow. When she did, it hurt. "Aspen," she said, the dryness of her throat making her voice crack. Her eyelids wanted to shut, but she kept them open. She rocked her hips subtly forward without permission from her higher brain functions. "That's not fair. I can't do this in a car at a movie like this. I can't. You're making me want to so badly, and I can't."

Aspen immediately drew her hand away. "Remington, I didn't— wow. I'm sorry. I won't tease."

Remington took a slow breath. "It's okay," she finally said, shaking her head to clear it. The credits were rolling. "You ready to go?" She forced her voice to sound casual.

"Yeah," Aspen said, adjusting to sit on her bottom and putting her seat belt on. "So, there's a football game Friday night."

"Isn't there a football game every Friday night?"

"There wasn't last night. We went to a party, remember?"

"Right," Remington said, mouth quirking at the memory of Aspen on Riker's bed.

"*Anyway*, do you want to come watch me cheer?"

If it were anyone else asking her that, Remington wouldn't have been able to think of anything she wanted to do less. But since it was Aspen, she considered it. "What time does it start? I have to work next Friday until nine."

"Oh," Aspen said, her face falling, but then brightening back up. "Well, it starts at eight, but we don't go on until halftime. You could still make it in time."

"Do you get to leave after halftime?" Remington crossed her proverbial fingers.

"No, but I can sit with you in the stands for the second half, and we can make fun of the jocks if you want."

"Ha! You realize you are a jock, right?"

"I am not! I'm a feminine, sultry cheerleader with no athletic ability whatsoever except dancing!"

"You're a jock, Aspen." Remington grinned. "But I like you anyway."

"Aww, you like me?" Aspen asked, putting a hand to her heart as Remington started the car. "My night is complete."

"Shut up, jock."

"Whatever, gangbanger."

"Gangbanger!" Remington nearly shrieked. "Hardly!"

"You wear leather and scare people off whenever you can. Gangbanger."

"Don't be stupid. To be a gangbanger you have to have a gang. I'm a loner, if you hadn't noticed." And honestly, where had that term even come from? Nobody said gangbanger anymore, ever.

"And I don't play sports."

"I can't believe we're actually having an entire discussion about this." Remington snickered, shaking her head as she pulled out of the drive-in. She started for Denna's house, where Aspen had left her car.

When she pulled up, she leaned over and gave Aspen a quick but gentle good-night kiss, keeping her tongue in her own mouth, not wanting to risk losing control again.

"So, Friday?" Aspen asked, leaning down to look through the door after she'd gotten out of the car.

Remington stared ahead, sucking one side of her bottom lip in thought, and then sighed, looking over at Aspen. "Okay. I'll be there by halftime."

Aspen grinned, blowing her a kiss. "I'll save you a seat."

CHAPTER NINE

Denna looked up from the table mid forkful of rice as Aspen burst into her house wearing a silly grin. "No, that's okay, no need to knock," she said, lowering her fork back to her plate. "Sorry, Dad."

Her dad chuckled. "You're not used to it yet?" he asked. "No, I guess you're usually in your bedroom when she comes in. It's a good thing we don't live in a dangerous neighborhood, Aspen, or we'd have to keep the door locked."

Aspen grinned wider and sat down, looking over the spread. "What are we having?"

Denna knew that her dad was aware of what kind of parents Aspen had, and she thought it was pretty cool of him that he never complained about her being over for dinner. Sometimes he even made a little extra. Denna doubted that Aspen's parents had ever cooked for her a day in their lives. They most likely had kitchen staff for that.

"Chicken and rice," her dad answered. "And broccoli."

Aspen made a face at the broccoli but spooned one tiny piece onto her plate. She loaded it with chicken and rice, though.

"Don't eat too much broccoli," Denna said, pointing her fork at Aspen's plate and then rolling her eyes.

Aspen kicked her under the table.

"Ow. If Raleigh were here we'd be getting a ten-minute speech thanks to you on chloroform or photosynthesis or some vegetable process and why you should always have a full serving with every meal."

Her dad choked on his chicken, turning away. "I think you mean chlorophyll, Den. Chloroform is what they use in movies to knock people out."

Aspen's glee was annoying. "And then after that, we'd be getting a twenty-minute speech, thanks to you, on the importance of paying attention to Raleigh's speeches so that you can avoid making mistakes like referring to chlorophyll as chloroform."

Denna stewed in silence for a few seconds, then frowned at Aspen. "I'm telling."

Aspen inhaled so hard that she basically choked, and she spluttered and flailed at Denna. "What are you, five?! Where is Raleigh, anyway?"

Denna's amusement faded and she set her fork on her plate, *feeling* like she was about five. "She's at a debate."

"Why aren't you with her?"

Now Denna turned sad, pitiful eyes to her father. "Because I'm grounded."

That, of course, amused Aspen no end. "What did you do?" The gleeful tone was not appreciated.

Denna refused to answer.

"I found marijuana in her room," her dad said. "Don't pout at me, Den. You'll be eighteen in a month and you can do what you like, but until then, you know I'm not going to put up with drugs in my house."

"I know," Denna said. "But I'm so annoyed. She really wanted me to go with her. Can I be excused?"

He waved his hand. "You're seventeen. You don't have to ask to be excused. But it's rude to leave Aspen at the table, don't you think?"

"Aspen can handle herself," Denna said, pissed that her dad wouldn't change his mind and let her go. Going late would be better than not going at all. She left her plate on the table and stalked off to her room. She could still hear them even after she slammed the door.

"I'm sorry, Aspen. I guess you're stuck with me. A poor excuse for company, I know."

"I'm used to her being grumpy when she doesn't get her way."

"Any advice?"

Denna couldn't believe they were talking about her like she wasn't twenty feet away.

"Don't interrupt her during—homework."

She knew Aspen was almost going to say *sex* and if she wasn't so pissed to hell she probably would have laughed.

"Homework?"

"She hates it when you interrupt her concentration."

"I'll keep that in mind. How's the chicken?"

"Ungh. Delicious."

Denna swore she could hear Aspen *chewing*. Maybe if Aspen kept *chewing*, Aspen would stop *talking*, and not almost mention sex to her dad.

The longer she sat there, the more restless she got, and she hadn't even realized she was crying until she felt her face was wet. She hated crying and everything was starting to go red. Another few seconds and she couldn't take it anymore. She stormed back out to the dining room and picked up her plate, then slammed it back down on the table. "It's not fair!" she shouted, slamming her plate again.

"Denna, that's enough," her dad said.

A tiny part of her, way in the back of her mind, registered that his voice was gaining an edge that didn't belong there. The front of her mind wouldn't let her care. "Or what?" she screamed. "You're going to hit me like Aspen's father, kill somebody like Remington's, or lock me out of the house like Raleigh's?!" Her vision was starting to blur.

"No," her dad said quietly. "Go back to your room and don't leave it until you're ready to apologize to me and your friend."

There was nowhere for the rage to go but out. She picked up her plate again and hurled it with all her strength at the wall. She felt a brief lull of emotion long enough for her to retreat to her room and throw herself on her bed.

Aspen watched her go, horrified.

Denna's dad turned to her. "I am so, so sorry, Aspen," he said, shaking his head. "Sometimes I don't know what comes over her."

"Me either," Aspen said. "It didn't used to happen this much, did it?"

"No," Arthur said. "It's gotten worse this year. Is there anything you know of that she might not have told her old dad about? Something bothering her?"

"The only stress I can think of is Jason's parole hearing coming up, but she hasn't said anything about being nervous for Raleigh about it, or anything," Aspen said, trying to think. "She's funny and rude, same as always." She wanted to tell him that she knew Raleigh worried about Denna, but she didn't want to bring up Denna's mom. She had talked about that with Denna before, but never with Arthur. It just seemed like none of her business and she didn't want Arthur mad at her for butting in. Denna's house was her sanctuary, and if she couldn't come here anymore, she didn't know what she would do. "So, I just, I don't know." She shrugged.

He gave her a moment, and then asked, "Your father hits you, honey?"

Aspen's stomach tried to drop out of her body. She could feel the motion, like being seasick. She tried to speak and couldn't find her voice, so she swallowed and tried again. "It was just once." Having to tell him that was humiliating. Why had Denna said that?

"Are you sure?" Arthur asked, his eyes searching her face, and when she nodded, he nodded. "All right. I hope you know you can come tell me if it happens again and you need someone to help you."

She nodded again. "Thank you. I'm going to go talk to her."

"That's not a wise idea, but I won't stop you if you're hell-bent on it."

"I am," Aspen said, resolved to give Denna a genuine piece of her mind. She took her plate and fork to the kitchen and washed them before going to Denna's room.

"Get out!" Denna shrieked, and Aspen ducked as something flew at her head.

"I will not!" she shrieked back, slamming the door behind her. "Do you have any fucking idea how lucky you are to have a father like that? ANY FUCKING IDEA?!" Tears streamed down her face. She seemed to have shocked Denna into stillness because Denna just sat on the bed and stared at her. "He doesn't hit you, he doesn't lock you out of the house, he doesn't yell at you, and he cares enough to give a shit whether you fuck your life up! And you treat him like that?! Like an ungrateful little bitch?! You should be ashamed of yourself! You should be on your knees thanking God that you don't have a father who parades you around in fancy dresses in front of his friends, trying to push you into the arms of the highest bidder and ignoring you the rest of the time, who never put any of your artwork on the fridge, never kept any of your Father's Day presents, never spent a moment of his time getting to know *anything* about you!" she screamed.

Denna was crying too by the time she was finished, mouth dropped open but no sound coming out. She turned and lay down, hiding her face in her pillows.

Aspen was about to keep yelling, but she noticed the tinge of red to Denna's cheeks and realized Denna had turned away out of embarrassment, not anger. She climbed into bed and pressed her body to Denna's back, draping one arm around her and squeezing tight. "Why did you tell him about my father?" she whispered after they lay there for a long, long time.

Denna was quiet for another long moment, then answered softly. "I'm sorry."

"But why?" Aspen insisted, wiping her hand over the dried tear tracks on her face.

"I wasn't thinking about what I was saying enough to stop myself. I'm really sorry, Aspen." And then in a tiny voice, sounding more unsure than Aspen had ever heard her, "Are you still my friend?"

"I wouldn't be in your bed if I wasn't," Aspen said.

"Would you mind waiting here while I go talk to my dad and clean up my mess?"

Aspen just nodded and wiggled around until she could pull the sheet and blankets up over her.

Denna took a deep breath and left Aspen in her bedroom. The first thing she did was carefully sweep up the broken plate and put it in the trash, then she made her way out to the living room where she knew her dad would be watching TV. "Dad?" she said, barely loud enough to hear over the football game. "I'll pay for a new plate."

Her dad shut off the television, and he looked like he didn't know what to say to her. "All right."

"I cleaned it up."

"Okay."

She was right. He didn't know what to say to her. "I'm so sorry."

"Sorry for breaking the plate or sorry for screaming at me and being hurtful?"

She started to cry again. "For both. I know you're being fair. And you always keep my Father's Day presents. Dad, please don't hate me, I'm so sorry."

"I could never hate you. Ever, Den. I love you to pieces. I just don't understand what goes on in your head sometimes. Why do you get so out of control like that? Is it a mistake I've been making since your mother left?"

The mention of her mother made her eyes go wide. They never talked about her. "No!" she said in a rush. "You're not doing anything wrong. I just get so mad when I can't have what I want. I don't know why. But I don't mean to hurt you, and I swear it's nothing you're doing. Maybe I need to see a therapist or something," she said, hiding her face in her hands.

"If you really want to, you know I'll pay for it, but maybe it's just a phase, a teenager thing." He stood up and hugged her. "Would it help to have a consequence?"

"Like what?" she asked, hugging him back tighter.

"I don't know. If you break something, you have to do a certain number of hours of housework to make it up, you can't just pay me back. And every time you scream at me you're grounded an extra day, and that means nobody coming over here, either."

"Okay," she said, nodding into his shoulder. "I think I'll hate that. But I don't want to keep hurting you, because you really are the best dad I know. I just—it's easy for me to take things for granted."

"Okay then, I'm glad we have a plan. You can spend the next hour cleaning your bathroom and your bedroom, and you can send Aspen home. No Raleigh tonight, either."

"We're starting now?" Denna said, looking at him pitifully.

He just shrugged and looked down at her. "It's up to you, Den."

She sighed and nodded, stamping her foot a little, but otherwise being gracious. "We're starting now," she said in resignation. She gave him another quick hug and then retreated to her room, flopping on top of Aspen. "You have to go home now. We worked out extra punishment."

"You worked out extra punishment," Aspen said, her face screwed up.

"Don't ask. Just go home." Denna groaned, rolling to the side so Aspen could get up.

Aspen snickered and got out of the bed, nudging Denna with her knee. "Bye, then."

"Bye."

"Can I come back tomorrow?"

"Ask my dad on the way out. I don't know."

She heard Aspen ask and she heard her dad say yes, and that was at least comforting. She liked having people here. Raleigh mostly, but Aspen too.

She texted Raleigh before she started cleaning her bathroom.

Denna: *hey baby, im so sorry but you cant come over tonight. im in trouble for yelling at my dad and breaking a plate and we came to a decision that being grounded means no one can come over here either. i wish you had been here. i miss you*

She started cleaning, and about a half hour later, when she knew the debate would be ending, she took a break to check her phone. Raleigh's message surprised her.

Raleigh: *Denna, you are very lucky I was not there. I would have left.*

Denna: *what? why?*

Raleigh: *Denna, I would have left because had I witnessed such a spectacle, my disappointment in the girl I love would have been too overwhelming to handle. My urge to KICK YOUR FUCKING ASS would have been too great to ignore. And seeing as how we do not have an ass-kicking agreement between us, I would have been forced to leave.*

Denna sat there, stunned, tingling to the roots of her hair. She couldn't believe Raleigh had used caps lock, among other things. All she could send back was—

Denna: *oh*

—before she quickly busied herself cleaning for the rest of her allotted punishment time. Her bathroom had never looked so nice.

After a shower, she noticed her message light blinking and opened her phone, melting onto the bed.

Raleigh: *Denna, I love you.*

She smiled at the phone, her heart fluttering, and quickly sent back a message.

Denna: *i love you too. so much. maybe we should talk about an ass kicking agreement*

Raleigh: *Denna, no.*

She laughed and snuggled with her phone in the absence of having the real Raleigh to snuggle with and climbed under the covers.

❖

Aspen couldn't sleep. It was like she couldn't find a comfortable position, or a comfortable temperature. Too hot with the blankets on, too cold with them off. Too hot with her socks on, too cold with them off. Finally, she gave up and stared at her phone, wondering if Remington might still be awake. It was almost midnight. But she had no idea how late Remington stayed up. A little text couldn't hurt, right? If she was asleep it probably wouldn't even wake her up.

Aspen: *psst. you awake?*

Her phone rang almost instantly.

"I am now."

"Oh, please. That was way too fast for you to have been asleep." Aspen grinned. Remington had called her like the very instant she texted. That was promising. Very promising.

"Okay, you got me. Why aren't you asleep?"

Aspen grunted her displeasure. "I can't get comfortable. I've been trying for an hour. I'm too hot, then too cold, then my pillow is too smothery, but I can't sleep without a pillow because it hurts my neck..."

Remington laughed. "That does sound like a problem. I'm sorry, it sucks."

"Yeah. So I just wanted to say hi, if you were awake." *You're stupid, Aspen.*

"Well, I'm awake."

"Yeah."

"So are you gonna say hi, or what?"

Aspen spluttered out a laugh and rolled onto her stomach. "Hi."

She could practically *hear* Remington grinning. "Hi."

She rolled onto her back again and tried to get comfortable. "Do you still like me?"

"You mean still as in I liked you earlier today and do I still like you the same night?"

"Uh...yeah."

Remington's laugh was sweeter this time. "Yes. I still like you. Do you still like me?"

Aspen didn't want to sound too eager, so she made herself wait until Remington finished the question. "Yes."

"Now that you know I still like you, do you think you can sleep? Or should I read you a story?"

The teasing made Aspen's stomach flutter and she closed her eyes. "I think I can sleep."

"Okay. See you tomorrow."

"Night."

Aspen held the phone to her chest after she hung up and settled down to try to sleep again.

❖

Raleigh checked on Danny and Joey to make sure they'd gotten to bed okay, then got ready for bed herself and lay staring at the ceiling. Denna's temper was getting worse. It was mostly little things, like clenched fists and gritted teeth, which wouldn't be worrying if there were good reasons for them, but she noticed it when anyone told Denna no. She noticed it when Denna dropped something and had to pick it up. She noticed it when someone barely bumped into Denna in the halls at school.

Now she was breaking plates?

Raleigh wished so badly that she could get inside Denna's head for five minutes just to feel what she felt. If she could do that, she would know how to help.

Why were there so many people in her life who needed help that she couldn't help? Was the universe trying to make her feel helpless for some reason? Aspen, getting hit and mistreated, and Denna, whom she wanted desperately to see a therapist, but she was afraid to suggest it because she didn't want to hurt the girl she loved. She didn't want to see the look on Denna's face that would say, "You think I'm crazy." Because she did not think Denna was crazy, and she would never even use that word, but that's what Denna would think. Raleigh did think, however, that Denna had something going on that she was not in control of. Whether it was a mental illness or it was something that could be helped with therapy, she just had to muster the courage to bring it up.

And then there was Danny. Jason's parole hearing was coming up and she knew Danny wanted to testify. But what if it traumatized him? What if it traumatized both of them? What if they both got up there and poured their hearts out and then the parole board let him out anyway? Would Danny regress and start wetting the bed again? Would Jason come for them in their sleep and hurt them for testifying? And what would he do to Joey? The same things, or would it be worse now that he'd been in prison for almost eight years?

Not for the first time, Raleigh wished that parole didn't even exist. The idea of Jason getting out of prison twelve years early was paralyzing. She could take care of herself now, mostly, but she wasn't home every hour of every day to protect her little brothers, and the thought nauseated her.

She tried to turn off her brain, but it wasn't a very accommodating brain. She rolled onto her stomach and put a pillow over her head, trying to drown out her thoughts, but they were internal, so it was useless. Everything was useless. Her life was basically in limbo until after the hearing, and that was not a nice place to be.

She wished Denna wasn't grounded. It was so much easier to stop thinking about the terrors in the night when Denna was lying next to her, in her arms.

It was well past two in the morning before she finally fell asleep.

CHAPTER TEN

When Aspen got to Denna's the next afternoon, her bedroom door was locked. That could only mean one thing. Who cared, though? She pulled out one of her credit cards, wedging it between the door and the doorframe, then slid it downward to trip the latch bolt and open the door.

Denna was in bed with Raleigh and snapped her head around. When she saw Aspen, her eyes narrowed and she let out a growl. "Aspen Allegra! I swear to God, how many times have I told you, if the door is locked, GO AWAY!"

"I'm bored," Aspen said, making sure the door was still locked when she closed it. "Entertain me."

"Just ignore her," Raleigh said through gritted teeth.

Denna scowled but returned to her task and Aspen flopped face-first onto the couch to wait. It wasn't too long before her friends stopped making out, Denna still scowling at her.

"I'm getting a deadbolt."

"I'll figure out how to use hairpins or something. Don't bother."

"Can't you get new friends?" Denna said, but Aspen knew she didn't really mean it. They said things like that to each other all the time.

"Sorry. I can't."

"Hey!" Denna said as Raleigh pulled a baggie out of her jeans pocket. "None of that in my room anymore, I told you."

"I promise not to leave it behind this time."

Denna shook her head. "Go outside. I am not getting grounded again because of something I didn't even do." As Raleigh sighed and turned to head for the sliding glass doors, Denna sat up straighter. "Wait! Let's make a deal. You can do it in here if you play your guitar for me."

"I'll be going outside," Raleigh said.

Aspen had a snicker fit and climbed off the couch. "I'm going with her. See you in ten." She slipped out the door after Raleigh and shut it.

"Who says I'm sharing?"

"I say. And I have a question for you."

"I'll alert the media."

"Oh, you're so funny I can't stand it," Aspen said, rolling her eyes.

"What do you wish to know?" Raleigh asked. She packed her very colorful pipe with a very delicious-looking bud and flicked her lighter, then took a long inhale.

"You play guitar?"

Raleigh held in the smoke and then let it out slowly. "I took one lesson, and the guitar has been collecting dust in my closet for three years."

"Then why does Denna want you to play it?"

"Because she has some rock star fantasy? I have no idea." Raleigh snorted. "Rock star I am not."

"You could still play her something."

"I can play three chords. My life's ambition does not include making the sounds of a dying cat with a musical instrument."

Aspen took the offered pipe and lit it up, sucking in as much as she could. Her lungs burned, but she held in the smoke until she had to breathe. She exhaled right in Raleigh's face. "You're a terrible girlfriend."

"Not true," Raleigh said, taking the pipe back. "I am merely waiting for something I want enough to trade."

"Blackmailer!"

"Please do study harder, Aspen. It's bribery, not blackmail."

"Speaking of using the wrong term, you should have heard Denna last night. She said chloroform instead of chlorophyll."

Raleigh made a very disapproving face. Almost a frown. "Oh dear." She took another hit. "She is so smart, it outrages me that she refuses to retain any academic knowledge outside the standard reading, writing, and mathematics."

"Well, now you have your blackmail. Or bribery, or whatever the fuck."

"I don't know that hearing me butcher 'Mary Had a Little Lamb' would be enough motivation for such a monumental task."

"And you won't know until you bring it up. Want me to test the waters, so to speak?"

"I do not, thank you," Raleigh said with urgency, turning the pipe upside down and tapping the ash out onto the ground.

Aspen laughed and moved to the door but stopped at her name.

"Aspen?"

"Yeah?" She turned back around.

"Was it horrifying?"

"Was what horrifying?"

"Last night, with Denna. Were you scared? Did she seem dissociated?"

"Oh. It was pretty horrifying, but I wasn't scared. And I don't know what dissociated means. I mean she flew into an irrational rage."

"Dissociated means your mind breaks off and takes you somewhere else while another part of you stays behind."

"Why are you asking that?"

Raleigh's eyes cast to the ground and her lower lip quivered. She looked different than Aspen had ever seen her. "From what Denna's told me about her mother, I think she was an undiagnosed schizophrenic."

"What?" Aspen knew there had been issues, but she didn't know enough about psychology stuff to come to any conclusions about Rose. "No," she said, sitting on the garden wall next to Raleigh. "She's not schizophrenic, Ral. She was just pissed off." At least Aspen thought she was just pissed off, but what did she really know about schizophrenia? Not really more than nothing. Her brows furrowed, wheels starting to turn that hadn't been turning before.

Raleigh shook her head and wiped at a tear. "I always worry."

Aspen hadn't ever thought she'd live to see the day Raleigh cried. "We all worry about people we love," she said, not sure what else to say.

Raleigh stopped crying as quickly as she'd started and pocketed her pipe, pushing off the wall to her feet. Aspen couldn't help feeling closer to her after being allowed to see past the veil, however briefly.

"The next time the door is locked, stay out," Raleigh said, and moved past Aspen, back toward the house.

"Ral?" Aspen asked.

"What?" Raleigh asked, vulnerability replaced by obvious annoyance.

Aspen paused, fumbling with the waistband of her jeans. "If Denna does have something wrong, you're not going to…?"

Raleigh's eyes flashed dangerously, and Aspen almost backed away. "What the fuck is wrong with you?" she said, hands clenching into fists at her sides. "I would never leave her. Ever."

"I'm sorry!" Aspen said. "I didn't think you would, but I had to ask."

"Go inside before the temptation to use your head as a bowling ball becomes too great to resist."

Aspen hauled her ass back into the house and scrambled onto Denna's bed, trying to wedge herself between Denna and the wall.

"What the fuck are you doing?" Denna asked, trying to get up, but Aspen wrapped her arms around Denna's waist to hold her in place.

Raleigh stepped inside and closed the door, flicking the lock, and walked to the foot of the bed. "You realize that what I am seeing right now is you in my girlfriend's bed with your hands on her."

Aspen dove out from behind Denna, throwing her hands in the air. "Hands off! Hands off! They weren't in any inappropriate places!"

"See to it that they never are," Raleigh said, fixing Aspen with a glare as she sat on the bed next to Denna. "Hello, dear." She smiled in a way that let Aspen know something terrible was coming. "Would you be so kind as to tell me the difference between chlorophyll and chloroform?"

Now Denna shot a glare at Aspen, and if looks could kill. "Chloroform is what they use in movies to knock people out." Denna repeated what Arthur had told her.

"Mm-hmm. And chlorophyll?"

Denna's face screwed up and her hands picked at her blanket. "Plants!" she finally blurted out.

"What about plants?"

"It's something to do with plants," Denna said, blushing.

Raleigh sighed. "All right," she said, and Aspen felt kind of bad for tattling. "You could know a hundred times more than that if you tried."

"Has it ever occurred to you that maybe I do try and I'm just stupid?" Denna asked, her voice raising a little with each few words.

"Not once," Raleigh said without missing a beat. "Don't give me that."

"I'm just not interested in things that don't matter."

"How can you possibly think that *any* type of knowledge doesn't matter?" Raleigh asked, clearly displeased. Aspen was totally with Denna on this one, though. Who gave a shit about chlorophyll? "I find that statement inane and offensive."

"And I find your condescension intolerable," Denna shot back. "If I don't feel like remembering what chlorophyll is, then I won't. It's a pointless piece of knowledge that I'd never need to use for anything as long as I live."

"Except to make your girlfriend happy," Aspen said.

"Shut up," Raleigh and Denna said at almost the same time.

Raleigh turned to Denna. She was quiet for several minutes before speaking. "I know three chords on the guitar."

"I'm sorry, did we just have a *Twilight Zone* subject switch?" Denna asked, shaking her head with an exaggerated blink.

"As highly amusing as I find your wit, please refrain," Raleigh said. "My point is simple. You want to hear me murder your ears with my guitar. I want you to do something for me too."

Denna's eyes widened. "Like blackmail." She almost breathed the words instead of spoke them.

"Oh, for the love of God," Raleigh said, putting her thumb and forefinger to the bridge of her nose. "Bribery, Denna. Not blackmail."

Aspen snickered. "I said the same thing," she stage-whispered to Denna.

"Well, aren't we ignorant," Denna stage-whispered back. But then she went from joking to, well, bubbly was the only word Aspen could think to describe the way she perked up and bounced on the bed. "What do you want me to do?"

Raleigh turned to Aspen. "Would you mind giving us a few minutes? Please?"

Aspen tried not to gape at the polite way Raleigh had just asked her to leave. Raleigh was never polite to her. This was obviously serious. "Yeah. Of course," she said, moving to the door. "Just come rescue Arthur from me when you're done talking?"

Raleigh actually smiled at her. "Will do."

"Okay then." She pulled open the door and stepped out, shutting it quietly behind her.

Raleigh waited until the door was closed and she heard footsteps receding before she sat next to Denna. Denna was staring at the bed and Raleigh could tell she was nervous. "Hey," she said, putting a finger under Denna's chin and lifting her head. "I love you. Don't be afraid just because I want to talk to you about something important."

Denna nodded and leaned forward, letting Raleigh hug her. "I'll try."

"It's nothing bad," Raleigh said, giving Denna a squeeze and then letting go. "I just wanted to talk about what I always sort of throw out there casually, which is you living up to your potential. We've never actually had a serious talk about it. Sometimes I wonder if you think I'm just joking, but I'm not, Den."

"I don't think you're joking, exactly. I just never know how to answer."

"Do you think if I made up some notes for you, you could study them? Would that be better than reading your textbooks? Because don't think I don't notice when you skip to the questions at the end without reading the chapters."

"The chapters are all so long," Denna said with a sigh.

"We're in twelfth grade," she said, giving Denna a look. "Of course they're going to be long."

"I guess I would rather look at notes from you than Methuselah-era textbooks."

Raleigh barked out a laugh. "Methuselah-era textbooks. Don't ever try to tell me you're stupid again, Denna."

Denna looked at her a little sheepishly but finally nodded. "I'll read your notes. I like that you want to help me. I just don't like science or history or English or math."

She stared. "I'll ask Mrs. Corcoran to move you to a music and nap time schedule."

"Perfect," Denna said with a purr, snuggling up to her again.

Raleigh kissed the top of her head. "But really, though, you'll try harder?"

"Yes, I promise."

Raleigh wanted to bring up her worries about Denna's temper, but when she opened her mouth to say something, she chickened out. "After you ace a few tests I'll get that nasty, dust-covered relic out of my closet and show you the *three* chords I know how to play."

CHAPTER ELEVEN

At 4:15 on Friday, Bryce Tanner and a bunch of other football players came into the diner.

"Hey, Remington," Bryce said with a smile and a little wave as they approached the counter.

Remington gave no reply, simply waiting for them to order.

"Hey," said one of the guys, who Rem thought was really short for a football player. He pointed at her. "Weren't you at the party last week with Aspen Wellington?"

Remington still gave no answer.

"Oh man, that chick is so loose." A third guy laughed, a big, beefy linebacker with greasy hair and a lecherous smile. Stefan Drumm. Remington was disgusted just by his presence.

"Dude, don't be like that," the short guy said, smacking Stefan's arm.

Remington's eye twitched. One of those little muscle spasms that she hated.

"What, jealous because you haven't got in her pants?" Stefan taunted her.

Remington slammed her palms down on the counter and all eyes snapped to her.

Stefan grinned wider. "You too, huh? Damn, she must've been on the rag or something. You know, you wouldn't run into that problem if you weren't a dyke."

"Shut up, Stefan," Bryce said.

Remington ached to rip off his balls, but unfortunately that would land her in jail, and she had a date tonight, plus a promise to her mother.

"What's the matter, Tanner? You haven't fucked the whore either?"

Remington vaulted the counter and was on him before he had a chance to duck out of the way. He was bigger than she was, but she was quicker, and craftier, and more ruthless, and she managed to break his nose with an elbow before he even got a hit in.

He was still reeling from her sucker punch, and Remington kneed him in the groin, making him double over. Enraged, he threw a fist at her chest, knocking her backward into the counter, clutching his balls with his other hand. She might not be able to rip them off, but she could at least injure them.

The other guys tried to pull him off once the two got going again, not daring to touch Remington. He managed to shrug them off and wrapped a hand around Remington's throat, squeezing.

Fury building by the second, she ducked her head and bit him, hard enough to make him let go, then quickly grabbed his right hand and bent two of his fingers back until she heard them crunch.

Stefan shouted, his eyes wide, but before he could lunge for her again, the other guys doubled their efforts to get him out the door, and they were finally successful.

Bryce popped his head back in. "You won't see him in here again. And I'm sorry about what he said. I think it's hot that you're a—I mean that you—" He shook his head. "Going now."

When the jocks were gone, a nice, quiet couple who had been eating at a corner booth stood up and made their way toward her. "Um, could we get a to-go box?" the man asked. "If it's not too much trouble."

"I am so sorry about that," Remington said, visions of losing her job floating through her brain. "Please enjoy your meal on the house, and I'll grab you that box right now."

"Your nose is bleeding," he said as she went back around behind the counter.

She grabbed a box and handed it to him with a nod. "Thank you. I'll take care of that. I'm really sorry again, sir."

"It wasn't your fault," he said, turning to shuffle back to his table.

Once the restaurant was empty, Rem glanced at the schedule to see who was coming to relieve her, then looked up his number on the phone list and called him. "Antonio?" she asked. "It's Remington. Can you come in like ten minutes early? Awesome, thanks. See you then."

She hung up, relieved. At least she'd have ten minutes to run home and change her shirt so Aspen didn't drop dead when she saw her.

She had to be careful, because now that the adrenaline had worn off, her face hurt like fucking hell.

❖

She got to the high school at twenty after nine, just about halftime; she saw there were two minutes left on the clock. Hands shoved into the pockets of her jacket, she made her way up into the stands, then down the side stairs to where she saw the cheerleaders sitting. "Hey," she said, sliding into an empty spot behind Aspen.

"Hey," Aspen said, leaning back between Remington's knees, draping her arms over Rem's thighs.

"How's the game going?"

"We're getting our asses kicked. Stefan isn't playing."

Remington tensed at the mention of him.

"What's wrong?"

"He called me a dyke. And you a whore."

"What are you—that was *you*?" Aspen said, sitting up and spinning around. "You kicked Stefan Drumm's ass? And lived? What did you do, shoot him?"

Remington blinked. "You doubt my hand-to-hand combat skills enough to ask if I shot him?"

"He's like a fucking giant bulldozer!" Aspen said. "Oh my God. You are so badass. I can't even." But then she frowned, reaching up to lightly touch Remington's cheek. "It looks a little swollen. Are you okay?"

Remington glanced around, trying not to flinch away from the touch because she knew it would upset Aspen, but they were in *public*. "I'm fine; it's fine," she said, unable to keep herself from leaning away just a little bit.

The whistle blew and Aspen leaned up to kiss her other cheek. "Gotta go. Make sure you watch, okay? The whole time. You can see that far, right?"

"I can s—" Rem stopped talking and just shook her head, giving Aspen's ass a smack as she stood up.

Aspen gasped and turned around, then straddled Remington's lap without warning. "If you do things like that to me in public I'm going to do things like this to you," she said, dropping her head and latching on to Remington's neck with her lips, sucking hard enough to leave a mark before Remington could push her off.

Denna snickered as she walked by on her way to the field, behind Raleigh. "I told you to eat before the game, Aspen."

"You know I'm always hungry," Aspen said back with a wicked smile, running her fingers through Remington's hair as she stood up again and followed Denna.

Remington watched her go.

When they were out of the bleachers and headed onto the field, Aspen relayed her new information to Denna and Raleigh. "You know my g—my f—Remington was the one who took out Stefan," she said, suddenly flustered. What the fuck had she almost just said?

"Your girlfriend? Oh, that is too rich," Denna said, laughing, but stopped when Raleigh reached back and pinched her. "Ow."

Aspen panicked to the point she almost forgot the routine, but once the music started it came flooding back to her and she performed for the team, the audience, but mostly for Remington. Even if she had almost called her her girlfriend.

Remington had a lazy smile on her face as she watched, reclined against the bench behind her, and Aspen wondered what she was thinking.

When the performance was over, Rem clapped and whistled for them, and when Aspen was back up in the stands, Remington grabbed her around the waist and pulled her down onto her lap. "You were awesome."

Aspen let out a little shriek of surprise before she settled. "Thank you," she said, grinding her hips down a little into Remington's thighs. If she was going to be sitting on Rem's lap, she was going to take full advantage. She leaned her head back on Remington's shoulder.

"Mmm. Can we leave now?"

Aspen growled. "I already told you I can't leave after halftime. And also? Just so you know? We're going to lose every game for the next six weeks thanks to you."

"Well, I'm not sorry," Remington said, her voice displaying how truly unapologetic she was. She shoved Aspen off her lap and Aspen knocked into an elderly gentleman two rows down as she fell.

"Oh my God, I am so sorry, sir!" She hoped she didn't dislodge his dentures. "Are you all right?"

The gentleman gave a grunt and shook it off, turning his head to peer at her. "What are you doing, young lady?"

"I'm so, so sorry. I lost my balance and fell. Are you all right?" she asked again.

"I'm fine, I'm fine." He waved her off.

She stalked back up and sat next to Remington, trying to dislodge Rem's brain from her skull with just a glare. "What the hell was that?!"

Remington stuck her tongue out, stood up, and left.

"What the f—" Aspen stood up and followed her, having to run to catch up. When she was behind the bleachers and got close enough, she reached out and grabbed Remington's arm. "Wait! What the hell is going on? Why are you leaving?"

Remington spun to face her, expression unreadable for a few seconds before a mischievous smile spread. "To get you to follow me."

"That's not funny!" Aspen gasped, horrified.

"It's a little funny," Remington said.

Aspen scrunched up her nose. "Just apologize for pushing me."

Remington gave a little snort of laughter, putting her arms around Aspen and giving her a squeeze. "I'm sorry I pushed you."

"Thank you, by the way. For not letting Stefan call me a whore. I'm sorry you got hurt."

Remington grinned. "It's not so bad."

Aspen let her hands wander under Remington's jacket to rest on the thin fabric of her tank top. Her black tank top. "Why are you wearing a different beater?" She could feel the warmth of Rem's skin through the shirt.

"I had a bloody nose," Remington said. "I had to run home and change."

"Can I kiss you in other places, since your face is so injured?"

"You can kiss my neck."

Aspen pressed featherlight kisses over Remington's jaw, then moved slowly down to her neck, letting her tongue out to graze the salty skin with a murmur of approval.

Remington gave a little noise from the back of her throat, rolling her head to the side, which offered more of her neck.

Aspen licked the mark she'd made earlier, then sucked it gently into her mouth. She stroked her hands up and down Remington's back under her jacket. "I'm not supposed to leave," she said, slowly pulling back. "But I want to go somewhere with you. Anywhere. Just us."

Remington closed her eyes, taking a few breaths, and Aspen got the sense she was fighting something. "Do you like the beach?"

"We don't have beaches here." She thought everybody knew that.

"I know of one," Remington said. "Do you want to go or not?"

"Yes." That was a no-brainer. "Where are you parked?"

Remington took her keys from her pocket and depressed a button.

Two beeps pulled Aspen's attention and she turned her head just in time to catch flashing taillights. "Close by, then."

Remington took her arm and dragged her toward the car. "Do you need me to stop in front of the locker room so you can get your stuff?"

"I didn't bring anything."

"No jacket? You're going to freeze."

"I guess you'll just have to keep me warm," Aspen said with a shrug, sliding into the passenger seat and buckling her seat belt.

Remington groaned and got in, then started the car.

They drove for about a half hour before Remington pulled up to a curb and shut off the engine. When they got out she locked the car and started leading Aspen down a steep slope through some trees. The air was cold, almost frosty, and Aspen clung to her for warmth and for support down the hill. She stumbled a few times in the dark and Remington laughed, making sure to steady her.

As they reached level ground, Remington led them through another patch of trees, and when they emerged Aspen could feel sand under her sneakers. She looked down, the moonlight illuminating the ground enough to see by now that they were out of the trees. It was just like a beach. There was a small lake, a sandy shore dotted with little rocks and larger boulders, the water lapping gently at the edges. "Wow." She shivered a little in the cool air and grinned when she heard the creak of leather and felt Remington's jacket being draped around her shoulders. "Thanks," she said. "This is awesome. How did you find it?"

Remington pointed across the lake, and in the distance there were houses. "I used to live over there."

"Cool," Aspen said, nodding, pulling the jacket tighter around herself.

"Sorry I don't have a blanket. I didn't plan on coming out here." Rem put an arm around her as they walked. "If it's too cold, we can go."

Aspen stopped and looked at Remington, tears brimming in her eyes. "No one has ever made me feel this special," she said.

Remington looked back at her. "No one's ever given you their jacket?"

It was a simple question that had far more than a simple meaning. She knew Remington was not just asking about a jacket.

"I think…" Remington stopped and brought her hands to Aspen's hair, running her fingers through. Aspen waited for her to continue, enjoying the feeling of fingers in her hair. "Do you want to come over for dinner Monday night? You can meet my mom."

Oh. Of all the things Remington could have said, that one was not even on Aspen's radar, but the invitation into Remington's life overwhelmed her with about a million feelings she didn't know how to process. She didn't say anything, afraid she'd cry if she opened her mouth, so she just nodded.

Remington smiled and kissed her.

CHAPTER TWELVE

"Did you ask your dad yet, about tonight?" Raleigh asked, reclining on the bed, taking Denna with her.

"Oh, crap, no. Hang on," she said, hopping up and heading into the living room. "Hey, Dad, can I spend the night at Raleigh's tonight?"

"Oh, honey, there's no supervision there at all," her dad said, making a face. "Why can't you both stay here like you usually do?"

"Her parents are out of town for business or something and she's taking care of her brothers. Please, Dad?"

"You can't be apart from her for one night?"

Denna put on her best puppy dog eyes and shook her head. "Please? I swear I won't do anything there that I'm not allowed to do here. I mean I know I'm not perfect, but you've always been able to trust me, haven't you? And I'm almost eighteen. Please?"

Her dad sighed and Denna was pretty sure the puppy dog eyes had done their job. "Will you call me to check in around ten?"

She grinned and hugged him, nodding in earnest. "I will. Ten on the dot, I promise. Thank you thank you thank you!" She bounced back to her room to tell Raleigh. "He said yes!"

Raleigh grinned. "Wonderful. And while Daniel and Joey are doing their homework, you can start studying the notes I've made for you."

Denna groaned. "Yippee."

❖

"Dennaaa!" Joey squealed when his favorite person in the world (because why would any child have a favorite person other than her?) walked into his house. He launched himself at her, throwing his arms around her waist and hugging her tight, then refused to let go so she had to walk with him wrapped around one leg.

"Joey!" She laughed, ruffling his chestnut hair so it stuck out everywhere. "Oh! There's something on me! Raleigh, help!"

Joey laughed hysterically, clinging tighter. "No, Rayray, don't help her!"

Raleigh shook her head, closing and locking the door behind her. "Danny?" she said, voice directed toward the far hallway where the bedrooms were. She set down her backpack by the entry table.

"In my room!" Daniel called back. "Doing my homework!"

"Excellent," Raleigh said, moving into the kitchen.

Denna made her way to Danny's room with Joey still clinging to her leg and poked her head into his doorway. "Yo, Danny! Are you staying in here all night like a loser or are you gonna come hang out?"

Denna knew Raleigh's brothers pretty well, not just from being Ral's girlfriend, but she had also babysat them a handful of times, and seriously, she wasn't sure how a tiny squirt and a teenager could be so much fun, but they always had a blast. One time, over the summer, she had come to pick up Raleigh, but instead she picked up all of them and took them to a carwash, and when no one was looking they snuck in and got washed and rainbow waxed and rinsed and dried. It was awesome. Except for the taste of the rainbow wax when some got in her mouth.

And another time, it was almost bedtime, and the boys had already brushed their teeth, but she made popcorn and ice cream sundaes and let them stay up late making prank calls.

Daniel groaned at her and gathered up his math book and note-book. Then his focus dropped to her new fashion accessory and he groaned again. "Joey, get off," he said, rolling his eyes. "She's not a stroller."

"I'm too big for a stroller." Joey made a sour face. "Are you crazy?"

"Are you crazy?" Daniel said, mocking the squirt.

Denna laughed and followed him, dragging one leg behind her because Joey was small, but the longer he sat there, the heavier he got.

Danny sank down onto the couch and spread his stuff out on the coffee table, going back to his homework.

"Thanks for trying to save me, Danny. I guess I'll just have to hit the self-destruct button. Three, two, one, beep, beep, beep." She started beeping like an intruder alarm and pulled Joey from her leg, making explosion noises as she threw him onto the couch next to Daniel. Then she jumped on top of him and tickled him until he begged her to stop and wheezed for air. "Do I win?" she asked, grinning.

"Yes!" Joey shrieked, batting at her hands.

"Awesome," Denna said, climbing off the couch and raising her fists in the air. "VICTORY IS MINE!" she bellowed, spinning in a slow circle, stopping when she saw Raleigh staring at her from the doorway to the kitchen. "I, uh, I won," she said, dropping her arms and giving a sheepish smile.

Raleigh lifted an eyebrow, arms slowly crossing over her chest. "They have homework to do," she said, making Denna shrink a little under the disapproving gaze. "And so do you."

"Technically, my homework is optional, because it was assigned by you," Denna said. Not that she thought that would get her out of it. But anything was worth a chance.

"Be that as it may, Daniel is already working on his, and Joey should be." She looked past Denna to Joey. "Go get your homework, Joe."

"No fun." Denna sulked. "How about we go for milkshakes inst—"

"Denna Delilah Ashford," Raleigh said, stepping into the living room. "Not only am I cooking dinner, but you are teaching my brother a bad work ethic and making me feel bad for objecting."

"He's six years old!" Denna said, though she did wince a little at the use of her middle name.

Raleigh moved close to Denna. "And who is going to teach him responsibility if you and I don't?"

That took the wind out of Denna's sails and she nodded. "You're right. I'm sorry. Can we go for milkshakes after homework and dinner?"

Raleigh smiled, took Denna's hand, and squeezed it. "Yes." Denna was relieved at both the answer and the forgiveness.

"WOOHOO, did you hear that, boys? We get to go for milkshakes after homework and dinner!"

"*Yes!*" Joey squealed, pumping his fist in the air. He handed Denna his backpack. "My homework is in there."

❖

"Okay Joey, it's time to get ready for bed," Raleigh said to her littlest brother, who was across the room playing cars with Denna.

"Aw, man!" Joey said, tossing his cars into their bin one at a time, crashing a few of them with Denna's on the way. She turned away when Denna picked Joey up and carried him upside-down to the bathroom.

"Brush. Your. Teeth," she heard. Denna's robot voice. That was one of Joey's favorites. How did she manage to have a girlfriend that was so amazing with her little brothers? She felt lucky and slightly envious at the same time. She knew she was good with them too, but Denna was *fun*. Raleigh wasn't fun with them. Maybe it was just as well, because this way the boys got balance.

"Danny," she said, turning to him. "Did you get all your homework done?"

"Seriously? When have I ever not done my homework?" He rolled his eyes, but he was grinning at her.

"I know. I'm ridiculous."

"Nah, just a broken record."

"I'm heading to bed. Don't stay up too late, okay?" Fourteen was a little old to impose a bedtime, and Danny was responsible, anyway.

"I won't."

"Good."

"Yeah, it is good."

She snorted a little laugh and went down the hall to her bedroom to get ready for bed and wait for Denna to finish up with Joey.

Joey came bounding in about ten minutes later, pajamas on and teeth brushed, Denna on his heels. "Can I sleep in here with you?" he asked.

"Sure, squirt!" Denna answered, just as she said no.

Joey had started forward, but stopped, looking between the two of them.

"Sorry, maybe next time, squirt." Denna backed off this time, for which Raleigh was grateful.

"I'm not a squirt," Joey said, sticking his tongue out. "G'night!" He turned and made airplane noises as he ran out of the room.

Denna got out of bed to close the door after him, then got back in. "Why did you say no?"

"He's not a baby; he does not need to sleep in here with us," Raleigh said, as if it were that simple, when in truth there was nothing simple about it.

"But he's a little boy, looking for affection, looking to know he's important," Denna said. "You won't even touch him. I've seen you hug Daniel, but not once have I ever seen you hug Joey. Not even a pat on the back. Why is that, Raleigh?"

Raleigh did not want to talk about that, and she could feel the tension coming over her muscles. She tried to temper her breathing, refusing to answer for a long time.

When Denna was reaching over to turn off the lamp, she finally spoke, without affect in her voice or in her expression. The flat tone was something she had used for a long time to protect herself. No emotion in your voice, no emotion in your body.

"You know what happened eight years ago. You know what Danny and I went through." She waited until Denna nodded and then continued. "Danny was six years old." The protection of her affect fled suddenly, and her voice was choked, filled with more emotion than she normally showed in a week. "When I look at Joey, I see six-year-old Danny and I ca—I can't," she said, her breathing speeding up, becoming shallow, her hands shaking.

"Oh God," Denna said, pulling Raleigh into her arms and holding her tight, and Raleigh melted against her. "I'm sorry. I didn't—I thought you'd…"

"Worked through it?" Raleigh asked, fairly clinging to Denna.

"Yeah," Denna said, squeezing.

"I have. I've worked through what happened to me, but there's no way for me to work through what happened to Danny. It helps that Jason's in jail, but it's not a quick fix." Her stomach churned with the urge to be sick. She hated talking about this; thinking about this, but who could she fall apart with if not Denna? Denna deserved to be let in, and she tried so hard. *So* hard. "I don't flinch anymore when men get near me. That took years, but it's progress. I doubt I'll ever be able to forgive myself for not being able to protect Danny, though. He seems okay, but what if he's hiding his feelings? What if he can't have a healthy relationship when he's old enough to date? What if he can never have healthy sex? I'm so lucky because I have you, but what if Daniel never finds the right person?" She knew she was speaking incredibly fast, but that was the only way to get everything out without shutting down. She let out her breath at the end, closing her eyes so she wouldn't have to see Denna's reaction.

"Daniel has the best person in the world in his corner," Denna said, her voice much quieter and more serious than usual. "If he struggles with sex and relationships when he's older, you will make sure he goes back to counseling. If he's hiding his feelings, they'll come out sooner or later, and you'll be there when they do. He wouldn't trust you and love you so much if this was your fault, Raleigh. It's not your fault. It's Jason's fault. It's your mother's fault. Don't blame yourself any more than you blame Danny. I know that you're not helpless now, but you were helpless then. And you have fought so hard to get past it, baby, and I know I never say it, but I admire you every single day because you're the strongest person I know."

Raleigh listened, Denna's words competing with the hammering pulse in her ears, and she tried to internalize what Denna was saying, that it wasn't her fault, but guilt was irrational and seldom able to be reasoned away no matter what Denna or anyone said. She was grateful for the sentiment, however, and she climbed under the covers, pulling them up to her chin, and laid her head in Denna's lap. "Thank you, baby. You're perfect, do you know that?"

"Perfect for you," Denna said, running fingers through her hair. "Your parents won't let him back in here if he gets out on parole, will they?"

The hearing was coming up soon. That was most of the reason for her frantic nerves and her difficulty suppressing feelings that she was typically able to suppress. "I don't know," she said. "He's still their son."

"You can all come live with me if they do. There's no way a judge will let them keep custody of the boys if they willingly let an abuser into the house."

"I don't want to talk about it," she said when she couldn't take it anymore, her body threatening to rip apart at the seams. She could not wrap her mind around the possibility of Jason stepping foot in this house, and she needed to be distracted from imagining it. She changed the subject. "How much did you learn about chlorophyll? Tell me."

Denna groaned. "It's green."

"That had better not be it, Denna."

Denna wiggled against her. "Give me some credit. I was poring over those notes for a freaking hour. It's used in photosynthesis, which is how plants get energy from light. It's a biomolecule. It's green because it absorbs red and blue light from the electromagnetic spectrum better than green light. The most common type of chlorophyll in plants is chlorophyll a, and the molecular structure of that is C fifty-five, H seventy-two, O five, N four, Mg."

"I told you you were smart," Raleigh said with a satisfied grin, nuzzling Denna's cheek with her nose.

"You're just underestimating how much I want my reward."

Raleigh rolled her eyes. "You'd say anything to get out of a compliment, wouldn't you?"

"Depends on the compliment."

Chapter Thirteen

By the end of school Monday, Aspen was nervous as hell. She had already asked Denna three times if she looked presentable enough to meet someone's mother.

Finally, as they reached the field for practice and Aspen asked again, Denna growled and kicked her. "Could you ask me after practice, when you're actually *wearing* what you plan to wear?"

Aspen flailed. "I'm sorry! I'm nervous! I've never met someone's mother before!"

"My dad doesn't count?"

"Shut it, you know what I mean!"

After practice she changed into the clothes she'd brought especially for meeting Remington's mother and asked Denna again. "Okay, how do I look?"

Denna blinked. "Like a monk. What are you wearing? Thank God I've never seen it before."

Raleigh narrowed her eyes. "While Denna's assessment is rather crass, I would have to agree that your choice of attire is rather concerning."

"I didn't want to look trashy!" Aspen shouted.

"But you want to look Amish?" Denna said.

A few silent seconds later, Remington came into the locker room, where they had planned for her to pick Aspen up. "Are you ready to—what the HELL are you wearing?" she asked, eyes wide.

"Fuck you guys!" Aspen scowled, ripping off the blouse and smacking Denna with it before she dropped it, then wriggled out of the skirt, standing in her bra and panties.

"Now that's more like it." Denna grinned. "Black satin? Good taste."

Remington bit her lip. "Just wear what you wore to school today, or your cheer outfit. I like your cheer outfit."

"But I'm meeting your mom."

"So? She's a person, just like us, and she's not going to judge you, especially not for what you wear. Be yourself. I wouldn't have invited you if I didn't want you to come."

Aspen felt a little silly now for having gotten so worked up about it. She pulled her cheer uniform back on, then checked her hair and makeup once more in the mirror before turning to Remington. "Okay, well, I'm ready."

When they were almost at the door, Raleigh stopped them. "Remington."

Remington stopped but didn't turn.

"Stefan Drumm. Thanks."

Remington gave a nod and continued out the doors, a slightly confused Aspen in tow.

"Do you know what her deal with Stefan is?"

"Besides the fact that he's a disgusting pig? I think it's something to do with Jason. But even if I knew for sure, I would tell you to ask Raleigh."

"You suck." Aspen made a lizard face at her.

"Whatever. Get in the car."

Aspen sat at the table, bouncing her legs up and down underneath it. She couldn't sit still. There was too much riding on this. Introductions had been made, handshakes exchanged, nice-to-meet-yous expressed, and now dinner was served. She followed Remington's lead, bowing her head while Mrs. Stone said grace. After that, she folded her napkin in her lap and smoothed it out, waiting for Remington to start eating before she would.

As Remington took a bite of lasagna, Mrs. Stone asked a question that made Aspen wish she could sink into her chair and disappear.

"So, Aspen, tell me. How did you work your way into my daughter's good graces?"

Remington choked. "Mama," she said, eyes wide.

Aspen felt like her head was going to explode and stared down at her lap. Remington's mother already hated her.

"Oh, I'm sorry, dear, I didn't mean to make you uncomfortable. I just meant, tell me how you two got to getting along."

"Can I go to the bathroom?" Aspen asked in a rush, and without waiting for an answer she fled from the table, locking herself in the bathroom when she found it. She sat on the toilet and put her face in her hands, trying to keep the tears at bay. This was a bad idea. She should've known she wasn't parent-meeting material. Why was she even trying to do a sustained relationship kind of thing? Fuck 'em and leave 'em hadn't failed her before, so why was she changing her MO?

A few moments later, there was a knock on the door.

"Just a minute," she said, trying not to let her voice shake.

"Aspen, honey, it's Catherine. Would you open the door please?"

Aspen didn't want to, but she was a guest in someone's house and she didn't want to embarrass Remington, so she stood and unlocked the door, allowing Mrs. Stone to open it.

Mrs. Stone stepped inside and shut the door behind her, gathering Aspen into a tight hug. "Now don't fuss, honey," she said, putting Aspen at arm's length and brushing some hair back from her face. "I'm sorry. I shouldn't have been trying to make jokes until we get to know each other better. I didn't think you would take my question at face value. Come back and have your supper."

It had never felt so good to be hugged, and Aspen allowed a sliver of hope to surface. "You don't hate me?" she asked, staring at the floor.

"Heavens, no! Don't be silly. Go on and eat before it gets cold." She opened the door and ushered Aspen out, to where Remington was waiting.

The rest of dinner passed with pleasant conversation. Aspen told about her parents, what little there was to tell, about what she liked to do, what subjects were her best in school, and Mrs. Stone reciprocated, telling about how she met Remington's father, how they'd gotten together, and a few funny stories about Remington as a toddler, during which Rem promptly asked to be excused and started washing the dishes.

By the end of the evening, they had talked more and played Scrabble and Monopoly. Remington won Scrabble and Aspen won

Monopoly. "I'm good with money," she said, as if she needed to explain her victory. "Probably because I don't have to pay for anything myself." She cringed. "That sounded really awful."

Remington snickered and Mrs. Stone laughed as they started cleaning up the pieces.

❖

Aspen quickly became a regular fixture for dinner and games, going to Remington's almost every night.

About a week after the first time, they ended up playing games much later than usual because Monopoly took forever and none of them would concede defeat until they were completely out of money and had mortgaged every single property they owned. Remington turned to Aspen after putting the game away. "It's late. You should just spend the night. Your car's at school anyway, so I can drive you in the morning."

"'Kay." Aspen nodded, excited butterflies making themselves known in her stomach.

"You can have the bed," Remington said. "I like the couch anyway."

Aspen blinked. "We're not sharing the bed?"

"No, you're not sharing the bed," came Mrs. Stone's voice from the kitchen.

Aspen ran her hands over her face. "Sorry," she whispered to Remington.

Rem just chortled. "I'll be on the couch if you need anything," she said, and leaned in to add into Aspen's ear, "until my mom goes to bed."

Aspen shivered. "Can I borrow some pajamas?"

Remington nodded and led the way to her bedroom, where she pulled a pair of boxer shorts and a tank top out of her dresser and handed them to Aspen. She grabbed another set for herself and kissed Aspen's cheek, heading toward the bathroom. "There's extra toothbrushes in the top drawer," she said. "And help yourself to anything in the kitchen if you get hungry."

Aspen nodded, watching her go, and let out a long breath, then changed into the pajamas, grinning at the way they smelled like Rem.

When Remington was finished in the bathroom, she dropped her clothes in the laundry and smiled as she passed Aspen. "It's all yours."

Aspen used the bathroom and washed her face, then brushed her teeth, and climbed into bed. She hoped she didn't fall asleep before Mrs. Stone did.

❖

Remington waited for a half hour at least after she'd heard her mother's door close and quietly slipped from the couch and into her bedroom, closing the door behind her without making a sound. She walked slowly toward the bed, intending to see if Aspen was still awake, but she didn't need to because sparkling eyes tracked her progress forward.

Aspen pulled the covers back as she reached the bed and she climbed under them, pressing her body to Aspen's, one hand rubbing up the front of her tank top while she brought their mouths together and kissed her. "We have to be quiet," she whispered, pulling back, putting a finger to Aspen's lips. "And stay above my waist."

Aspen nodded and let her hands wander. She slid them under Remington's top, flattening her palms against Rem's lower back and moving firmly up to her shoulder blades. At the same time, she opened her mouth, took Remington's finger into it, and bit down softly.

Remington sucked in a shallow breath, arching her body tighter against Aspen's, holding in a moan at the warm, wet pressure on her finger.

Aspen sucked Rem's finger farther into her mouth, swirled her tongue back and forth across it, and then pulled back, climbing onto her hands and knees over Remington, gently pinning each wrist to either side of her head. She let go and moved her hands to the hem of Remington's tank top, starting to push it upward. "I want to—can I— please," she said, stopping the tank top just below Rem's breasts. She lowered her head to kiss and lick and suck Remington's annoyingly quivering stomach.

Remington groaned, her skin jumping under Aspen's mouth. Should she say yes? Probably not. But was she going to say no? Probably not. Finally, she nodded, giving permission.

Aspen shoved the tank the rest of the way up and stared. And okay, Remington could get used to being stared at like that because Aspen looked like she was about to start drooling. "You have a seriously amazing rack."

Before Remington could complain about the terminology, Aspen dropped her head and left a feathery kiss on one breast.

Aspen's mouth was somehow more powerful than she'd expected, and just that one tiny kiss made Remington grip the headboard behind her and arch her back with another quiet groan. She didn't look down; she couldn't handle seeing Aspen's head against her chest. She'd explode. When Aspen kissed her other breast she threw her head to the side and whimpered, wishing they were home alone because Aspen was making her want to go all the way.

Aspen grinned down at her and gave a hesitant lick. "Is this—am I doing it right?"

"Yeah," Rem said, nodding.

Aspen gave another lick, firmer and less hesitant, then moved to her other breast and pulled in a mouthful. She slid a hand teasingly downward, and when her fingers curled under the waistband of Remington's shorts, Rem jerked beneath her, sending the bed into the wall.

A few seconds later there was a knock on said wall. "Remington! Go back to the couch!"

"Fuck!" Remington glared at Aspen. "This is your fault." And then, louder, she called to her mother, "Okay!"

Aspen groaned, running her hands over her face as Remington got up.

"I am not coming back in here tonight," Remington whispered in a huff.

"I hope you know I'm going to masturbate in your bed," Aspen said back, just as huffy.

"Fine!" Remington said, trying not to show how much the idea made her tremble. She quickly left the room.

Ten minutes later, she heard her bed hit the wall again and her eyes went wide.

"Remington Stone!" Mama yelled, and she heard footsteps coming from her mother's bedroom, a door opening.

"I'm on the couch!" Remington squeaked, kneeling up so she could look over the back of it and prove she was there.

"Well, then what—? Oh. Oh!" Mama frowned, going to Remington's bedroom door.

Remington could only watch in complete and utter horror.

Her mother rapped sharply on the door. "Aspen Wellington," she said. "Some of us in this house are trying to sleep! See to it you respect that, young lady!"

Remington wanted to *die*. Although really, it was Aspen's own fault. She flopped back down on the couch and laughed.

"I'm sorry!" Rem heard through the door, and she could picture Aspen's desperate blush and body language, and practically see the accompanying wide green eyes.

"I should hope so! You mind your manners. If you want to do that, do it quietly. Now good night, *both* of you." Mama went back to her room.

Remington couldn't even say good night, she was laughing so hard. But quietly.

❖

Remington woke first and folded her sheet and blanket, then decided to make breakfast. She grabbed some bacon from the fridge and fired up a pan with canola oil. When it started bubbling, she dropped in enough for the three of them and let it sizzle.

Aspen still hadn't come out by the time breakfast was on the table and Mama was seated, reading the newspaper, waiting for Rem and Aspen to join her.

"I'll get Aspen," Remington said, wiping her hands on her shorts and padding to her bedroom. She knocked quietly and pushed the door open, peering inside. She was surprised to see Aspen, dressed in her cheer uniform, shoes on, hair brushed, and makeup applied, just sitting on the bed. "Aspen? Come on, breakfast."

"I can't go out there!" Aspen said, blushing bright red.

"Oh my God. Come on. It's just my mother."

"Exactly! It's your mother!" Aspen whined, sinking backward to lie on the bed.

Remington moved forward and leaned over the bed, kissing her cheek. "Get your ass out of bed and face the music."

"Will you give me head real quick first?" Aspen asked hopefully.

Remington licked her cheek instead and pulled her up off the bed. "I made bacon and to—"

"No eggs?!" Aspen shrieked, wiping the saliva from her cheek.

"Bacon and toast and eggs," Remington said. "If you would have let me finish."

"I'm sorry I got us busted. I wanted to make out with you all night."

"Next time you want to put your hand down there, make sure we're not twenty feet from my mother."

"Ooh, is that permission to put my hand down there?"

"In the broadest possible sense."

"Smells good out here," Aspen said as she stepped into the dining room. "So, is there anything interesting in the paper this morning?"

Mama looked over her glasses at Aspen. "Stop trying so hard and eat your breakfast. You girls are going to be late for school at this rate."

Aspen grumbled and sat down, then pulled her chair closer to the table and started to eat.

❖

When they got to school, Remington leaned over and gave Aspen a kiss before they got out of the car. "I have to work until six," she said.

"Okay, pick me up at Denna's?" Aspen asked as they walked to homeroom.

"M'kay," Remington agreed, resisting the urge to hold her hand. "I should be there by six thirty. I'll text you if it's later."

"'Kay."

She was in trouble. She was seeing Aspen every day, and she really, *really* liked seeing Aspen every day. This was not what she had expected when she had agreed to go to one party. She had expected to not even really have a good time, let alone start to get to know Aspen Wellington, whom she had always avoided like the plague because hello, rich and snooty? Not exactly Remington's type.

Thinking of her type made her think of her freshman and sophomore summers. Made her think of Layla. She still missed Layla once in a while, but who didn't miss their first girlfriend? It wasn't a pining, yearning kind of missing, it was just a little flare in her chest of nostalgia from time to time.

They had met while working as counselors at a summer camp for underprivileged kids and had shared a cabin. They'd clicked instantly and one thing led to another, and they had spent every night for two entire summers exploring each other. Layla had always been very handsy and very confident, and very vocal about the fact that Remington wasn't her first. She had taught Rem a lot about sex. All the things that the birds and bees speech didn't cover and all the things that Remington hadn't even known she would like. But she did like them. A lot. And now she liked Aspen a lot and wanted to do *everything* with her.

❖

After practice Aspen swung by Taco Bell on the way to Denna's and picked them all up something. "I checked for tomatoes," she said as she pushed Denna's bedroom door open farther with her hip and glided into the room. "And meat," she added, pulling the Mexican pizza out of the bag and handing it to a starved-looking Raleigh. "Jesus, Raleigh, you look like Gollum."

Raleigh stroked the box affectionately and hissed in a creepy whisper.

"NEVER AGAIN," Denna said loudly, eyes wide. "Ever."

"Did you forget to feed her?" Aspen asked, handing Denna her taco.

"We skipped lunch." Denna looked just as starved as she tore into the taco.

"Why?"

Two sets of eyebrows raised in her direction.

"Nice."

"It was, it really was," Denna said, dramatically fluttering her eyelashes. "We messed around under the bleachers."

"And we never will again if you insist on sharing the experience with others," Raleigh said.

"Aspen, did you know that Raleigh is a closet exhibitionist? Right before she kissed me, she said she wished you were watching."

Aspen froze, her eyes almost crossing at the thought of it, but the twitch of Denna's lips let her know Den was just fucking with her. "Oh my God."

"Aspen," Raleigh said, her feathers appearing unruffled to the naked eye, but Aspen knew something sinister was coming. "Did you know that Denna secretly enjoys sleeping outside on the cold, hard ground without a pillow?" She paused to finish the last bite of her pizza, then continued. "Naked?"

Denna choked, gasping for air, her face going bright red as she flailed wildly for something to drink. She ended up grabbing Aspen's soda and sucking almost half of it through the straw, swallowing rapidly. "What the FUCK?!" She wheezed, handing Aspen back her soda. As if she wanted it back now, with probable taco bits floating everywhere?

She had never seen Denna so flustered in an embarrassed sort of way. It was kind of awesome, actually. "No pillow, Denna?" she asked, tilting her head to the side. "The rest I can see, but why no pillow?"

Denna shoved her hard enough to make her drop her drink, and it spilled on the carpet. "Your fault your fault your fault!" She panicked, running to Denna's bathroom for a towel.

When she came back to clean up the mess, Denna folded her arms across her chest, still clearing her throat every few seconds. "Now it's your turn, Aspen. Embarrass yourself or I'll think of something."

"I have you both beat by a hundred yards," Aspen said, tossing the towel into the laundry and the empty cup into the trash. "Especially since yours were both untrue."

Denna and Raleigh both looked like they'd won the lottery.

"Remington's mother caught me masturbating in her bed last night."

"What the fuck were you doing in Remington's mother's bed?!" Denna gaped at her.

"Remington's bed! Remington's bed, you fucking dumbass!" she shrieked. "God, it was so—I can't even."

"Don't call me a dumbass," Denna said. "You're the one who got caught jerking off in your girlfriend's bed."

"That's amazing," Raleigh finally said.

"How did you get caught? Were you way loud?" Of course Denna would assume she was loud.

"*No*," she said, lifting her chin. "I knocked the bed into the wall."

A split second of silence, and then—

"Bwaahahahahaha!" Denna burst out laughing, toppling onto the bed and rolling around in a fit of hysterics.

Raleigh just smirked. "What did Catherine do?"

"She may or may not have told me to mind my manners and that if I wanted to do *that*, to do it quietly."

Denna smooshed a pillow over her head, squeezing it around her temples, and when she finally stopped laughing, she rolled onto her back. "You're a fucking idiot, Aspen."

"Love you too." Aspen snorted.

"You know I love you. And you're not really a fucking idiot. That story is epic, though. Eh-pic."

Aspen's phone buzzed and she grinned as she read the message. "She's here, gotta go. See you guys tomorrow."

"Bye," Denna said, and Raleigh echoed, both giving a wave.

CHAPTER FOURTEEN

"You girls had better have your homework finished by dinner," Catherine called from the kitchen.

Aspen froze mid-channel change and stared toward the sound. "How long until dinner?!"

"About forty-five minutes," Catherine said, poking her head into the doorway. "Why, do you have a lot left?"

Aspen's stomach churned. "Allofit," she said, annoyed at Remington's snort of amusement.

"All of it? It's seven o'clock and you haven't even started your homework?" Catherine asked.

"I…" Aspen didn't even know what to say.

"Well, if you want to eat, get on it," Catherine said, gesturing toward Aspen's backpack.

Remington snickered. "Mine's done. I'll just be watching some TV while you slave away. Give me the remote."

Aspen looked at her pitifully. "Help me," she said, unzipping her backpack and taking out her notebook.

"I don't think so."

"Please? I have science homework and I don't understand it."

"How do you know that if you haven't even started it?"

"Because I don't understand science. And you're getting an A, aren't you?"

"I'd better be getting an A," Remington said, her eyes narrowing. As if Aspen's mere mention of an A meant that there might be another grade lurking somewhere.

Aspen opened her textbook and flipped through it until she got to the part she was supposed to be learning. "This. What the hell does it mean?"

"What does what mean?" Remington asked, glancing at the page.

"All of it!"

Rem leaned over closer to the text. "*What is a chemical bond?*" she read. "*It is a bond between electrons from different atoms. The valence electrons on the outer shell are the only electrons involved in chemical bonding. When two atoms get close enough together, the valence electrons of one atom interact with the protons of the other atom, and vice versa. When the electrons and protons meet, they induce a chemical reaction that results in two or more atoms being bound together.*" Remington looked at her.

"I have no idea what you just said."

Rem's eyes widened. "None?"

"Atoms have shells?"

"I—yes. They have layers of shells."

"And what. I have no idea."

Remington took her notebook and drew a picture of an atom. "This is the center. It's called the nucleus. Think of it as the sun." She pointed to the first ring around the nucleus. "This is the first shell. Think of it as Mercury, orbiting the sun."

"The planet, I'm assuming."

"Yes, the planet." Rem pointed to the outer shell. "This is the outer shell. Think of it as Venus, orbiting the sun, farther away than Mercury."

"Got it." At least she understood the order of the fucking planets.

"Now, on the outer shell, whatever electrons are there are called valence electrons, and they can be used for bonding to other atoms. So, the people living on Venus have social skills."

Aspen laughed but nodded. That made sense.

"The people living on Mercury are dull and boring, and don't bond with anyone. When their universe meets another universe, they do nothing, they just go about their business as it serves their own universe. They're the electrons on the inner shell or shells. When their atom meets another atom, they do nothing, they just sit there."

"And the outer ones, the valances—"

"Valence electrons. Valence, not valance."

"Right. Interior decorating I could pass with flying colors. *So,* the valence electrons are the popular guys, and do all the dating and eventual marriage to protons on other atoms, bonding their little universes together?" How could something so difficult become so simple? It was like she had never *not* understood it.

"Yes, exactly."

"You're a fucking amazing teacher," she said. "That was so easy to understand."

Remington looked at her, and was that judgment? "It would help if you paid attention in class. You might learn something there too."

Nope, not judgment, just teasing. Aspen resisted the urge to tackle her or otherwise torture her in some way.

Remington went on to explain ionic and covalent bonds in terms of sexual tension and hand holding, and when Aspen wasn't quite getting it she had them act it out, standing in front of each other. She explained that if they were to form an ionic bond, she would be a negatively charged atom and Aspen would be positively charged. Remington then kissed her to symbolize giving Aspen her extra electron, to neutralize their positive and negative charges. Aspen did not want to stop kissing, but Rem moved a few inches away to show that they could stand without touching while still being drawn together. If they were a covalent bond, the draw would be more powerful, and they would be constantly pulled into each other's space. She pressed her body against Aspen's to illustrate.

Needless to say, Aspen liked covalent bonds. And she actually finished the assignment with enough time to complete her English assignment before dinner!

❖

"Oh! I brought something," Aspen said while she helped Rem do the dishes. "I brought my Xbox 360."

What? Aspen played Xbox? "You play Xbox?" she asked. "You should have asked if I have one before you brought one over."

"*You* play Xbox?" Aspen asked. "Were we hiding that from each other or something?"

Remington snorfled and handed Aspen the last plate to dry.

When everything was put away, Rem followed Aspen into the living room. Mama was on the sofa.

Suddenly, Aspen clapped. "Let's play *Lips*."

"Aspen!" she choked, glancing at her mother in alarm.

Aspen doubled over with laughter, shaking her head. "It's a *karaoke* game, Rem."

Mama turned her head to hide her chuckle, but Rem heard it.

She scowled and opened the bottom cabinet of the entertainment center to reveal her game system. "Fine, put it in."

Aspen grinned and searched through her backpack until she found the game, then opened the box and put the disc in the player. She tried to explain how to play, but Remington shook her head. So did Mama.

"Just show us one round, then we'll start it over," Remington said.

"Okay." Aspen chose "Battlefield" by Jordin Sparks, and when the little circle thingy started bouncing across the screen by the lyrics, Aspen started singing.

She pointed at the screen as she sang, showing with her finger how the circles filled in if you hit them at the right time and on the right note. Rem didn't think any of the circles would fill in when it was her turn.

Aspen was swaying her hips with the music, even dancing a little. Remington stared at her in awe and so did Mama, but Rem was the only one with her mouth hanging open and a hundred inappropriate thoughts running through her head.

Mama reached over and gently closed her mouth with a hand under her chin.

A few seconds later, it was open again.

Remington's pulse was pounding in her ears, her heart racing, and she quite possibly had never been so turned on in her life without being touched. Aspen sang so beautifully, so amazingly, so perfectly, she couldn't believe she had never heard her sing before. If she was this good, she should be doing something with her talent.

Aspen finished the song and directed the game back to the menu, then turned around. "Who wants to go first?"

Remington shook her head, just as vehemently as Mama. "There is no way I'm singing after that," she said. "Where in the—? How did you? Do you have any idea how amazing that was?"

"I'm not singing either," Mama said to Aspen. "Honey, you should be onstage."

Aspen stared at Mama for a second, and then at her for a second, and then blushed bright red. "You guys are crazy," she said, turning away. "That's so embarrassing."

Rem opened her mouth to apologize, but Aspen turned back around so she shut it.

"You really think so, though?"

Did they really—seriously? "Did you not see the looks on our faces?" she asked. "I can't even."

"Remington is not often speechless," Mama said with a wink to Aspen. "Congratulations."

Remington grumbled and shot a look at her mother, then got up and hugged Aspen, whispering in her ear, "Listening to you sing made me want to jump you a little."

Aspen's arms tightened around her. "Can I have the couch tonight so I don't bang the bed into the wall?" she whispered back.

Remington snickered.

"All right, you two, I'm off to bed. I have to work early tomorrow." Mama stood and gave her a kiss on the head, then Aspen. "Good night, and behave."

"Good night," Aspen said.

"Night, Mama," Rem said, and squeezed Aspen tighter. "You can have the couch. Just this once."

Chapter Fifteen

Another week went by, and Aspen spent every night at Remington's. She only went back to her own house to get clothes and things.

Tonight, they were having an early birthday party for Denna, whose birthday wasn't for another two weeks, but some of her friends were going to be out of town then, so she had told Aspen that she'd just have two parties. This party was at some girl's house. Aspen didn't know her very well.

She walked with Remington up to the door and rang the bell, taking a moment to admire Rem in her usual attire of jeans, a white ribbed tank, and her leather jacket, complete with shitkicker boots. Aspen had specifically chosen a blood-red dress that flowed everywhere with the intention of trying to tempt Remington's hands constantly onto her body. It worked, because Remington kept touching it in one place or another.

The door opened and a brunette stood staring at them. "How do you expect to help set up in those heels?" she asked Aspen, glancing at her shoes.

"These are Manolo Blahniks," Aspen said, "and I'm Denna's best friend."

The girl moved out of the way and impatiently let them in. "We need you in the backyard. I hope one of you can grill steaks. One of you will load the ice chests and then fill them with drinks according to type. Whiskey in one, vodka in one, et cetera, et cetera. If you can handle that. Can you handle that?"

"Can you handle a broken face?" Remington asked.

Aspen bit her lip to keep from laughing and stepped on Remington's foot.

The girl just waved toward the backyard and walked away.

Rem stepped on Aspen's foot in retaliation and snickered, pulling her close for a kiss. "What did the brand of your shoes have to do with her question?"

Aspen laughed. "Nothing. I was just name-dropping."

"Oh my God," Remington said. "You are ridiculous."

❖

After cake, Denna opened presents, and just as Raleigh lit up a joint and took a puff, there was a knock at the door.

"Aren't you going to get that?" someone asked the hostess when another knock came.

"No. They can either let themselves in or go fuck themselves, I don't care."

A throat cleared and Remington looked up. There were two uniformed police officers standing in the living room, looking unimpressed.

"Oh. Hi," the hostess said. "How can I help you fine officers?"

Most of the kids started inching their way toward the door, some of them flat out running. A handful got away, but the officers quickly moved to block the door, the female one drawing her baton. "Who lives here?"

"I do. Might I inquire what you think you're doing, preventing my guests from leaving? My father will have your badges, you know."

"You can call him from lockup," the female officer said. "You seem to know the law quite well; I'm sure you're aware you only get one phone call."

"You can't arrest me. I've done nothing wrong. Get out of my house."

"You're under arrest for the possession and ingestion of marijuana, disturbing the peace, and underage drinking," the female officer said.

"I'm seventeen. You can't arrest me without my parents."

Remington stared. This girl really did not know when to quit.

"I can't question you without your parents," the officer said. "I can arrest you any time I like."

The other officer was an older man with white hair, his face clean shaven. Remington knew him. He was friends with Mama and Daddy; he used to be by the house all the time and had kind of watched her grow up. She hadn't seen him since she was like twelve, though, because he'd gotten married and his new wife hadn't been quite so friendly. So while he looked the same, she looked different, and she hoped he wouldn't recognize her.

He did. "I'll handle this one," he told his partner, pointing at Remington while the female officer called for a parade of squad cars to transport the rest of the partygoers.

Remington slumped down in her seat, not looking forward to this.

"What the hell?" Aspen asked. "Why is he picking on you?"

"He's not picking on me. He's a friend of my mother's."

The officers stood at the door until their backup arrived, and then moved toward the kids.

"Officer Cannes," Remington said when Marc reached her, giving him a hopeful look. "I—"

"Save it, young lady," he said. "Come with me."

"And her!" Remington said almost desperately, pulling Aspen up beside her as she got to her feet. "And those two. Please?" She pointed at Denna and Raleigh, since they were Aspen's best friends. If she could keep them out of jail, she would.

Marc regarded her for a moment, then nodded. "I assume none of you are fit to drive?"

"We are," Remington said, indicating herself and Aspen. "We haven't had anything to drink."

"Or smoke," Aspen said.

"Very well. You may drive yourselves home, the two of you, and I will escort these two ladies myself. You are very lucky I was nearby when we got this call, Remington."

"Yes, sir," Remington said, staring at the floor. "Aspen and I came in one car."

❖

Remington waited until Marc put Denna and Raleigh (and all of Denna's presents) in the back seat of his squad car, and then drove herself and Aspen home.

Marc followed, and when Remington realized he was going to wake up her mother, she nearly tore the steering wheel from its base with her grip. "Oh God," she said, pulling into her side of the driveway and shutting off the car. She got out and started up the walk, Aspen beside her.

"You two stay put," Officer Cannes told Denna and Raleigh. He walked with Remington and Aspen up to the door and rang the doorbell before Remington could stop him.

"I would have gotten her up for you," she said, again staring at the ground. Somehow she just felt that a gentle shake to her mother's shoulder would be nicer than a blaring doorbell. She glanced at her phone. Almost one in the morning. Great. "I am so completely fucked," she said under her breath.

Aspen found her hand and squeezed.

Mama answered the door, fully dressed, and raised her eyebrows at the scene. She was already awake? Marc must have called ahead. Rem wasn't sure if that was worse or better.

"Mama," she said. "I'm—"

"Hush," Mama said. "Get inside."

Remington tried to let go of Aspen's hand to go inside, but Aspen followed her in.

Mama thanked Marc and closed the door, clicking the deadbolt into place. "Aspen, go on home," she said.

Aspen shook her head.

"What?" Remington asked. *What in the actual fuck?* "Go home!"

"No," Aspen said, her lip quivering. "I feel more like a part of this family than my own, and I should be in trouble too."

Mama looked slightly dumbfounded as she glanced back and forth between her and Aspen. "Very well. Both of you get into your nightclothes and come to the living room."

When they were in her bedroom with the door closed, she turned to Aspen. "Are you insane? Go home!" she whispered, turning away to pull out some boxers and a tank top.

"No," Aspen said, reaching around her to pull out some clothes for herself as well.

"Maybe you've forgotten that we just almost went to jail, but—"

"And maybe you've forgotten what kind of parents I have."

Aspen interrupted her. "I wish I had your mom. No matter what kind of punishments you get, it's better than what I've got."

Remington stared, letting realization seep slowly into her of what it must be like for Aspen at home. No wonder she chose to spend every night here, even though there were rules and restrictions. She quickly pulled her clothes off and slipped into her pajamas.

Aspen got out of her dress and changed as well, shaking her head. "Even if I didn't feel like part of this family, I still wouldn't let you get in trouble alone. I—" She stopped and stared into Rem's eyes. "You're really important to me. Like, the most important person in my life besides Denna and Raleigh."

Remington's shock gave way to a warmth in her body and a feeling of belonging, and she kissed Aspen, hard. "Same to you, you know," she said. "Which is why I think you should leave."

"I'm not leaving," Aspen said, pinching her on the arm.

"Ow!" Rem squealed, batting her hand away.

"Girls!" Mama called, apparently having heard them fooling around.

Remington immediately turned and opened the door, and Aspen followed her out.

Mama motioned them to sit on the sofa and addressed them both. "I understand from Marc that neither of you had anything to drink or smoke," she said. "Is that correct?"

"Yes, Mama," Remington said.

"Yes, Mrs. Stone."

"That's good. But being at a party where drugs and alcohol were present? Putting yourselves in danger like that? It is unacceptable," she said, a stern expression on her face. "I will not allow it. Both of you, give me your car keys."

Remington's stomach fluttered nervously as she handed over her keys. Not for herself, but for Aspen. She was nervous for Aspen. She wanted to make her leave, but at the same time she understood what Aspen was thinking and knew that Aspen had to make her own choice. *Had* made her own choice. She just hoped Aspen didn't get angry at her even though she'd warned her more than once to go home. She had no idea how Aspen would react to having her car taken away.

She watched Aspen disappear silently into her bedroom, then

come back with her keys. Aspen separated the car keys from her other keys and handed the car keys to Mama.

Once Mama had both of their keys and they were both sitting on the sofa again, she spoke. "If Marc hadn't been on that call, I would be bailing you both out of jail right now."

"I'm sorry," Remington said. "We didn't break the law, though. Aspen and I, we didn't, Mama."

"You should not be around drugs, young lady, whether you're using them or not," Mama addressed her specifically. "That is a bad element, which I hope you can see by the trouble it's gotten you in. Cops don't care if you have good intentions. Look what happened with your father."

Remington nodded that she understood. And she did. Her daddy had been saving a woman's life, but he was still convicted of manslaughter and sent to prison. "You're right, Mama."

"Do you have any idea how afraid I am of losing you?" Mama asked, her voice shaking along with her hands. "When Marc called, before he could explain, I almost threw up, baby. Please, please don't scare me like that ever again."

Remington felt sick now too. Her mother was always so together, and while she was never dishonest, and she had admitted to being scared of things, Remington had never seen her shake like that. "Please, I'm sorry," she said, tears in her eyes.

Mama pulled her to her feet and hugged her for a long time.

Remington wanted to kick Raleigh's ass, but then she remembered when and why Raleigh had started smoking in the first place, and her anger completely vanished.

"I was so scared," Mama said again, squeezing her harder, and Remington was horrified to see tears.

It hurt to make her mother cry. Nobody ever liked to see their parents cry, but being the cause of it was *really* horrible.

After a few minutes, Mama kissed her head, then let her go. "I love you so much, Rem."

"I love you too, Mama." She was aware of Aspen's eyes on them, but it didn't change any of her responses to her mother.

Aspen felt tears sting her eyes, watching and listening to them. She thought about Catherine's reaction. She was angry, yes, but she hadn't yelled or called them stupid, or ignored them. It felt strange to have someone treat her like that, and as crazy as that might make her, she liked it. It was strange, but good. Like she was important enough to have her behavior corrected, by an adult. She knew her friends cared about her and that Remington did, but that was different.

Then when Catherine sat next to her and hugged her, she started to cry. She cried harder when she felt Catherine rubbing her back. She cried, and cried, and cried, letting out everything she'd bottled up over the years, and prayed Catherine knew it wasn't anything to do with her car.

After a few minutes, when Aspen still hadn't calmed down, Catherine spoke softly to her. "It's okay, honey," she said. "You just cry, and I'll be here, and I promise not to let go."

Aspen did just cry, and she clung to Catherine, feeling like she had a mom for the first time. She never wanted to move. She really hoped that Remington was okay with her hugging her mom.

Catherine didn't let go, as promised, and as she started to calm, Catherine hummed softly to her.

Finally, reluctantly, Aspen pulled back and lifted the hem of her tank top to wipe her face. "I don't want to bother you any longer. Can I go to bed now?" she asked, starting to get up.

"Bother me? Don't be silly," Catherine said. "But yes, I think it's time for bed."

Relieved beyond anything she could remember feeling, Aspen quickly shuffled out of the living room and into Remington's bedroom, where she climbed into bed.

Remington came in a few minutes later and flopped onto the bed next to her.

"Am I weird because being punished made me feel safe?" she whispered.

"Yes," Remington whispered back, snorfling when Aspen batted at her shoulder. "No, I'm just kidding."

Aspen dug a fingernail into Remington's arm in retaliation for her totally rude answer.

"Sorry," Remington said, leaning down to kiss her. "See you in the morning."

"Night." Aspen watched her leave the room. When Rem was gone, she closed her eyes, exhausted, and after such emotional turmoil, sleep came easy.

❖

Raleigh helped the police officer carry Denna's presents to the door and then went back for Denna.

Getting a drunk and half-passed-out Denna to the door was harder than carrying armfuls of presents. She held Denna up with one arm and used the other to search for keys. She found them in Denna's jacket and unlocked the door, pushing it open as quietly as she could.

"I'll need to speak to her father," the officer said, and Raleigh grimaced. She had been hoping to let Arthur sleep.

"Of course." She maneuvered Denna inside and to bed, then took a breath and returned to the foyer and the officer. "I'll get Mr. Ashford now," she said, extremely unhappy at having to go to her girlfriend's father's bedroom door in the middle of the night and knock. If she didn't know Arthur so well and know that he would never hurt her or Denna, she would not be doing this. But it was still nerve wracking and uncomfortable. The door was open most of the way so she had to reach across the threshold, and she knocked lightly. "Arthur?"

She saw movement under the blankets and then Arthur was sitting up. He blinked in the dim light and peered at her. "Raleigh?"

"Yes. There is an officer at the door needing to speak with you." That was even harder to say than she had anticipated.

He got up quickly and crossed to her. "Is everything okay? Are you okay? Is Denna okay? Where is she?"

"She's fine, she's—" *Do not say drunk.* "Sleeping." She moved out of the way so he could get by, and she waited in the living room while he talked to the officer. They weren't loud so she couldn't hear what they were saying, but it wasn't hard to figure out.

Arthur looked so tired. He shut the door and ran a hand over his face, and Raleigh couldn't hold her confession in anymore.

"It's my fault!" she said, watching him look at her.

"What? How can Denna's poor choices be your fault?" he asked, walking closer to her.

"I'm the one who had the pot," she said in a rush. "And it was my pot that you found in her bedroom. It was never hers, and I'm sorry I didn't tell you before, but I was afraid you wouldn't want me to be here anymore and—"

"Raleigh," he said, shaking his head. "It's okay, honey. Take a breath."

She tried.

"I'm not going to kick you out of our lives for having marijuana."

She breathed a little.

"I would prefer you not to have any on you while you're here, but that's probably just because I'm old-fashioned and grumpy."

She got a full breath. "You're not grumpy."

Arthur grinned. "Tell that to Denna tomorrow when I ground her."

Raleigh knew he was trying to be funny, but her nerves were still jumping around too much to let her guard down. "I'm just going to bring in her birthday presents and go to bed, if that's all right."

"You go on to bed, I'll bring in the presents," Arthur said, waving her off.

She nodded, looking over his shoulder toward Denna's bedroom. "Thank you."

"Good night, honey."

"Good night."

CHAPTER SIXTEEN

Aspen woke the next morning and rolled over with a stretch, a smile on her face until she recalled bursting into tears last night. *Dude.* She snuck out of the room to find Remington on the couch and sat down unceremoniously. "Do you think Denna and Raleigh are okay?"

"Morning," Remington said, turning to kiss the side of Aspen's head. "I don't know, but why wouldn't they be okay?"

"I'm sure they're fine," Aspen said. "Just, if that policeman told Denna's dad what happened, then she'll be grounded."

"That sounds pretty normal to me."

Aspen had to remember that Remington didn't know Denna that well. Not like she did. "I guess I'm worried about her reaction to getting grounded. Last time she got grounded she started screaming and smashed a plate."

Remington's mouth opened.

"She's always had kind of a temper, but Raleigh started worrying that it's worse lately, and that made me start worrying too."

She could tell that Rem didn't quite know what to say. "Why don't you call her?"

Aspen nodded. "Yeah. I think I will."

It went straight to voice mail.

❖

"I'm sorry, Dad."

"You were drunk, Denna."

"I'm almost eighteen."

"And the legal drinking age is twenty-one. I do not want you drinking."

"It's not really your decision, is it?"

"I am your father, and you are seventeen for another week. You are grounded for that week."

"No!" Denna screamed.

Raleigh heard the scream, then a crash and darted out of the bedroom. The dining table was flipped on its end and Denna had a chair held over her head, prepared to smash it to pieces. Fight-or-flight kicked in and she rushed forward, grabbed the chair and dropped it, and forcibly restrained Denna against the wall.

"That is enough!" she said into Denna's ear, her voice a heated whisper.

Denna froze.

"Are you calm?" she asked.

Denna took a breath and then nodded.

"Apologize to your father and go to your room."

Denna nodded again and Raleigh released her. She turned to Arthur but didn't look at him. "I'm sorry, Dad," she said as she walked quickly past him and into her room.

Raleigh righted the table and sat in one of the chairs, her face in her hands.

She heard Arthur sit across from her. "Thank you, Raleigh," he said after a minute.

She took her hands away from her face to look at him. "Really?"

"Yes. When she gets like that I don't know what to do. I'm glad you came out."

"I would never hurt her," she said, feeling the need to explain herself.

"I know." Arthur gave her a smile. "I might be a little jealous that one word from you calmed her down," he said with a chuckle.

"I didn't mean—"

"I'm just kidding, hon. I could take a few pointers from you, that's all."

She nodded, folding her arms on the table and resting her head on them. She was shaking lightly, both with the fading rush of adrenaline and the shock of seeing her girlfriend like that. It terrified her. The worst part was the blind rage in Denna's eyes.

"Are you okay, hon?" Arthur asked after another minute.

Raleigh didn't know how much she should say or not say to Denna's father. "I—I worry," she finally said quietly, picking up her head, because talking to him with her head on the table would be rude.

Arthur let out a sigh, staring at his hands. "Yeah. So do I. I'm guessing she's told you some things about her mother, and that's why you worry?"

Raleigh knew the subject was sensitive. "She hasn't told me too much." She attempted damage control just in case.

"It's okay," Arthur said. "You should probably know, since I'm fairly sure the two of you are going to be together forever. Something happened to Rose when Denna was little. She got mugged one night on her way home from the grocery store. It was right down the block, so she always walked there and back." He ran his hands over his face. "It triggered something when they hit her in the head. She changed. She started having these delusions, sometimes thinking she was sent from God to save humanity and other times screaming that people were after her, trying to kill her. She did dangerous things that made no sense to me, and one night she lit Denna's curtains on fire. Thank God I was just in the living room and I took care of the fire before it spread, but that was it for me. I couldn't have Denna in danger. I tried to talk to Rose about getting some help. I knew something had happened, a brain injury from the mugging at the very least, but she wouldn't even entertain the idea of going to the hospital for a scan. She was gone when I got up the next morning. Denna or I haven't seen or heard from her since."

Raleigh hadn't realized she was holding her breath until Arthur stopped talking and she let all the air out of her lungs in a rush. Hearing the whole story just made her exponentially more concerned and she fought valiantly not to cry in front of Denna's father. "Thank you for telling me," she choked out. "I'm going to—" She cut off speaking and glanced toward Denna's bedroom door.

"Of course, hon. I'll go in the living room since you're—" Now he cut off speaking and just got up from the table, disappearing into the living room, and *shit*, because she realized she was in a tank top and underwear.

She took a shuddering breath and went to be with Denna.

Denna had been crying in bed, face pressed into a pillow, for what seemed like forever. Finally, she heard her bedroom door open and close and prepared herself for the chance that Raleigh would break up with her. But Raleigh crawled into bed behind her, and soon she felt Raleigh's body shaking against her. She gasped in surprise, guilt flooding through her, and squirmed until she was facing Ral, putting her arms around her. "No," she breathed. "Please, no." She had never seen Raleigh cry. Not even watery eyes. But Raleigh was sobbing now.

"Denna," Raleigh said, burying her face in Denna's neck and returning the embrace, holding tightly. "I'm scared."

"Scared of me?" Denna asked, a feeling of dread coming over her.

"No," Raleigh said, still shaking. "I'm scared you could be—I'm scared you might be sick."

"I'm not sick," Denna said, confused. "I feel fine now. I was just mad."

Raleigh cried harder. "Not that kind of sick," she said, her voice choked and raspy.

"Oh." Denna exhaled, the dread growing stronger. "Like my mom?" She could barely hear herself she spoke so quietly.

"Yes," Raleigh said, squeezing her tighter. "You were out of control. You—you lost it, completely. That scares me more than anything else."

"But I stopped when you held me." She knew it was a weak offering. "Doesn't that mean I can control it if I have to?"

"That's not fair to your father, if that's true," Raleigh said. "Why should you stop yourself for me and not for him?"

Denna didn't have an answer for that and shrugged, shaking her head. "I don't know."

"And if you're not sick, then your behavior was so far beyond unacceptable that I don't even know where to begin," Raleigh said after a minute of quiet.

"I'm sorry," Denna said.

"You should be. You should be ashamed of yourself, Denna Delilah." Raleigh paused, and Denna did indeed feel ashamed. "Unless—unless you're sick. I need you, do you understand me? You are not allowed to be sick. You're just not allowed." Raleigh squeezed her again. "But if you are, you know I'm not going anywhere, right?"

Denna shivered at the thought of losing the person she'd fallen so helplessly in love with, but she knew that Raleigh would never, ever lie to her, and if she said she wasn't going anywhere no matter what, then it was true. Undisputable. "I believe you," she said, wiping at her own tears. "I need you more than anything."

"You have to go see someone," Raleigh said after just lying there with her arms around Denna for a long time. "To find out for sure."

"I actually talked about that with my dad. He said he would pay for a therapist."

Raleigh squeezed her so tight that she wondered just how long Ral had been wanting her to see a therapist.

"I think that's a really good idea. I will go with you if you want and stay in the waiting room."

"Okay. I'll call first thing on Monday, before school even. I'm so sorry, Ral."

"While I appreciate the sentiment, it is not me you should be continuing to apologize to. You are hurting him, Denna. He is lost about what to do."

"I'll fix it," Denna said, her lip quivering. "He's the best dad ever."

"I can't disagree with that," Ral said. "If my father was even half as attentive as yours, he might have realized—it—he might have stopped—"

"He might have stopped Jason," Denna said, finishing for her when Raleigh couldn't seem to say the words. She knew that Raleigh's father was aloof and neglectful, and her dad was just the opposite, and she hated that she was hurting him. After a while she tried to lighten the mood, hoping Raleigh would let her. "Um, you know you're wearing a tank top and underwear, right?"

"I am aware of that, yes."

"And my dad saw you in a tank top and underwear?"

"It was not the first thing on my mind at that particular moment."

❖

Monday came around too quickly for any of them, and Denna leaned over to whisper in Aspen's ear after the homeroom bell rang. "I have to go see a therapist tomorrow."

Aspen snorted. "About damn time."

"Like you're the poster child for sanity."

"I'm saner than you. At least I don't attack my parents."

"No, they attack you."

"Ow," Aspen said, hand over her heart. "Hit below the belt, why don't you?"

"You asked for it," Denna said in her own defense.

Aspen rolled her eyes and shifted in her seat, then looked different. "Are you nervous?"

"I—what?" Denna's heart started racing.

"You know, I mean because with everything, and like about Ral, and I just maybe thought you might be nervous."

Denna stared at her. "That was a train wreck of a sentence." Being funny was so much easier than being vulnerable, and she was glad she could find something in Aspen's reaction to make a joke out of.

"Come on," Aspen said, regrettably not taking the bait.

Denna was not used to this side of her. "Of course I'm nervous," she said, irritation bristling her skin. She slumped down a little as if her desk could protect her from the harsh realities of life. "What if they tell me I have a really serious mental illness?"

"Then all that will have changed is that you'd have a name for your temper. Them telling you something doesn't make it suddenly true, Den. Whatever's true is already true. But whatever it is or isn't, you know you will always have me and Raleigh. I know we're assholes to each other, but you're my best friend. I wouldn't run away over a label."

Denna's throat felt tight and her vision was a little blurry, and she couldn't believe that Aspen had just made her tear up in homeroom. She didn't know what to say, and the tension in her body was thick enough that a regular knife wouldn't disperse it. Maybe a machete?

She blew out a slow breath and blinked back the tears. "That's good, because I haven't run away over all of your labels," she said, needing diffusion.

Aspen snorted, and Denna knew she'd gotten away with being funny this time. She was grateful for that.

"Fuck you," Aspen said. She slowly extended her middle finger toward Denna. "So did you get grounded? After the party, I mean? I called you but it went straight to voice mail."

"And you didn't leave a message. That's called stalking." Denna sulked at the mention of being grounded. "Yes, I'm grounded. It's good that I got an appointment so soon, because I flipped over the dinner table and Raleigh had to come out and hold me against the wall." She wasn't sure why she was telling Aspen that.

Aspen didn't look surprised, which told Denna a lot about how her friends viewed her outbursts. She was especially glad now that her appointment was tomorrow.

"But the good news is that my dad saw her in her underwear, so we were both embarrassed."

Aspen shrieked. She covered her mouth, but it was too late. The teacher was paying attention now.

"Ladies," he said with a stern look.

Remington chuckled from her seat in the back corner. Several heads turned to look at her, including Aspen's.

She watched Aspen rise from the desk and walk toward her. "You think that's funny?" Aspen asked, leaning on Rem's desk, bracing herself with her hands.

Remington still didn't like to talk in front of the general student body, and so she simply folded her arms across her chest.

Aspen leaned closer, so close that she finally had to lean back in her chair to avoid their faces touching. "Would you think it was funny if I kissed you right now?"

She stood up and growled, giving Aspen a warning glance.

"Ms. Stone!" the teacher said, and Remington realized that maybe growling like a fucking grizzly bear was not the best idea.

Aspen grinned, then sauntered to her desk and slid into her chair.

"Detention, Ms. Stone," the teacher said, adjusting his glasses. What else was new?

Rem's amusement faded, replaced by a menacing glare, directed at both the teacher and the back of Aspen's head. Aspen would regret this.

After school she sat in detention, twirling her pencil, counting the ticks of the clock. Counting the ticks until she would have her revenge. She didn't care that her thoughts sounded like a Lifetime movie. Aspen was going to be sorry.

❖

During a break from practice, Aspen flopped onto her back in the grass, crossing her ankles in Raleigh's lap.

Without looking over at her, Raleigh lifted her feet by the laces of her sneakers and dropped them a few inches away.

Aspen put her feet in Denna's lap instead and was satisfied when they stayed there. "So, Ral, your girl's seeing a therapist?"

"I hardly think you are in a position to judge. I believe you willingly accepted a punishment this weekend, did you not? You and Remington took the bus to school?"

Raleigh still hadn't looked at her. "So?"

"So it seems to me that the old adage 'pot calling the kettle black' would apply in this situation."

"I took the punishment because it was the right thing to do, and it was fair," Aspen said, kicking Denna's thigh in an attempt to rally some backup.

Denna raised one eyebrow at Aspen as if to ask, "Do you really think I'm going to side with you against my girlfriend?"

"Of course you did," Raleigh said, offering a smile as she finally looked at Aspen.

"What's that supposed to mean?" Aspen did not like the implication, whatever the implication might be. And that smile was totally fake.

"Are you really in denial, or merely stupid?"

"Fuck you." Aspen stuck her tongue out and pulled up a handful of grass, tossing it toward Raleigh's face. It scattered in the wind and blew away, not a single blade reaching its intended target.

"Watch it," Raleigh snapped.

"Oh, I'm quaking in my designer sneakers," Aspen said, faking a shiver. "And I'm not in denial."

"Admit it, then." Denna finally spoke up.

"Admit what, bitch?"

"That you wanted a punishment because of some fucked-up psychological need for parenting!"

"Fine," Aspen said, rolling her eyes. "Happy now?" she asked them both.

"Quite," Raleigh said, rising from the grass when the coach called them back over.

❖

The cheerleaders were mostly all still in the locker room getting changed or finishing up showers when Remington walked purposefully in, letting the door slam behind her. Everyone looked over at the resounding sound of metal on metal, and all but three sets of eyes were wide and shocked to see her in their locker room.

She thought Aspen looked nervous. At any rate, she stopped dressing, standing in a fitted T-shirt and panties, a pair of jeans clutched in one hand.

True to form, Rem didn't speak. She stood in the doorway and pointed at Aspen's jeans, then to the bench behind Aspen.

Aspen set her jeans on the bench.

Remington twirled her finger in the air and watched as Aspen turned to face the row of lockers. As she took a few steps into the locker room, several of the girls skittered past her to leave. She didn't care about them, only about Aspen, and teaching her a lesson. If she wanted to push Rem to interact with her in front of the other students, it would be on Remington's terms.

She stepped up behind Aspen and forced her against the lockers.

Aspen gasped. So did several other people. She could hear the rest of the girls scrambling to leave.

Raleigh cleared her throat, taking Denna by the hand, but Denna grinned and shook her head. "I have to see this," she said. Rem didn't care one way or the other.

Raleigh let go of Denna's hand. "I'll wait outside."

They were alone enough now that Remington felt comfortable speaking, but still she kept her voice low and only for Aspen's ears. "Detention?" she asked, breathing against the skin of Aspen's neck.

"Sorry?" Aspen squeaked.

"No," Remington said, shaking her head. "Sorry isn't good enough."

"But what can I say besides sorry?"

Remington bit her on the shoulder, leaving a mark. "That's for detention. Get dressed."

Aspen stood, rubbing her shoulder. "Are you mad?"

Remington picked up Aspen's discarded jeans and thrust them at her chest. "An hour, Aspen. An *hour*. Sitting there, bored as fuck, twirling my pencil, for an *hour*."

"Remington, please," Aspen said, not moving from her spot against the lockers. "I'm sorry. I'll never get you detention again."

"Damn right you won't," Remington said grumpily, folding the jeans into one of Aspen's hands. "Get dressed."

"Rem, I'm sor—"

"Get dressed or I'm leaving without you." She was about to leave when she saw tears in Aspen's eyes. What? What the—? Did Aspen seriously think she was that mad? "No, come on, don't cry," she said, instantly sorry, wiping Aspen's tears.

Aspen leaned into her hand and then dropped her forehead on Rem's shoulder. "But you're mad at me," she said.

"No," Remington said, stroking her hair, turning to kiss her temple. Two things hit her at once—one, yes, Aspen did seriously think she was that mad, and two, being mad at Aspen was something that would make her cry.

"Yes," Aspen said. "You're mad at me."

"I'm not," Remington said, lifting her Aspen's head to look her in the eye, brushing some hair back from troubled green eyes. "I was just being an ass to pay you back for what you did; I'm not mad at you."

"You're not?" Aspen asked, her eyes becoming less worried. "You're not just saying that?"

Remington hadn't seen so much insecurity from Aspen before. "If I was mad at you, you'd know. I'm not mad, Aspen." She kissed Aspen's forehead. "I'm sorry I made you cry. That really sucks."

Aspen laughed a little and shook her head. "It's not your fault. I'm sorry about the detention. I was just playing around. I shouldn't have said it. I was a little asshole."

Remington grinned and kissed her again. "Okay, little asshole, get dressed."

CHAPTER SEVENTEEN

Joey shoved gummy bear after gummy bear in his mouth and chewed rapidly, his eyes glued to the movie screen. Every so often he sipped his grape slushy. Denna hoped he didn't spill any because purple on a white T-shirt would be hard to get out.

Daniel sat with his feet on the chair in front of him and munched popcorn. She had asked him to be ready to cover Joey's eyes if there was any nudity.

Denna sat on the other side of Daniel, engrossed in the horror flick (with the exception of checking on the boys every few minutes) even though it was completely unrealistic and unimaginative. But the boys had wanted to see it, so she gave it a shot, and now she was anxiously waiting for the conclusion even though she had figured out who the killer was within the first twenty minutes.

"Excuse me, miss?" Someone tapped her shoulder.

Denna turned to look over her shoulder. "Yeah?"

"I was just informed that you have children under seventeen with you?"

"Is that a question?" Denna asked, appreciating Daniel's chuckle.

"No, it is not," the theater manager said with a frown. "I'll have to ask you to take them out."

"The law clearly states that children under seventeen are permitted into R-rated movies if accompanied by a parent or guardian. I am their guardian for the evening. I know what they can handle better than you do. And if you kick us out now, I will demand a full refund. I have an expensive lawyer on retainer."

Daniel turned to smile at the man. "Dalton Carmichael. He works for our father," he said, and Denna wondered if that was true or if he was just familiar with her evasive tactics when it came to authority figures.

"I don't care who you have on retainer. That child is not permitted to be in this theater." The theater manager nodded toward Joey.

Denna glared at him but finally sighed and stood up. "Come on, boys. This guy hasn't gotten laid this week, so he's kicking us out."

Daniel choked on a piece of popcorn and started laughing as he got up and tugged Joey with him. "Come on, squirt."

"I'm not a squirt," Joey mumbled with a mouthful of gummy bears. He grabbed his garish purple slushie on the way out. Denna would not be upset when that cup was safely empty.

❖

The Hunters were still not there when Denna brought the boys home. Raleigh would be back from her debate soon, but it was past Joey's bedtime, so she went about the routine with him, making sure he brushed his teeth and got into pajamas.

"Good night, squirt," she said, tucking Joey into bed and kissing his forehead. She turned off his lamp and his nightlight glowed.

"G'night, Denna," he said sleepily, and she figured he was too tired to protest the nickname. It was a half hour past his bedtime, after all.

When she got back to the living room, she was about to find something for her and Daniel to watch on TV when he said something that almost made her drop the remote.

"I know why Raleigh hates Joey."

Denna froze, carefully setting the remote on the coffee table so she could focus her full attention on him. She turned to face him and shook her head. "She doesn't hate him, Danny."

"She does," Daniel said, staring at his hands, which were picking at the hem of his T-shirt. "Because of me. Because when she looks at him, she sees me. And she thinks she should have protected me, but she couldn't."

"I know," Denna whispered, folding her hands in her lap. "She partly blames herself for what happened, for not stopping it sooner."

"But she couldn't," Daniel said. "She was only ten. She was only little. She couldn't do anything. Like I couldn't do anything either. I know I was only six, but I wanted to protect my sister too. It's not just her that feels responsible."

"Have you told her any of this?"

Daniel shook his head. "I'm afraid to upset her."

"I think this is something she'd like to hear," Denna said with a smile. "You should tell her."

"Do you think you could tell her for me? And then if she wants to talk to me, she can?"

Denna nodded without hesitation. "Of course."

"Denna?"

"Yeah?"

"Are you, um, are you my sister's girlfriend?"

"Would that bother you?"

"Nah." He shook his head. "I'm too young for you anyway, and my sister deserves somebody awesome."

Denna grabbed him and pulled him into a hug, ruffling his hair. "Okay, what do you wanna watch?"

❖

Raleigh got home from her debate around midnight and quickly got ready for bed, then crawled in with Denna and snuggled up behind her. She was grateful to Arthur for releasing Denna from her grounding for one night to babysit. Her parents would have gone to the opera anyway, and Raleigh hated the boys being home alone.

Denna stirred, mumbled sleepily, and turned over, nuzzling into her. "I have to tell you something."

"You took my brothers to a strip club," Raleigh guessed without affect.

"We couldn't get in." Denna snuggled closer.

Raleigh snorted. There was no other appropriate response to that.

"No, it's something serious," Denna said with a sigh. "Daniel thinks you hate Joey."

"What?" The hair on the back of Raleigh's neck stood on end. "Daniel thinks *what*?"

"I told him you don't, but he thinks you hate Joey because you see *him* when you look at Joey. He said that—Ral, he said that he knows he was only six but that he hated not being able to protect his sister. That you're not the only one who feels responsible."

"Why hasn't he said this to me?" Raleigh felt the walls closing in. Was she that unapproachable to Danny? After all they'd been through together?

"He's afraid to upset you. He asked me to tell you so that you could talk to him about it if you wanted and he wouldn't upset you by bringing it up."

She was quiet for a long time, letting that sink in. So she wasn't unapproachable, exactly, he was just being considerate of her comfort level. "Thank you, Den."

"I love you, baby."

"I love you too."

"Eh," Denna said, making a noise that sounded like a buzzer when someone got the wrong answer on a game show. "Sorry, folks, but you're wrong! Denna's father has grounded her until her actual birthday, so her party has been moved to next Friday night."

"Game show announcer is not the career path for you." Aspen frowned. "Do you want me to make new fliers?"

Denna nodded, shoving the last bite of her lunch into her mouth and standing, practically knocking Aspen off the bench as she wriggled out of her spot. "Gotta go," she said with her mouth full. "Gotta catch Mr. Waller before class so I can—" She stopped talking and just ran.

"Swallow first!" Aspen yelled after her, then turned to Raleigh with a snicker. "When did you say you were going to teach her table manners?"

Raleigh stared at her, unamused. "Right after you join a convent."

"I'm on my way, you know," Aspen said, puffing up a little with obvious pride. "I've only been with Remington since our first date."

Raleigh was impressed, and shocked, but she didn't let it show. She kept her face a mask of indifference, as it usually was. "Which news channel shall I notify first?"

"National Geographic," Aspen said. "It's a miracle of nature."

"National Geographic is more known for being a magazine."

"Yes, let's split hairs on this fictional notification, please." Aspen rolled her eyes.

Raleigh wasn't going to respond anyway, but the bell rang and she cleaned up her lunch, then headed off to class before Aspen had even finished chewing.

"Uh-huh. Yeah. See ya!" Aspen called after Raleigh pointedly in the absence of a good-bye, or even an acknowledgment that they had been speaking before the bell rang. She huffed to herself and threw out her trash, then stood and turned to go to class, bumping smack into Stefan. He smiled down at her, and when she moved to go around him, he stepped sideways to block her path. "What do you want?" She was not in the mood for this.

"Why are you so bent outta shape at me? I didn't do nothin' to you," he said, his smile turning into a scowl. He held up his broken hand, putting the cast right in her face. "Stupid dyke friend of yours fucked me up."

Aspen wanted to rip his balls off and couldn't believe she'd ever been with him. What had she been thinking? God, ew. "So do you have to take it in the ass from the other jocks now that you've had your balls handed to you by a girl?"

Stefan's face went red, his entire body tensing, and for a second Aspen was sure he was going to hit her, but she heard footsteps behind her, and Stefan stood down. It didn't sound like Remington's footsteps, and when Aspen turned, she saw her science teacher, Mrs. Zavalier, standing calmly with her arms folded over her chest.

"This isn't over," Stefan said.

"Are you not even as much of a man as my stupid dyke friend?" Aspen taunted him, hands on her hips. She knew she should be quiet, but she was pissed off now. "She practically mauled me in front of the entire student body." Okay, that was a total exaggeration. "And you won't even *hit* me in front of a teacher?"

Suddenly Remington was at her side and Aspen wondered where in the hell she'd come from. "Back off, Drumm."

Stefan actually looked a bit nervous. "I was just trying to find out why she suddenly hates me," he said to Rem.

"Because you're—"

"I got this," Aspen said, laying a hand on Remington's arm and catching her eye before turning to Stefan. Something about the way he said that got to her. Like he actually thought she hated him and couldn't understand why. Maybe he *didn't* understand why. Would it be the worst thing in the world to try to actually talk to him, since he was being exceptionally human at the moment? "I don't hate you. It's not really you, specifically, anyway. I've just been realizing a lot of things about myself lately, and you know my history, you're a part of it, so you know there's a lot there for me to be humiliated about."

Stefan shifted his weight and nodded but didn't speak. He didn't look as mad anymore, though.

"I definitely don't like it when you call Remington names, though. That makes me want to hate you."

Stefan's eyes darted to Remington and back to her. "Can we talk alone for a minute?"

Aspen felt Remington tense like a bowstring and she squeezed Rem's arm. "It's okay, Rem. I'll see you in P.E."

Remington turned to her, looking pained. "Are you sure?"

Aspen took a chance on kissing her cheek, then pulled back and nodded. "I'm sure."

Remington pointed a finger at Stefan. "If you touch her I'll fucking kill you."

Did Remington really just say that in front of a teacher?

"Remington," Mrs. Zavalier said, and Rem spun around, giving Aspen the impression that she hadn't actually noticed there was a teacher behind them. "Come on."

"I'm not gonna do anything," Stefan said, though it was more of a mumble than a statement.

"It's okay, Rem, really. I'll meet you in the principal's," Aspen said, figuring that's where Rem would now be headed.

Remington looked extremely uncomfortable but finally sagged a little and gave her cheek a return kiss before walking away with Mrs. Zavalier.

Stefan sat down and Aspen joined him. He looked at her, then stared at the table. "I just like you," he said. "I don't understand why you switched teams. I thought you liked fucking. You know, fucking me."

Aspen almost cringed at the terminology even though a few months ago she would have put it that way herself. And Stefan *liked* her? What? "It's not that I didn't like it." She would try to explain and hope he could get at least some of it. "I did like it. But there were never any feelings with it, it was just sex. All you guys were fine with that and never asked me for anything else."

"I thought that's how you wanted it."

"It was. Or at least I thought it was."

"But Remington?"

"Remington is the first person who's ever said no to me," Aspen said with a huffy kind of laugh. "So it felt like a challenge. Do whatever I had to do to get her to say yes."

"And she said yes, I guess."

"Not in the way you're thinking." Aspen sighed. "She makes me feel good about myself, Stefan. Like I'm worth more than sex. Like what's inside my heart and my brain actually matters. I know you never meant to make me feel the opposite, and it wasn't your fault, it was mostly my fault, but that's not good enough anymore. I like Remington, a lot, and I like myself for the first time ever."

He stared at his cast. "So there's really no chance, then."

"We can be friends, if you stop being a dick."

"That's asking a lot."

Was he making a *joke*? A funny joke instead of an asshole joke? She made a sort of chortling sound at the very idea of it. "Why are you such a dick? You're obviously capable of having a normal conversation," she said, indicating herself and then him with one hand.

"You did most of the talking, actually."

Was that another joke? She snorted and shoved him. And then it occurred to her that she could get a firsthand answer to a question that had been constantly burning in the background. "Why does Raleigh hate you?"

His half smile vanished, and he put his uninjured hand over his face. "I was drunk at a party a couple years ago and kissed her. She completely freaked out like I'd tried to rape her or something and so I freaked out back and said a lot of nasty things about her brother. Like, I asked if he tried to kiss her too and that's how he ended up in jail. But I swear I didn't know what happened, I only found out after that night when Tanner cornered me and lit me up for it. He told me, you know, and she's hated me ever since."

"Why the fuck didn't you just apologize?"

"Because it's easier to be a dick. Nobody expects anything from a dick linebacker."

"Well, it's never too late. You should just apologize."

He moved his hand from his face to the back of his neck, scratching with one fingernail. "I don't know about that. I'll probably just still be a dick."

"Then she'll just continue to hate you even though you obviously feel bad about it. That's stupid, Stefan. Don't be that guy. I mean if I can be monogamous, you can say the word sorry."

He actually chuckled. "We'll see."

"Just do it." Aspen stood up and rolled her eyes. "I gotta get to class. Thanks for talking, though, like a real human being."

He didn't answer and she walked out of the cafeteria, feeling like she was floating. Holy fucking shit, that felt like ten years of growth condensed into one conversation. Not only had she solidified her feelings of self-worth and said them out loud to someone besides Remington, but she had also gotten to know a little bit about the literal *worst* guy in the school that made her understand some things about him and why *he* behaved the way he did.

She couldn't wait to talk to Rem.

❖

Remington was still waiting for Mrs. Corcoran when Aspen came into the office. "Are you okay?" She shot out of her chair.

"Yeah, we just talked. Like normal people. He's a dick because he likes me, but I told him I'm with you and that I'm not having any more casual sex."

Remington almost choked and opened her mouth to make some kind of attempt at a response, but it would have to wait because Mrs. Corcoran came out of her office.

"Remington. Aspen."

"Suspended, right?" Remington sighed.

"No. S—"

"Oh God," Remington said, her stomach flipping. "Am I expelled?"

"No," Mrs. Corcoran said, raising her eyebrows. "S—"

Remington groaned with relief.

"Ms. Stone! Let me finish!"

Remington was pretty sure her face turned red.

"Stefan has been a problem at this school since he enrolled here," Mrs. Corcoran said. "And in light of the fact that you were concerned for Aspen, your threat, while inappropriate, was understandable. Do not let it happen again, is that clear?"

"Yes, ma'am," Remington said. Thank God she would not have to explain getting suspended to her mom.

"Can we have the rest of the day off?" Aspen spoke up suddenly.

Mrs. Corcoran eyed her, then Remington. "I can't do that. But I want you girls to know something."

Remington stared at their principal. What could she possibly want them to know?

"Remington, you have always been a good student, even with the occasional bout of misbehavior." She turned to Aspen. "Aspen, even a principal can tell when one of her students starts making better choices than she had been before. I can't just give you the day off for no reason, but I want you both to know I'm really very proud."

Remington had no idea what to say.

"Thank you," Aspen said, and Rem could hear the surprise in her voice.

Yes, that seemed like a good response. "Thank you," she said to the principal. "That's—I don't—"

"It's all right, dear. You'd better get to class."

Aspen dragged her out of the office. Why did it feel so weird for the principal to say she was proud? Maybe because Rem spent her entire high school career trying not to be noticed.

❖

Aspen was still riding high on the way home after school. She glanced sideways at Remington, wanting to do something nice for her. Remington had been so sweet in the cafeteria, so worried about Stefan hurting her, and she wanted to show her appreciation. "So, what's your ultimate fantasy?"

Remington pulled to a stop at a red light and looked at her. "What?"

"No one's ever been so protective of me before," she said. "I've fantasized about it, but I never thought it would actually happen. I want to make a fantasy come true for you."

Remington looked stunned "Oh. I thought you were being naughty." She was quiet for a minute. "I don't think I have an ultimate fantasy like that," she finally said.

"That's okay, it can just be any fantasy you've ever had, then. Sexual, domestic, academic, I don't care, I'll do it. I *want* to do it." She leaned over and kissed Remington's cheek as the light turned green. "Think about it for a while; there has to be something."

Remington opened her mouth and shut it, turning her eyes back to the road. "I want you to get better grades."

Well, that certainly was not what Aspen had expected to hear. "What? Why?"

Remington shook her head. "Nothing, never mind."

Aspen mentally smacked herself and reached a hand over to rest on Remington's knee. "No, I'll do it, if that's your fantasy," she said. "I don't know how I'll do it, but I'll do it. I'd probably do pretty much anything for you," she added. "I know it sounds silly, but you've changed my life."

Another red light and Remington stretched, wrapping her right arm around the back of Aspen's seat. "Yeah, I know I have," she said, grinning.

Aspen groaned, smacking Rem's leg with the back of her hand. "Arrogant much?" When the light turned green, she slid her hand up between Remington's legs and squeezed. "Can I give you head while you drive?"

"Sure, go ahead."

"Really?!"

"No."

"Tease!"

"You're not putting your head down there," Remington said.

"Okay, I'll use my hand. Undo your pants."

"You know how people in movies crash the car when they try to have sex? That's not going to be me. Get your hand away from there."

Aspen snatched her hand away and sulked. "So why the grades thing? I'm still doing it! I'm just curious."

Rem pulled into the driveway and shut off the car. "You might need them to get into college. I know you're not exactly the plan for the future type, but it's been drilled into me since I could talk, so I just share the wealth?"

Rem looked a little apprehensive and Aspen didn't want her to feel self-conscious. "I haven't thought much about college. Or what I want to do for a living."

"Give my mom another month. You will." Rem was grinning now and Aspen relaxed.

"She'll have her work cut out for her."

Remington laughed and got out of the car. "You said you're going home to get some stuff, right? I'll be at work until nine, so meet back here then?"

Aspen got out and shut the door, moving to Remington and giving her a kiss. "See you around nine."

"See you, hot stuff."

Chapter Eighteen

The first thing Aspen noticed when she pulled up to her towering palatial estate was that her parents' cars were there. That was unusual in and of itself, for them to be here during the day. The next thing she noticed was a blood-red Porsche Boxster with gold trim parked behind her father's car. She didn't recognize that car. Its presence was even more unusual than her parents being home.

She parked behind her mother and got out, set the alarm, and walked up the drive before letting herself into the house. The light in the sitting room was on. Obviously, her parents had an important guest. She would just sneak up to her room and stay out of the way.

"Daughter!" her father called, snapping his fingers from the sitting room when he noticed her.

Shit. "Yes?" she asked, stopping in the foyer, just in front of the grand staircase, without turning to face him.

"Come in here," her father instructed.

She exhaled a frustrated breath and turned, walking into the sitting room, her heart dropping into her stomach when she saw the guy from her parents' party sitting on one of the settees.

"Aspen!" her mother gasped, putting a hand to her mouth.

Her father stood and rushed to her, pulling her out of the sitting room and shaking her by the arms. "What have you been doing? Why are you so unkempt? How dare you come home looking like that when we have a guest!"

Aspen was tired of being pushed around and threw her arms up, twisting out of her father's grip. "I didn't know you had a guest!"

"How dare you talk back to me!" her father raged, grabbing her by the hair and putting his face so close to hers that she could see the blood vessels in the whites of his eyes. "You are going to march in there, apologize for your appearance, and invite our guest to have something to drink!"

"He's not my guest," Aspen said, her skin going suddenly clammy. "I'm not. I am not going to have a drink with him." She shook her head, trying to back away.

"Listen to me, you ungrateful—" He stopped and shook his head. "I do not have time for this. Your mother and I are about to lose everything, and so help me, daughter, if you do not make a good second impression on Mr. Hadley after failing miserably at a first," her father warned her, letting the threat trail off as he used his grip on her hair to propel her back into the sitting room. He squeezed once more before finally letting go.

Tears in her eyes, Aspen turned and fled the room, just barely getting past her father, and ran up the stairs, not stopping until she was in her bedroom with the doors shut and bolted. She grabbed a backpack, tears streaming down her face, and started shoving things into it.

She had always known her parents didn't think much of her, but to have it so blatantly thrown in her face like that still hurt. And what did he mean, about to lose everything? She was desperate to know, but it wasn't like she was going to go back down there and ask him. He probably wouldn't tell her, anyway. She was nothing more than a trophy, a pawn to gain her parents the political prestige they wanted by pushing her in the direction of some affluent and powerful family. She had never hated them more than she did at that moment.

"Aspen!" Her father banged on the door so hard she was afraid he would break the deadbolt.

Dread seeping into every bone in her body, she moved faster, taking her favorite things and some clothes, and her laptop. She had never been more grateful to have left her school stuff in the car. She slung the backpack over her shoulders and pushed open the window, then climbed out onto the trellis and scrambled down as fast as she could. She jumped the last ten feet, and pain exploded in her left ankle when she hit the ground off balance. She didn't care, though. She had to get away. She was not going to be used, not by *anyone*, not anymore.

She straightened and ran across the gardens and down the drive, her hands shaking as she unlocked the car and got in. She locked the doors before she even tried to get the key in the ignition. Her ankle throbbed. It took her three fumbling attempts before the key finally slid home and she turned it hard, then shifted into drive and peeled out of the estate.

She drove straight to Remington's even though Remington was at work. She hoped Catherine was home. She left her things in the car and went up to knock on the door, still shaking from the adrenaline rush and near-paralyzing fear.

Catherine opened the door with a smile that faded as soon as she saw Aspen. "Dear Lord, honey, come in," she said, ushering Aspen inside and closing the door. She took them to the living room and sat Aspen on the sofa, crouching down in front of her and holding her hands. "You just relax here for a minute and I'll make you some cocoa."

Aspen burst into fresh tears and threw her arms around Catherine's neck, clinging to her. "No," she said, burying her face in Catherine's shoulder.

"Okay, all right, shh now," Catherine said, sitting beside her on the sofa, arms going around her. "I'm not going anywhere, honey."

Eventually, Aspen was able to tell her what happened, and couldn't believe her ears at the curse that left Catherine's lips when she finished. It made her laugh. "I've never heard you curse before," she said, wiping her tears. "My ankle really hurts."

"There's a first time for everything," Catherine said, shaking her head. "And what happened to your ankle?"

"I landed too hard on one side when I jumped off the trellis." Another curse. This one more mild, but still! Aspen laughed again. "Stop making me laugh," she said.

Catherine kissed the top of her head. "You want some cocoa now?"

"Sure, thanks." Aspen nodded, finally relaxing against the back of the sofa. "Can I maybe stay here tonight?"

"Of course, Aspen, don't be silly," Catherine said. "You can stay here any night you want. Every night, as far as I'm concerned. It doesn't sound too safe for you at your parents' house."

Aspen thought "at your parents' house" was an interesting thing to say instead of at home. "I'm afraid to go back. I don't really have to throw myself at this guy, do I?"

"You sure as heck don't," Catherine said with a frown. "This isn't the Middle Ages. Your parents can't force you to be with anyone. Let me ask around and find out what your father meant when he said he was about to lose everything."

Aspen jumped as her phone started ringing. She glanced at the screen and bit her lip. "It's him."

"Give me that," Catherine said, snatching the phone and bringing it to her ear. "Hello?"

"Who the hell is this? Where is my daughter? You put her on the phone right now!"

Aspen could hear him yelling, and she grimaced as she imagined how loud that must be right in Catherine's ear.

"Now you listen to me, you self-righteous son of a bitch," Catherine snapped into the phone. "You'll be lucky if I don't report you for child abuse. You keep your hands off of Aspen or you can be sure the police will be involved, as will the local newspapers, and I doubt a man of your status wants a public scandal. Especially since you are about to lose everything. She is not your daughter until you treat her like one." And she hung up.

Aspen sat staring in awe, her mouth hanging open. She already loved Catherine, but that was so epic she didn't even know which way was up.

"Now," Catherine said, her tone of voice completely back to the gentle, supportive one Aspen was used to. She handed Aspen back the phone. "How about that cocoa?"

Aspen nodded mutely, and when Catherine moved into the kitchen, she sent a text to Remington.

Aspen: *OH. EM. G. your mom is so totally and completely made of win*

A few minutes later she had a reply.

Rem: *what*

Aspen: *she told off my dad!*

Rem: *what? why was she talking to your dad*

Aspen: *i'll explain when you get here just wanted to tell you shes epic*

Rem: *are you at my house*

Aspen: *yeah*

Rem: *why*

Aspen: *tell you when you get here its too long to text. come home soon k*

Rem: *im off work in 20 min*

Aspen: *see you then. love you*

Rem: *love you too*

❖

When Remington got home, Aspen told her what happened, right up to the telling-off, which she was still in awe about, and then they cuddled on the couch with her leaning against Remington, Rem playing with her hair.

"Don't go back there, okay? Not alone."

"Okay."

"You swear it?"

Aspen nodded.

"Say it though, please?"

"Okay, I swear I won't go back there alone."

"Good," Remington said, nuzzling her. "How's your ankle feel?"

"Like I got stepped on by a horse," Aspen said.

"Do you want some Advil?"

"That would be nice, actually," Aspen said, wishing she would have thought of that before. "Thanks."

"And my mom said you can stay here as long as you want, right?"

"Yes, but are you sure that's really okay?"

"Of course it is. But we don't have a spare bedroom, so we'll have to take turns on the couch."

"I want to sleep in your bed with you," Aspen said just as Catherine came into the room.

Catherine looked at her, then at Remington. "All right, here's the deal. As long as you behave, you can share the bedroom."

Aspen squealed and moved out of the way so Remington could get up and get the Advil. "We will! I'll wear pajamas, I promise."

Catherine coughed. "I should hope so."

Aspen was too happy to even be embarrassed, and she stood and threw her arms around Catherine. "Thank you."

"Mm-hmm," Catherine said, hugging her back and patting her shoulder. "But if I hear that bed hit the wall one time, all bets are off."

"Mama." Remington groaned.

"I mean it, young lady," Catherine said, raising her eyebrows at Rem.

"We understand," Remington said in a sort of a grumble. "We'll behave. I'm going to go crawl into a hole now and die of embarrassment. After I find Aspen some Advil."

"Aww, you'd help my ankle before you go die of embarrassment?" Aspen asked, hands to her heart, snickering softly at the look on Remington's face.

"I think she's the one you need to convince to behave, not me," Rem said, pointing a finger at Aspen while looking at Catherine.

"I am quite aware," Catherine said, turning her face away.

"Ganging up! What is this?" Aspen whined, flopping to the couch with an arm draped over her forehead.

She watched out from under her arm as Remington went off in search of a remedy for her ankle.

Catherine sat next to her and nudged her. "Sit up. I made some calls while you were talking to Rem."

Aspen sat up, interest piqued, and Catherine handed over her phone, which had an internet article pulled up on the screen. Her eyes bugged as she read the headline. Her parents were being investigated for tax fraud?

She looked at Catherine, jaw dropped. "So since he knows they're about to lose everything, that must mean they're guilty."

"I was thinking that, yes," Catherine said.

"And the Hadleys are filthy rich, so he wants to siphon their money by wedging his daughter into their family. No wonder he lost his fucking mind!"

"Aspen!"

"Oh my God. Sorry. I'm sorry."

Catherine chuckled. "It's fine. I can't disagree."

"He's always been a jerk, you know, but I never seemed important enough to hit. This at least makes sense of that. He's desperate. Suddenly, his livelihood depends on me instead of on him and my mother."

"Well, that is no excuse for what he did," Catherine said, kissing the top of her head.

"No, I'm not saying it is. I'm just glad I understand, because I didn't, you know?"

Catherine nodded just as Remington returned holding a pill bottle.

Rem looked back and forth between her and Catherine. "What'd I miss?"

CHAPTER NINETEEN

Remington must have relented because Aspen was sitting next to her in homeroom. Denna watched Aspen take advantage of that and use it as an excuse to put her desk right up to Remington's, and then five minutes into the ten-minute class, Aspen slid out of her own desk and onto Remington's lap.

"You're lucky you're injured," Remington said, settling her arms around Aspen's stomach, "or I'd push you on the floor."

Denna was a little jealous that she didn't have Raleigh in the one class where they could get away with sitting on laps.

"Would my injury still save me if I kissed you?"

"No."

"Damn."

The bell rang a couple minutes later and everyone filed out.

As they stopped at their lockers, Remington kissed Aspen's cheek, then took her leave.

Aspen flushed and grinned, ducking her head into her locker, and it was very amusing.

"Hey. She kissed your cheek in public, that's impressive," Denna said, rolling her eyes and slamming her locker shut after she had what she needed for science.

"Shut up," Aspen muttered. "Oh, how did yesterday go?"

Denna wished someone would run up and down the hall dragging a stick over the lockers so Aspen couldn't hear her answer. "The therapist wanted me to talk about my mom."

"Ah. Sorry."

"It's okay. It's probably good, really. How else am I supposed to make progress, right? If she just wanted me to talk about Raleigh, there would be no problems to work through."

"Well, that's true. Are you ready for the science quiz?"

"Yes, actually." Denna was grateful for the subject change. The air smelled fresher to her somehow, knowing that she would ace the quiz.

Aspen stopped in the doorway, causing Denna to crash into her. "Wait, what?"

"I studied."

Aspen backed into Denna, forcing her out into the hall again, and spun on her. "Betrayer!"

Denna's jaw dropped. "Not!" Didn't Aspen know she had made a deal with Raleigh?

"Oh my God, you are so dead to me."

"Come on! Don't hate. I thought you knew Ral made a deal with me. She promised to play her guitar for me if I work on my grades."

Aspen's face went from faux anger to abject despair. "Oh no. Fuck. I promised Remington I'd work on my grades. I completely forgot. God, I'm horrible. Can I cheat off you?"

"I don't care." Denna shrugged, holding her hand up, palm facing outward as she stalked past Aspen into the classroom.

"No, I can't do that," Aspen said from behind her.

❖

After class, Denna approached Mrs. Zavalier's desk, leaning her hip against it. "You wanted to see me?"

Mrs. Zavalier waited until the rest of the students were out of the room before she held out Denna's quiz, with 15/15 marked at the top in red.

Denna grinned wildly, but her excitement faded at the look on her teacher's face. "What?"

"The highest mark you have ever gotten on a quiz in my class is three out of fifteen."

"So shouldn't you be like jumping for joy right about now at your teaching abilities?"

Mrs. Zavalier laid the paper on the desk when Denna didn't take it from her hand. "From whom did you copy?"

Denna's mouth went slack. She had never cheated on a test in her life, not ever. "No one," she said quietly before she could stop herself from sounding hurt. She quickly schooled her surprise and glowered at the teacher.

"And why should I believe that?"

Her shoulders slumped a little. "I don't know."

"I just find it hard to believe that you have gone from less than twenty-five percent to one hundred percent with nothing in between."

"Everyone thinks I'm stupid," she said, "but I'm not. I just never tried hard before now."

Raleigh went skidding into the room, quickly surveying the scene and sighing with relief at the absence of overturned tables. When Aspen had come running to tell her Denna was held after class, she'd feared the worst. Her assessment changed from relief to concern, though, at the wounded look on Denna's face. "Denna?"

Denna spun, tears shining in her eyes. "I didn't cheat," she said. "You know I studied."

Raleigh smiled. "Does that mean you got a good grade?" she asked, squeezing Denna's waist.

"I got a hundred percent," Denna said, looking and sounding a little confused at her reaction.

"Of course you didn't cheat," Raleigh said, leaning in to kiss her, unmindful of the hawk-like eyes watching their every move. "Go wait in the hall. And close the door."

Denna returned the kiss with a little noise of contentment and left the room.

When the door clicked closed, Raleigh turned on Mrs. Zavalier. "Sheila," she said, snatching up Denna's paper.

"Ms. Hunter," the teacher said coolly.

"She studied for this quiz."

"So you say."

"If you accuse her of cheating again, without irrefutable proof, of which there will never be any given the fact that Denna is not a cheater, I will go to the school board with something you will not like." They were both very much aware of what Raleigh was alluding to—a gambling habit. Mr. Zavalier worked with Raleigh's father, and Raleigh had overheard plenty of conversations she wasn't supposed to have overheard during business meetings in her kitchen.

Mrs. Zavalier's eyes widened almost imperceptibly, her hands trembling as she shuffled papers around on her desk. She tossed her hair back over one shoulder, trying and failing to adopt an air of nonchalance. "We will not have a problem."

"No, I didn't think we would," Raleigh said, staring her down another moment before turning to leave.

"Ms. Hunter," Mrs. Zavalier said when Raleigh had almost reached the door. "How did you get her to study? I have failed at that all year long."

Raleigh turned and pressed her lips together for a second. "The answer would not be appropriate for me to share with you." She turned back and left, not caring whether the door stayed open behind her.

"What happened?" Denna asked, bouncing.

"She knows you did not cheat," Raleigh said, taking her hand and walking with her toward their next class. It was the only class they had together—P.E.—because Raleigh was taking all advanced placement courses.

Aspen and Remington had the same class, and they met in the locker room, Denna and Aspen chatting idly while they all dressed out and headed for the gym.

She spoke quietly to Aspen as they lined up for stretches. "Remington looks ridiculous with that jacket on over the P.E. uniform. Please ask her to remove it at your earliest convenience."

"It's her security blanket!" Aspen gasped, her expression scandalized.

"Then she should refuse to dress out. The combination is utterly abhorrent."

"She doesn't want to fail. She gets straight As, you know, just like you."

Raleigh was not happy about her P.E. grade. "I have an A minus in P.E."

Aspen grinned. "Maybe you should wear a leather jacket."

"Have I mentioned how little I like you?"

"Not in a while, actually. I was starting to wonder if you were slipping." She stretched her calf muscles in a lunge, then switched legs.

"No, no, I still dislike you," Raleigh assured her. "No need for concern."

❖

On Monday morning Denna burst into homeroom and threw her hands in the air. "I'm eighteen!" she shouted, tumbling into a roundoff and then sliding into her desk with a squeal.

"Ms. Ashford!" the teacher said, stepping back to avoid her.

"I'm eighteen!" Denna said, flushed with excitement. "Do you have any idea how long I've been waiting for this day?"

"I still don't want to be kicked in the face," the teacher said, straightening his tie. "But happy birthday."

The whole class, except for Remington, started singing "Happy Birthday" to Denna. It was the worst rendition of the song she'd ever heard, but it made her giddy and she kicked her feet rapidly against the tiled floor. "Thank *you*," she said, clutching her backpack to her chest with a beaming smile. "Party at the Farm on Friday night. No drugs, we got busted last time."

"Ms. Ashford!" the teacher said.

Denna had mostly forgotten he was there. "What? I said *no* drugs."

"What's the Farm?" A girl in the back row spoke up.

"You know, that abandoned farmhouse off the highway," Denna said.

"Why is it called the Farm?"

Denna stared at the girl. Was that a real question? "Because it's a farmhouse."

The teacher covered his face.

❖

"Cartwheels? In homeroom?" Raleigh asked at lunch. Unfortunately, it was quite easy to picture.

"Don't face-palm, Ral," Aspen said.

"Please do not use netspeak when talking face-to-face," she said, the term almost physically painful. "I don't even approve of it textually."

"What, face-palm?" Aspen asked. "That's a totally valid word. It's not even an abbreviation."

"Yeah, baby, don't face-palm," Denna said.

"I am willing to let that go in light of the fact that you aced two quizzes last week, provided that it does not insert itself into conversation again in my presence." She lightly flicked Denna in the shoulder.

Aspen rolled her eyes. "I think you were a dictionary in a past life."

"The dictionary was my favorite book as a small child." She would sit on her bed all hours of the day looking up words. She remembered hiding it under her pillow when she wasn't reading it so her mother wouldn't find it. Her intelligence had always been difficult for Darlene to handle.

"How small are we talking?"

"Four."

Aspen groaned.

Denna took her arm. "Don't be jealous because my girlfriend is a genius."

"I'm not jealous. Remington's a badass."

They were about to head to their respective classes when Raleigh was called to the office over the loudspeaker. Her stomach dropped. The counselor was probably here. "Come with me?" she asked Denna.

"Catch up with you later," Aspen said, heading off in the opposite direction as she and Den.

❖

Raleigh recognized Jazlyn even though it had been years. She had been a good counselor, and she was a nice person, but Raleigh really did not want to see her.

"Hello, Raleigh," Jazlyn said, standing from her chair.

"Hello," Raleigh said. "What can I do for you?"

"Can we talk in one of the conference rooms? Your principal assured me that would be okay."

Denna stepped in between them. "Does she have to do this now?"

Raleigh made no attempt to stop her, both because she appreciated the intervention and because she was frozen in fear.

"It's just a routine visit, but it is important," Jazlyn said to Denna.

With shaking hands and staying well behind Denna, Raleigh took out her phone and texted Remington.

I need you in the office.

There was a silent standoff for roughly fifteen seconds before Remington flew through the door, surveyed the situation, and stood in front of the counselor. "Get out," she said and growled, baring her teeth.

Raleigh was shaken from immobility at the tone of Remington's voice. "Rem, it's okay, she was my counselor."

Rem spun around, looking at her. "You said you needed me."

Raleigh swallowed and nodded. "I do. I wanted you to come in with me."

Remington looked embarrassed and put her hands in her pants pockets, slowly turning back to face Jazlyn. "Sorry," she mumbled, barely audible.

"It's fine," Jazlyn said, seemingly unaffected. "I'm glad that Raleigh has such good friends."

"I'm her girlfriend," Denna said, and Raleigh didn't miss the note of possessiveness in her voice. That rarely surfaced, but she always loved it, and it almost made her smile now.

"Well then, I'm glad Raleigh has such a good friend and such a good girlfriend," Jazlyn said, and then looked at her. "Are you okay to proceed? They are more than welcome to come in. It's entirely up to you. I'm not here to try to make you uncomfortable. We can reschedule, but the—"

"It's fine," Raleigh said, not wanting to hear the rest of it. "I want them with me. The conference rooms are over there." She nodded toward the back part of the office.

"Thank you. I'll try to make this quick."

She still felt shaky and light-headed. She gave a subtle nod, not trusting her voice, and took Denna's hand on the way to the conference room.

It didn't turn out to be as daunting as she'd thought upon first seeing Jazlyn. The counselor just wanted to prepare her for the logistics of Jason's parole hearing, who would be there, what the order of things was going to be, and her rights and responsibilities. Most of it she already knew, but she found that she didn't mind hearing it again.

It really was quick and relatively painless, because Jazlyn didn't bring up anything about the abuse directly, and she was much more relaxed by the time she said good-bye and walked Jazlyn out.

She turned to Remington. "Thanks. Sorry to scare you."

Remington shrugged her off. "Don't even worry. Are you okay?"

"Yeah. It wasn't as bad as I thought it would be. But really, thanks. See you later?"

"Later," Rem said, and left the office.

Raleigh laid her forehead on Denna's shoulder. "I liked that little possessive bit. I'm her *girlfriend*." She grinned against Den's shirt.

"You noticed that?" Denna asked, whistling.

She nodded. "I noticed that." And then suddenly she shot upright. "Danny," she said, and moved to the doorway of the principal's office. "Mrs. Corcoran, would you call the middle school and make sure they don't let her talk to my brother until I get there? Daniel Hunter."

"Of course," Mrs. Corcoran said, already moving to make the call.

"I hope she didn't go there first," Raleigh said, wringing her hands.

"I'll find out," Mrs. Corcoran said as she dialed and put the receiver to her ear. "Hi, Susan? It's Joyce, over at the high school. Fine, how are you? Listen, has anyone been to the school today asking for Daniel Hunter? No? Okay, great. If a woman does show up, can you please have her wait until his sister, Raleigh, gets there? Okay, thanks, Susan. Yes, she'll be on her way in just a minute. You too. Bye-bye."

Raleigh sighed with relief as she listened to Mrs. Corcoran's side of the conversation. "Thank you," she said when the principal hung up.

Mrs. Corcoran nodded. "My door is always open."

Raleigh managed a small smile. "Thank you."

"Baby, do you want me to go with you?" Denna asked softly, rubbing her hands up and down Raleigh's arms.

A few more slow breaths and Raleigh had regained the rest of her composure. "You're not getting out of class," she said. "But I appreciate the offer."

Denna kissed her forehead and sighed. "Can't blame a girl for trying."

"I'll be fine. I was just shaken. I'm over it."

"See you after school?"

"See you after school," Raleigh said, squeezing Denna's waist and then moving quickly out of the office and down the hall.

❖

"Jazlyn Hyte came to my school today," Raleigh said in the middle of dinner. It was just her and her mother—Danny was at baseball practice and Joey was at Cub Scouts, and her father was still at work.

"Is she a friend of yours?" Darlene asked, not taking her eyes from the book she was reading as she ate.

Raleigh put her hands in her lap, squeezing her knees as she answered, trying to keep the anger from her voice. "No. She was Daniel's and my counselor."

"Why do you sound angry at me? I have no control over that."

If there was ever a time when Darlene didn't miss the point of something, Raleigh would drop dead. "Did you know she was coming?"

A pause, then a shrug. "I can't be expected to remember what other people have told me they're going to do."

"I'll take that as a yes. You're supposed to tell me about these appointments."

"Don't get flippant with me."

"Do you not love me? Or Danny? Is that it, Mother?"

"Don't be ridiculous. Of course I love you, you're my children."

"Then what is it? You just love Jason more? Or maybe you don't believe he did what he did?"

Darlene finally put her book down and looked at Raleigh. "I'm sorry about what happened, you know that, but what am I supposed to do? He's my son, too."

"You're supposed to protect us now since you didn't back then!" Raleigh yelled, tears filling her eyes as she stared pleadingly at her mother. She hated showing weakness, especially in front of her family, but if there was any way to get her mother to stand up for them now, then she had to at least try.

"You stop it!" Darlene shouted, pounding her fist on the table and standing up. "I sent you both to counseling. What else do you want me to do?"

"I want you to fire that attorney and let him have a public defender. I want him to stay in prison for his full sentence and not get out on parole. I want you to never let him step foot in this house again!"

"He's your brother, Raleigh!"

A single tear finally rolled down her cheek and she dropped her head in defeat. "He hurt us, Mother. Over and over and over again. He may be your son, but he is not my brother." She took a deep breath before continuing, still staring at the table. "If he gets out of prison and you allow him back in this house, I will petition the state for custody of Daniel and Joseph and take them away from you."

Darlene gasped. "You have no idea what you're saying."

Raleigh lifted her head at last, her gaze calm and cool. "I am smarter than you and my father and all your business associates combined and multiplied exponentially. I know what I'm saying, Mother."

"Watch your mouth," Darlene said. "You don't know the first thing about raising children."

"Don't I? What do you think I've been doing for the past six years?"

"You'd have nothing. Your father and I work so hard to provide for you kids. We make sure you have the nicest things."

Raleigh's eyes hardened past cool to cold. "Wearing secondhand clothes is a small price to pay for feeling safe in your own home."

"You wouldn't have a home."

"I always have a home with Denna."

Darlene threw her hands up. "There you go, talking about that girl again. What is it with you and that girl?"

"The point is, Mother, that the state is not going to permit you to keep your children if you willfully allow a sexual predator into their home."

"Don't threaten me, Raleigh. And there's no use discussing this until after the parole hearing anyway."

"You make me sick," Raleigh whispered, standing from the table and leaving the house before Darlene had a chance to answer.

CHAPTER TWENTY

The day before Denna's birthday party, which Remington had explicitly requested not to be forced to attend but which she was attending anyway, she found herself alone with Mama after school while Aspen was at cheer practice. There was something she had been wanting to bring up for a while but hadn't gotten the chance. Okay, so she'd chickened out whenever she did have the chance, but that was beside the point. The point was that it hadn't been discussed yet, and it needed to be. "Hey, Mama?" she said, standing in the doorway between the kitchen and the living room, where her mother was reading the newspaper.

"Yeah?" Mama asked, looking up.

Playing with one of the zippers on her jacket, Remington moved into the room and sat on the couch next to Mama. "I wanted to talk to you about something."

"Something nerve wracking, obviously," Mama said, putting the paper down on the coffee table and turning to face her. "What is it, honey?"

"Well, Aspen and I have been going out for a while, and..." She trailed off, losing her nerve at her mother's raised eyebrow. "Never mind," she said quickly, her face flushing as she resolved to get up and run.

Mama laughed, grabbing her arm to anchor her to the sofa. "Remington," she said, shaking her head. "I know where you're going with this. At least I think I do." She sighed. "You're pretty much all grown up, and you have a girlfriend you love. At least I hope you love her; you'd better. And I have forbidden you from being physical with each other in the house. Is that what you want to discuss?"

Remington's face was burning, something she was highly unused to, but she nodded. "Yes."

Mama sighed again. "I knew this day would come. I just didn't know when. I told myself that if you came to me about it, I would do my best to be flexible. It's just hard for me, thinking of my little girl having sex."

Remington thought she might try to crawl under the couch and wait for an apocalypse before crawling back out. "It's just that we don't have anywhere else to do it," she forced out, her voice much higher than usual. "Not that we've done it yet. And we're both eighteen."

"I'm not going to roast you over a spit. Would you relax?" Mama laughed. "Give me a little credit. I just..." She shook her head and ran a hand over her face before continuing. "If you rearrange your room so your bed is not against my wall, I'll allow it. Just please, make sure you're ready. And make sure *she's* ready? Remember what you told me when we first talked about liking her?"

"Yes, and I didn't try to fix her, but she doesn't sleep around anymore. She hasn't been with anyone since we went to that party together. You know, the one with the leather pants."

Mama laughed. "If you're sure you know what you're doing, Rem. Go ahead."

Remington muttered a thank you and fled the room, intending to hide out in her bedroom until her face stopped burning. While she was at it, she moved her bed to the far wall.

About an hour later, she was finished rearranging and had showered and dressed in boxers and a tank top when a soft knock came at her door.

"Remington?"

"Come in."

Mama stepped in, a smile on her face. "I have to go to work, hon," she said, moving to give Rem a hug. "One more thing about our conversation? Please get a lock for your door."

Remington had been almost over the embarrassment, but it flared anew and she squeaked at her mother, who just chuckled and left for work.

When she was alone, Remington flopped on her bed with a groan, then got up and pulled her phone out of her jacket to text Aspen.

Rem: *can you stop by the store on the way home and get a lock*

Aspen: *what*

Rem: *a lock for the bedroom door. get one on the way home okay*

Aspen: *k*

Remington flopped on the bed again, and then got up, *again*, when something occurred to her. She riffled through Aspen's drawers until she found what she wanted and grinned. The bra might be a little big for her, but not enough to matter. They were Aspen's favorite set. Red lace. Very sexy, revealing red lace. She undressed and slipped on the panties, shivering at the feel of the lace against her skin, then put on the bra, satisfied that it fit well enough to look good. She checked herself in the mirror, grinning, and pulled the boxers and tank back on over the lingerie. She hoped Aspen would like it as much as she thought she would.

❖

Aspen let herself in with the key Catherine had made her. "Hello," she called.

Remington poked her head out of their bedroom. "Come in here."

"No objections," Aspen said with a grin, dropping her backpack and just taking the bag with the lock in with her. "Hey, what did you do?" She blinked as she looked around at the changes. "I'm totally going to trip over things when I get up to go to the bathroom in the middle of the night. I finally got the layout mapped in my subconscious!"

"Close the door," Remington said, reclining on the bed.

"Okay," Aspen said, closing the door.

"We're allowed to make out and stuff," Remington said, folding her hands under her head. "That's why the bed is moved."

Aspen crawled onto the bed over Remington. "Really?" she asked, leaning down for a kiss. "You're not just trying to get me in trouble?"

"Really." Remington unfolded her hands to bring them around Aspen's neck, winding into her hair. "You're so beautiful," she said, pulling Aspen down for another kiss.

"So are you," Aspen said back. She ran her hands up Remington's sides, stopping when she felt underwire. "Are you wearing a bra with pajamas?"

Remington didn't answer, just raised her arms so Aspen could pull off the tank top.

It was a little hard to maneuver the top off with Remington lying down, but Aspen tugged until she got it, then gasped as she let the shirt fall from her fingertips to the floor. "Oh my God," she whispered, running her hands reverently over Remington's breasts, encased by her favorite lacy red bra. She had to close her eyes for a minute against the sight—pale skin offset by the deep red lace, blue eyes staring at her with a mixture of desire and vulnerability, blond hair fanned out over the sheets and the pillow beneath Rem's head. "Are you wearing my panties too?"

Remington bit her lip and nodded.

Aspen's breath came in a rush and she scooted backward, hooking her fingers in the waistband of Remington's boxers and slowly inching them down over her hips, then sliding them the rest of the way off in one smooth motion. "Remington," she said, running trembling fingertips over Remington's knees and up her thighs.

Remington squirmed, watching her.

Aspen's eyes went unfocused.

"Is it okay?" Remington asked.

Aspen groaned, her eyes raking over Remington's body. "How can you even ask?" Her voice came out rough around the edges. Like she'd swallowed sandpaper. "I want them to stay on you forever, but I want them off." She dropped her head to place wet, open-mouthed kisses along Remington's quivering stomach. "I'm conflicted." And something occurred to her that made her breath catch. "Don't move."

She went to the door and peeked out to make sure they were still alone, though she knew they would be, and then quickly darted out, grabbed her backpack and hurried back into the bedroom, closing the door. She rooted around in her bag until she found her phone and pulled it out, climbing onto the bed again and watching as Remington blushed. "Please?" she asked. "No one else will see them."

Remington licked her lips. "You like this that much?"

"Yes. God, yes," Aspen said, opening her phone's camera. When Remington didn't roll away or cover up, she snapped a picture, then stood up on the bed to get a full-body shot.

At first, Remington looked uncomfortable, but the second the flash went off, Aspen could see something change. A glint in her eyes, maybe.

Aspen took shots from a few different views before she dropped back down, straddling Remington's knees. She reached out with one hand to tug the panties down on one side, just far enough to reveal a hint of soft hair. She snapped another picture.

Remington gasped at that shot.

She took one of Remington's hands and slipped her fingertips just barely inside the waistband of the panties, where they started to angle down, and shivered when Rem let her take another picture. "You're amazing," she said with some difficulty. Her chest felt constricted.

"Are you done?" Remington asked, biting the inside of her cheek, keeping her hand where Aspen had placed it.

Aspen could feel sweat prickling at the back of her neck. "Just one more. Please?"

When Remington nodded, she pressed the button, then moved a little to get a better angle and took another.

"You said one more," Remington complained.

"Okay, just one of us kissing and that's it," she said, lying down next to Remington and holding the phone above them.

Remington acquiesced and kissed her, slow and sweet, opening her mouth to accept Aspen's tongue as the flash on the phone went off.

As promised, Aspen lowered her arm behind her and set the phone on Remington's nightstand. "I like that you wore this for me."

Remington grinned at her. "I can tell." She grabbed for her boxers and started pulling them on. "Can you get my shirt? You dropped it on the floor."

Aspen leaned over and grabbed the shirt, holding it out. "Okay, but not just because it's sexy," she said with a snort. "Also because it means you thought of me, you know? Thought about what I might like and went out of your way to do it." She was trying to say something here, something she wasn't used to and had no frame of reference for. "You make me feel really important." *There. Not so bad.* "Getting to know you has turned my life upside down, in the best way I can imagine."

Remington was looking at her a certain kind of way—one of the ways she could never read. Was it shy? Was it happy? Was it embarrassed? Was it affectionate? What *was* it?

"I make you feel important because you are," Remington said, moving a hand into her hair and scratching lightly at her scalp, which felt amazing. So maybe that look was affectionate, then. "I've never really felt this comfortable with someone before. You make me feel like it's okay to be myself, and to want things, and to put myself out there a little more."

Aspen put her hands on Remington's waist. "Before I met you, I wouldn't have cared where I ended up, or where anyone else ended up. But you've—you've somehow taught me to value myself, and I do, Remington, I really do. My parents may not, but the more I'm with you, the less I think about them."

Remington growled. "I'd like to take a swing at your father."

"Hey. I value you too. I know you're a badass, and I love that about you, and I'm not trying to suggest that you should be any less badass, just please don't throw any punches unless you're protecting yourself from like, physical harm."

Remington was just staring at her in awe as the seconds, minutes ticked by. Finally, lips pulled into a tight line, eyes almost brimming with tears, Remington just nodded.

"Thank you," Aspen said, allowing herself to relax, her lips parting in a relieved smile. "Okay, I have homework to do before dinner."

Remington blinked. "You're willingly admitting to having homework?"

Aspen gave her a sheepish look. "Well, I promised you to work on my grades."

Rem grinned. "I wasn't complaining, just surprised. And impressed. Do you need any help?"

Aspen shook her head. "No, it's not science. I've got history and math. I paid attention in class today, so I know the material."

Remington sighed, and Aspen thought it sounded really happy. Like they were on a beach in Hawaii on their honeymoon. "Okay. I've got some physics. I'll join you."

They did homework until dinner, sprawled on their stomachs on the bed, propped up on their elbows. "I'm going to ace the test on Monday," Aspen announced as they closed their books.

Remington smiled. "You think so?"

"Mm-hmm," Aspen said. "And then if I do, in celebration, you can take me out to dinner."

Eyebrows lifting, Remington's smile grew. "I can? Thanks for the permission, Your Highness."

Aspen groaned at the teasing. "Your spurs are showing."

"You think I'm riding you?" Remington said into her ear.

Aspen sat up and pulled until Rem was straddling her. "Ride me," she said, suddenly a bit breathless.

Remington pressed down, arms going around her. "We have to go eat dinner."

Aspen flopped backward dramatically and threw an arm over her eyes. "You're the worst."

Remington blew her a kiss and left her there.

Aspen got up a few seconds later and wandered to the kitchen to ask if there was anything she could help with.

CHAPTER TWENTY-ONE

A re you nervous, honey?" Mama asked, straightening Remington's shirt and fussing over her hair.

"No," she said through clenched teeth. "I hope he rots in hell."

"Are you sure you don't want us to come with you?" Aspen asked, wringing her hands and biting her lip as she stared at Remington, who was dressed very professionally in slacks and a nice blouse. Without her leather jacket. She knew Aspen loved the jacket, and since she couldn't wear it to a parole hearing, she was letting Aspen wear it instead. It smelled like her, which she knew because Aspen had mentioned it no less than three times in the last ten minutes, and Aspen was hugging it tight to herself.

Rem shook her head. "No. I don't want either of you to hear what I'm going to say." She did not want Aspen to hear her give her account of what she'd seen. "I just want to tell them what I saw so he doesn't get out early." She had of course told her mother at the time, but that was different. She'd been ten years old and unfiltered. It was a different kind of language back then.

"Nail him to the wall, honey," Mama said, grabbing her face and kissing her forehead. "I love you, and I'm proud of you, you know that, right?"

"I know, Mama," Remington said, giving her a quick hug, then hugging Aspen and kissing her cheek before she picked up her keys from the coffee table and headed out of the house.

Aspen watched her go, hugging the jacket even tighter and leaning her head down to smell it until she felt eyes on her and looked up to see

Catherine with a hand over her mouth. "It smells like Rem," she said, quiet but not quite embarrassed. "I'm nervous."

Catherine roped her into a one-armed hug and ruffled her hair. "Let me tell you something about Remington. She is very good at doing what needs doing. She'll be fine, and she'll make sure that Raleigh and Daniel are okay too."

"What if he gets out?"

Catherine shook her head. "I don't know, honey. As they say, we'll cross that bridge if we come to it."

"I guess." Aspen nodded, but she couldn't help being nervous.

❖

"No!" Raleigh shouted, slamming her fist down on the kitchen table. "You can't bring Joey! Denna will watch him. She already said she would!"

"I'm not leaving him with that girl." Darlene scowled, snatching up her purse and checking her coiffed hair in the mirror.

"She's a better mother than you are!" Raleigh retorted, furious.

"Shut your mouth," Darlene said, breezing out of the kitchen to where Raleigh knew her father and brothers were waiting, dolled up in suits, and she followed. "Let's go," Darlene said, lips pursed into a thin line.

"I'm riding with Raleigh, remember?" Daniel said, taking a step toward Raleigh.

"Me too, me too!" Joey piped up, obviously having no idea of the nature of the event they were attending.

"Let them ride with her, Darlene. What does it matter?" her father said, pulling on his coat.

"Come on," Raleigh said, taking her brothers by the hand, one on each side, and rushing them out the door before Darlene had time to change her father's mind.

"She's going to take him to that girl's house," she heard Darlene say as she ushered the boys into her car and got in.

"Joey," she said as she buckled her seat belt and locked the doors, "how would you like to go hang out with Denna?"

"YES!" Joey squealed, pumping his fist as if he'd just won the best prize a six-year-old could ever win. Raleigh could hardly disagree. For a minute, she had been so focused on thwarting Darlene's efforts to be an even worse mother than she already was, but now that she knew Joey would be safe, she had time to be terrified of what she was about to do.

❖

"He won't be in there," Remington said as she caught Raleigh's shaking hands in her own and squeezed.

Raleigh exhaled a shuddering breath and pulled Daniel closer, feeling as if she were about to be sick all over the tiled floor. She nodded to Remington, grateful for her supportive presence, and for so many other things that they never talked about. When she saw Jason's attorney her stomach lurched and she shoved Danny into Remington's arms, darting into the bathroom at the end of the hall. She threw up into the trash can, and when the dry heaves finally stopped, she washed her face, rinsed her mouth, and slammed her hands on the counter. She had to get it together. She was eighteen years old now. There was no way Jason could ever hurt her again; she'd kill him first. But she was worried for Daniel. And for Joey if Jason was granted parole. She knew her parents wouldn't protect her little brothers. They had already proved that once. She didn't know what she would do if they let him out.

She paused at the door, listening to Remington and Daniel just outside it.

"This sucks, for all of us," Remington said. "It's okay to be freaked out."

"Are *you* freaked out?"

"No, I'm just pissed off." That almost made Raleigh smile.

"I guess I should be freaked out for *him*, then, if you ever see him again," Danny said.

"Exactly."

Raleigh came out of the bathroom wiping her hands on her slacks. "Let's just get in there," she said. "Before I decide I can't do it."

"You have to do it, Raleigh," Daniel said. "And I have to do it. This is the time the counselor told us about, remember? The time we'd have to take action? This is how we stand up for ourselves. And even if he gets out of jail, or prison or whatever, at least we did our part. She said we won't regret testifying even if he gets out."

"I know." Raleigh sighed, scrubbing her hands over her face and taking a slow breath. "Can we just—is the door open yet? Can we go in?" She glanced over just as an officer emerged from the small room they were going to be gathering in.

"They just opened it. Let's go," Remington said.

❖

Denna knocked on the door, and Aspen opened it looking strung out on not-exactly-legal pills, but she didn't comment. She felt much the same way and she knew Aspen hadn't really self-medicated. Not in Mrs. Stone's house, that was for damn sure. That woman scared Denna. But not in a bad way. Not like a cringe-when-you-see-someone kind of way, but like a be-on-your-best-most-politest-behavior-around-them kind of way. She hugged Aspen tightly and then moved into the house, Joey trailing happily behind her.

They had decided to all hang out at the Stones' house while they waited to hear something from Remington or Raleigh. Aspen had suggested it when she found out Denna was watching Joey because she had thought the little man might want to play some Xbox, and Denna had readily agreed.

"Joey, this is one of my best friends, Aspen. Aspen, this is Joey, the coolest six-year-old on the planet."

"Last week it was only the coolest six-year-old in the country!" Joey said, wide eyed.

"Well, you got cooler!" Denna said, rolling her eyes. "Duh!"

Joey giggled and hugged her waist. "Well, you're the coolest girl on the planet!"

"Thanks, squirt!" Denna said, picking him up and spinning him around as Aspen laughed and shut the door.

"Okay. So, Joey. What's your favorite Xbox game?"

"I dunno," Joey said as Denna set him down. "Never played it."

"What?!" Aspen shrieked, putting a hand to her heart. "Oh no, we can't have that. At all. Come look through my games and pick one. Why haven't you ever played?" She led them to her game collection, which was quite extensive if she did say so herself.

"We don't have Xbox." Joey shrugged.

"Hm. Remington has some good games too, but mine are better,"

Aspen told him as she started pulling them off the shelves so he could look through them. Denna noticed that she left some of the more gory ones up, figuring Aspen didn't want Raleigh to kill her.

"There's so many!" Joey said, his eyes lighting up as he started turning the cases over and looking at the pictures on the back. "I want this one!" he said after only looking through a few. "Sup, super, sss-muh-a-sh brothers. Brothers! I know that word, brothers!"

"Hey, good reading, squirt!"

Joey groaned, flopping his head into Denna's lap. "I'm not a squirt!"

"Okay, *Super Smash Brothers* it is!" Aspen said. "Catherine! *Super Smash Brothers* in five, four, three…"

Catherine appeared in the doorway before Aspen got to two. "I'm here!" She hurried over to sit with them and hooked up the controllers. "You must be Joey."

"That's me. Who are you?"

"I'm Catherine. I live here, with Remington and Aspen."

"Ohhhh, you're their mom," Joey said.

"Cool *and* smart!" Denna told him, smiling at Remington's mother. She hadn't been around her much and she had to admit she was nervous. Of course, she was already nervous about the hearing, so maybe it was more that. So many things could go wrong; there were just so many variables. She had been trying to squash her litany of what-ifs all day. Maybe being nervous around Remington's mother would give her something else to worry about. "Hello, Mrs. Stone, thanks for letting us come over."

"Call me Catherine," Catherine said with a dismissive little wave, and picked up a controller. "Okay, what are the teams?"

❖

Remington kept a reassuring hand on Raleigh's knee as everyone filed in and took their seats around them. They had been the first in the door, and now were just waiting for people to finish arriving and for the proceeding to begin. Finally, an older gentleman with graying brown hair seated at the table in the front of the room reached over and turned on a tape recorder.

"In the matter of the parole suitability of Jason Hunter, we begin the proceedings on the record. I am Commissioner Julian Claybourne, C-L-A-Y-B-O-U-R-N-E. I would ask each of you in attendance to state your position and name for the record and spell your last name." He nodded to the woman seated at the table next to him.

"Commissioner Emily Wright, W-R-I-G-H-T."

Next was Mr. Carmichael, at the end of their row to the right. "Attorney for inmate Hunter, Dalton Carmichael, C-A-R-M-I-C-H-A-E-L."

"Assistant District Attorney Janet Cain, C-A-I-N."

"Interested member of the public, Henry Ludlow, L-U-D-L-O-W."

Commissioner Claybourne held up his hand. "And what is your interest, Mr. Ludlow?"

"I live down the street from the Hunters. I have young children, Commissioner."

"Thank you." He nodded to Remington, who was next.

"Witness, Remington Stone, S-T-O-N-E."

Claybourne held up his hand again. "Witness for inmate Hunter or opposing early release?"

"Opposing early release, Commissioner."

"Thank you." He looked at Raleigh.

"Witness opposing early release, Raleigh Hunter, H-U-N-T-E-R."

"Could you spell your first name, please?" Commissioner Wright asked.

"R-A-L-E-I-G-H."

"Thank you."

"Witness opposing early release, Daniel Hunter, H-U-N-T-E-R."

The rest of the people were in the back row so they started again at the right, with Darlene. "Inmate Hunter's mother, Darlene Hunter, H-U-N-T-E-R."

"Inmate Hunter's father, Jackson Hunter, H-U-N-T-E-R."

"Interested member of the public, Jazlyn Hyte, H-Y-T-E."

"What is your interest, and could you please spell your first name?" Commissioner Claybourne asked.

"J-A-Z-L-Y-N. I provided counseling services for inmate Hunter's victims after the fact."

"Thank you." He glanced to the guard at the door.

"Correctional Officer Henry Mann, M-A-N-N."

"Thank you. I have a few more questions and then we will begin," Claybourne said, turning to her father and Darlene. "Mrs. Darlene Hunter, for the record, will you be speaking on inmate Hunter's behalf?"

"Yes, Commissioner," she said without hesitation.

"Mr. Jackson Hunter, for the record, will you be speaking on inmate Hunter's behalf?"

His response was not so forthcoming. Silence reigned, Darlene's eyes going wider with every second that passed, and finally Jackson shook his head, tears in his eyes. "No, Commissioner."

"What?" Darlene said, whirling on him. "He's your son!"

"Mrs. Hunter, please do not speak out of turn," Commissioner Wright sanctioned her, "or you will be asked to leave."

Darlene managed to control herself, even if she was still fuming obviously.

Raleigh's throat was too dry to swallow comfortably, and she turned away from her parents. She wondered if her father said no because he felt guilty for what had happened or just because he didn't want to talk about it. Either way, her chest burned with gratitude for him, for this one small fatherly act.

"Thank you," Commissioner Wright said when it was silent again. "We will hear from inmate Hunter's attorney, Mr. Dalton Carmichael, first. Mr. Carmichael, have you prepared a written statement for your client's file?"

"Yes, Commissioner. I also have reports from the prison psychologist and inmate Hunter's cellmates."

"We do not accept reports from third parties, but you may hand in your written statement now," Wright told him, indicating the file folder in front of her.

Jason's attorney rose and set a piece of paper in the open folder, then returned to his seat.

"Let the record show that Mr. Dalton Carmichael has just placed his written statement into the appropriate folder," Wright continued. "Do you wish to speak at this proceeding as well?"

"No, Commissioner. My written statement will be sufficient."

"Thank you, Mr. Carmichael."

Claybourne handled the next order. "District Attorney Janet Cain, have you prepared a written statement for inmate Hunter's file?"

"Yes, Commissioner." She did not wish to speak either, and Darlene was called on next.

She hadn't prepared a written statement and wanted to speak.

"Please give your statement for the record," Commissioner Claybourne said after making the appropriate notations in the file in front of him. "And state your name again."

"Mrs. Darlene Hunter," Darlene said. "I would like to start off by saying that my son was always a good boy, and—"

Claybourne interrupted. "Please be more specific, Mrs. Hunter. You have three sons."

Indeed.

"Jason," Darlene said. "My son, Jason Hunter, he was always a good boy. He got good grades, he never got into any trouble. He would, well, he would look out for the kids that other boys bullied, you know? He had a way of talking to people that got them to realize what they were doing was wrong. He had so many friends growing up, even into high school he was always surrounded by friends. He helped out around the house, helped take care of his little brother and sister when Jackson and I had to work. He's a very helpful boy."

Take care of his little brother and sister? Did she forget what this fucking hearing was about? Raleigh wondered if she was trying to convince the parole board or herself. She felt Remington squeeze her knee and gave a tight smile of thanks.

Darlene went on and on about how helpful Jason was and what a nice boy he was who cared for others, blah blah blah. Raleigh had to tune it out or she was going to scream.

Finally, it ended and there were no more people who wanted to speak on Jason's behalf. Remington was next.

"Remington Stone, witness opposing early release," Commissioner Wright addressed her. "Have you prepared a written statement?"

"No, Commissioner."

"Would you like to speak at this proceeding?"

"Yes, Commissioner."

"Please give your name again for the record and then you may make your statement."

"Remington Stone," she said, taking a slow breath. "I grew up next door to the Hunters. Raleigh was my best friend since we were four years old. We did everything together and told each other everything. After her tenth birthday party, I noticed a change." She bit down on the bile in her throat at the memories. "She didn't tell me everything anymore and she never wanted to do the things we used to do. She—we loved swimming, but she told me she didn't like bathing suits anymore. We used to climb trees together, but she said it was babyish. I believed her then, but now I know it was because she was hurt, and she—" Her voice choked with emotion and she cleared her throat, hardening her resolve. Her voice was emotionless when she continued. "She couldn't sit astride the branches. We used to play baseball, but she told me she got too out of breath running the bases. I knew something was wrong, I just didn't know what it was." The room was dead silent, and Remington renewed her resolve again before she went on. "I went over one day, and nobody answered when I knocked on the screen, but the door was open so I just went in. I heard crying from her bedroom and ran back there, and—" She swiped a hand over her face, trying to block out the picture in her mind.

"Take your time, Ms. Stone," Commissioner Claybourne said gently.

Remington brought her anger to the surface, to override the nausea. "Daniel was on the floor next to the bed, naked, huddled in a ball crying. He was six years old. Six! Raleigh was ten. She was a sweet little girl and he tortured her!" she yelled, losing control of her temper before she could rein it in. But the commissioners didn't seem to mind. They didn't ask her not to yell. "Jason was holding her by the hair, forcing her to—" Her voice cracked, and she clenched her fists. "Do I have to say it?"

"It is up to you what you wish to say," Commissioner Claybourne replied. "Your testimony is for the parole board to review, and for this case that includes myself and Commissioner Wright. If you feel we will understand your meaning without explicit language, I don't see the need for you to use words you are uncomfortable with."

"Thank you," she said, clearing her throat again. "He was forcing her to have him in her mouth. She was crying, and she tried to pull away, and I saw him pull back and slap her, then start again, until I started throwing things at him and screaming. He tried to calm me down. He told me it was okay, that he was their big brother and was just looking out for them." Her voice was dripping with acid now. "I kept screaming, at the top of my lungs, until he took a swing at me, and I kicked him in the groin hard enough to knock him down. I wrapped Danny and Raleigh in blankets and dragged them to my house, and my parents called the police."

She could hear choking behind her and turned to see Mr. Hunter with tears streaming down his cheeks. She didn't have the energy to feel anything for him, though.

She turned back and addressed the commissioners again. "Raleigh was so sad after that, for so long. Her spirit was crushed, and she hated herself for not being able to protect Danny. It took years of therapy before she was even partly back to her old self. Even now she still seizes up at the mention of his name and comes close to panic attacks when she's put in situations like the counselor coming to the school to talk about her testimony."

Commissioner Wright spoke when Remington had been silent for a minute. "Is there more to your statement, Ms. Stone?"

"Only that Jason Hunter is a manipulative bastard and if he is released on parole, well, you know the recidivism rate for child molesters and I'm sure you also know that the Hunters have a six-year-old son at home as well as his two previous victims."

"Thank you, Ms. Stone."

Remington nodded.

Commissioner Claybourne spoke up, to the room at large. "We will take a five-minute break and return for the remaining testimony."

She had to spend all five of those minutes convincing Raleigh not to leave. In the end it was Daniel who convinced her anyway.

"Don't leave me here, Raleigh," he said. "I need you."

Raleigh hugged him fiercely and returned to her seat with him and Rem despite how shaky and sweaty she was. She looked like she was about to faint. "I can't talk in front of all these people. I can't, I c—"

"Shh," Remington said as the commissioners filed back in and turned on the tape recorder, stating they were back on the record. "Write a statement. You don't have to talk." She turned around and whispered to Mr. Hunter. "Give me a notepad and pen from your briefcase."

He did as she asked, handing over the requested items, and she gave them to Raleigh.

With a shaking hand, Raleigh started to write.

"Ms. Raleigh Hunter." Commissioner Wright began the second half of the proceedings. "Have you prepared a written statement?"

Raleigh was writing furiously and didn't answer the question.

"She's writing one now, Commissioner," Remington replied for her. "She panicked at the thought of talking in front of an audience."

"Let the record show that Ms. Raleigh Hunter is writing a statement for the board's review and will not be giving verbal testimony." Wright spoke into the tape recorder. "Mr. Daniel Hunter, have you prepared a written statement?"

"No, your Hon—I mean Commissioner. I haven't. I want to talk."

Commissioner Wright smiled at him. "Of course. Please give your name again for the record and then you may make your statement."

"Daniel Hunter. And I want to say first that I know my sister thinks she should have protected me, but it wasn't her fault. He was hurting her too and she tried her best, and it wasn't her fault. The first time it happened, she tried to make him stop, and he hit her in the stomach and made her throw up. He said that was for trying to help me and it would be worse next time if she wasn't a good little bitch and let him do what he wanted."

Raleigh curled farther into herself, putting her feet up on the chair and hugging her knees with one arm while she wrote. Rem laid a hand on her shoulder.

"My sister was really sad all the time after it started. I think I was too young to understand what was happening, I just knew it hurt, but Raleigh knew, and it made her so sad. She always had straight As but she got all Ds in fifth grade. I know her teachers called the house a few times, but I always heard Mom saying everything was fine. I remember thinking it wasn't fine, but that I couldn't say so because Jason would hurt Raleigh more. He promised that if we ever told anybody he would hurt us so much worse than he already did. The counselor told us that happens a lot. She told us that people like Jason threaten their victims to keep quiet because they don't have any power once their secret is out. I wish I was smart enough to know that before, but I was only six. The same age as my brother Joey is right now. You can't let Jason near him, you just can't. Please, keep him in jail forever. He'll hurt Joey, I know he will. He's sick, the kind of sick that nothing can fix. He would get so excited when we cried. We tried not to cry, but he'd just do more things to make us cry, and then get excited. He never hit our faces;

he said it was because then people would ask questions, and besides that, he liked to look at our pretty faces when he…" He glanced at the commissioners. "Can I say 'fucked'?"

"There are no limitations on your testimony here," Commissioner Claybourne said.

"When he fucked us. He liked to look at our pretty faces when he did that. Look, he ruined our childhoods. Please don't let him ruin anyone else's. It's too late to protect us, but you can protect Joey. I know our mom will let him in the house; she doesn't care what happens to anyone but her first baby. I know she knew what was happening, I know that now. And she didn't stop it, she didn't even try. And my dad? I don't know about my dad. I don't think he knew. He wasn't home a lot. He still isn't home a lot, and he doesn't seem to care much about us, either. He can't protect Joey if he's not there. Just, please. He's a danger to society, to Joey, to Mr. Ludlow's kids down the street. Don't let him out. He'll never change. He abused us for almost a year before Remington found out and stood up to him. He wouldn't have stopped. Keep him away, please." He took a breath. "That's all I have to say."

"Thank you, Daniel," Commissioner Claybourne said. "You are a very brave young man and I applaud your candor." He stood. "I would like to thank everyone for coming and everyone who testified in this matter. We adjourn this meeting, and pending Ms. Raleigh Hunter's written statement, Commissioner Wright and I will convene and come to a decision. If you wish to be informed of the decision, please submit a request in writing to the clerk's office. They will show you what form to fill out. End record." He turned off the tape recorder.

Remington waited with Raleigh while she finished writing her statement and turned it in to Commissioner Claybourne, then walked her and Danny to their car. "Everyone's at my house," she said. She'd had a text from Aspen waiting when she turned her phone back on. "I was thinking, why don't you two head straight over there and I'll pick up ice cream on the way and bring it home?"

Danny grinned. "Chocolate fudge caramel rocky road swirl with bubble gum?"

"That's disgusting." Remington made a face.

"Okay, okay. Just chocolate."

"Deal."

Raleigh didn't say anything as she got in the car, gripping the steering wheel until her knuckles turned white.

Remington bent down and talked to her quietly. "Are you okay to drive?"

Raleigh nodded, her voice choked when she finally spoke. "I need Denna."

"She's at my house. You'll be with her in five minutes. Okay?"

Raleigh nodded again. "Yes."

Rem waited until Raleigh's taillights disappeared before she got in her own car and headed for Cold Stone.

❖

Joey's fingers were like lightning as he slammed the buttons at an amazing speed, his character flipping and kicking and using all the special moves at once. Aspen growled out an angry whine and threw her controller on the floor as he kicked her ass yet again at a game she was wicked good at!

Denna and Catherine had long since tired of the stiff competition and were now just watching as Aspen and Joey battled it out on different stages and Joey won every single time. They both kept laughing and whispering to each other, until Aspen threw her controller and Catherine cleared her throat. "Aspen, is that any example of how to behave?"

Aspen had forgotten about her audience since she couldn't hear what they were whispering, and bit her lip as she picked up the controller. "I, uh…" She was saved from having to think up a reasonable excuse by a knock on the door.

Denna jumped up and ran to the door, then flung it open. Aspen could see Danny and Raleigh on the porch. Danny was grinning, but Raleigh looked like she was going to be sick. "Hi, Danny. They're playing Xbox. Go grab a controller!" Denna said.

When Danny rushed over to her and Joey, Denna pulled Raleigh inside and into Rem's bedroom, shutting the door.

"Where's Remington?" Aspen asked Danny. "You must be Danny, right? I'm Aspen."

"Rem's getting ice cream. Nice to meet you, Aspen. Did you just lose to Joey?"

Aspen scowled at him. "He's a *Super Smash Brothers* hustler, did you know that? Pretending he's never played before and then kicking my butt over and over and *over*."

Danny laughed. "Wow. Who would've thought, my little brother, the video game king."

Joey squealed with laughter too. "I haven't ever played before!" he said. "Swear!"

Aspen heard Raleigh break into sobs and froze. She caught Danny's eye, both of their gazes flicking to Joey and back, and Aspen reached over to turn up the TV. "REMATCH!" she shouted.

"I'm in!" Danny said loudly. "And I'm Donkey Kong!"

"I'm Yoshi!" Aspen yelled.

"I'm Link!" Joey said, joining in the shouting, and as far as Aspen could tell, he didn't know why they were all being so loud. He had learned the names of all the characters as he played, but he always chose Link. Aspen wondered if she would win if she got him to play a different character.

"You look more like Pikachu," Danny said.

"Hey! I'm not fat and yellow!"

"Pikachu is not fat!" Aspen said, staring at Danny in horror.

"He kind of is, if you think about it," Danny said, pressing his lips together in an obvious attempt not to laugh. "He's almost as wide as he is tall."

Aspen grumbled and they started the round while Catherine went into the kitchen to make hot chocolate for everyone.

Roughly ten minutes later, Remington came in with a giant Cold Stone bag. "Who wants ice cream?" she asked, and Aspen watched as Joey abandoned the game mid-battle to run for the kitchen.

"HA! I win!" she nearly screamed in triumph as she smashed Joey's immobile character off the screen.

"That's just pathetic," Danny said, shaking his head.

Aspen stuck her tongue out at him, then bounded over to Remington and kissed her cheek. "Hey," she whispered. "Are you okay?"

"I'm fine. Raleigh's not."

"I know. We turned up the TV so Joey wouldn't hear her crying."

❖

Raleigh had started sobbing as soon as she hit Denna's arms, clinging to her desperately, face buried in her neck.

Denna didn't say anything, she just let Raleigh cry and held her. It seemed like the only reason she finally stopped crying was because all possible moisture had left her body. She felt drained and empty, in a fairly good way, but mostly she felt safe in Denna's arms. She always felt safe there. "I love you so much," she whispered at last.

"I love you too, baby," Denna whispered back. "Are you gonna be okay?"

Raleigh nodded. "I just needed to cry. I feel exponentially better already. And of course being close to you helps."

"Now I know you're okay. You said exponentially." Denna grinned. "I think they're having ice cream out there. I heard someone yell about ice cream a few minutes ago. You want?"

Raleigh licked her lips. "I do want. Are my eyes red?"

Denna peered at her. "Of course they are. You were crying. It's okay, it's human," she said, giving Raleigh a kiss.

Raleigh leaned into the kiss. She put her arms around Denna's back and ran her hands up and down. "Sometimes I don't want to be human."

"But you're so very good at it."

"What I wouldn't give to be inanimate right now. With no concept of humanity."

"Inanimate!" Denna screwed up her face. It was one of Raleigh's favorite expressions.

"Yes, inanimate. If there was some way to temporarily become a rock…" She loved to rile Denna up on occasion. "No?"

"No."

"And here I thought I was a genius, coming up with that."

"You are a genius, Ral. That's why the world can't lose you to inanimacy."

"That isn't a word." Raleigh rolled her eyes and pushed off Denna to stand up, giving a stretch and a yawn in an attempt to shake off the night's stress. "All right. Ice cream."

CHAPTER TWENTY-TWO

Denna had decided to postpone her party again, this time until after the parole board made their decision. Raleigh had submitted an official request to be notified by email the moment the decision was reached and recorded, and they were both on alert every time Raleigh's phone beeped.

They typically weren't allowed to have phones on during class, but Mrs. Corcoran had given her permission and notified the teachers, without letting them know the reason, which Raleigh was grateful for. She had just left Denna's side after lunch and was settling into calculus when her email notification went off. When she saw it was from the court, her heart started hammering, her air flow constricted, and she looked desperately up at the teacher.

Her teacher moved to her side and leaned down. "What is it, dear?" she asked discreetly.

"I need to go get Denna," Raleigh managed to whisper, and when the teacher nodded, she all but flew from her seat, leaving her things scattered on her desk as she headed for Mr. Waller's room.

Denna was reaching into her backpack for a piece of gum, but when she saw Raleigh appear in the doorway she shot out of her chair, at Raleigh's side in an instant. "Did you read it?"

Raleigh shook her head.

"Let's go to the office and I'll read it for you, okay?" Denna said, and when Raleigh nodded mutely, Denna led her to the office, and Mrs. Corcoran let them use the empty conference room for some privacy.

Raleigh sat and handed Denna her phone.

Denna sat next to her and navigated the email screen, opening the document. When it loaded she started reading aloud.

"D. HUNTER–FSID #77514G5F. DECISION. COMMISSIONER CLAYBOURNE: Parole denied, hold forty-eight months. Next appearance is April 2024."

She looked up at Raleigh.

Raleigh had been holding her breath and let it out in a long, relieved sigh, her entire body relaxing. "Four years. We don't have to deal with this again for four years," she said, leaning forward to rest her forehead on Denna's shoulder. At least Joey would be ten in four years, which was better, but not ideal. If Jason had to serve his entire sentence, which was twenty years and two months, Joey would be eighteen when Jason got out, and Raleigh could live with that. "Thank God. I don't know what I would have done."

Denna put her arms around Raleigh, squeezing tightly. "This is fucking awesome news," she said. "Do you want to hear the rest?"

"Not right now. I'll read it later. I just wanted to know." She grinned and lifted her head, kissing Denna. "I feel like celebrating."

Denna blinked, handing back the phone. "Now?"

Raleigh nodded.

"You mean to tell me that you, Raleigh Hunter, are suggesting we don't go back to class?"

"I—no. I most certainly am not." Except she was.

❖

Denna swiped a pile of passes from the secretary's desk on their way out, then pulled a pen from her backpack and scribbled a note to get Raleigh out of class since she had to go back in to get her stuff. Then she wrote one for Remington and Aspen, collecting them from their classes as well, and the four of them piled into Denna's SUV.

"Where do you want to go, Ral?" Aspen asked, getting into the back and bouncing.

"You're shaking the car," Denna said, turning to look over her shoulder.

Remington was more subdued than Aspen, but even Denna could tell she was happy.

"I want to go to the beach and get so drunk I can't walk a straight line," Raleigh said, grinning.

So Denna stopped at a local quickie mart and flirted shamelessly with a random guy to get him to buy them some whiskey, and then headed out to the beach. There were none nearby, except the tiny one across from where Remington and Raleigh used to live, so it was about an hour drive, but she didn't care. None of them cared. They rolled the windows all the way down and let the wind wreak havoc on their hair, blasting music and singing at the top of their lungs.

❖

They drank. A lot. And when the sun set they gathered sticks and built a fire.

"Rocks!" Raleigh shouted out of nowhere as the flames sprang to life. "Put rocks around it."

"We're in the sand," Denna said. "Sand doesn't burn. And it's wet."

Aspen had never seen Raleigh so carefree. It was awesome. She knew it probably wouldn't last past today, but it was still awesome. She looked over from her position on her back in the sand a few yards away. "We should go get some of that clay stuff by the wall over there and paint ourselves."

"Yes!" Denna shrieked, pointing at Aspen and making her feel like a genius. "But it'll mess our clothes."

Aspen meant to ponder that but ended up spouting the first thing that came to mind. "Get rod of them. Rid of them. Take 'em off!"

"*Yes*," Denna hissed, stumbling over to the wall in question, a freestanding stone wall separating the sand from a cement walkway into the woods. The sand around it had hardened into a sort of clay over the years, and Denna dug both hands in, then carried a big pile back to their little campsite.

Five minutes later, they were all naked, though Remington insisted on wearing her leather jacket. Aspen didn't mind because as everyone and their mothers knew, she loved that jacket. She and Denna had Remington and Raleigh lie on their backs while they slowly, painstakingly drew clay lines across their faces, chests, stomachs, thighs, shins, and ankles. Remington and Raleigh, for their part, were good subjects, lying still while she and Denna painted them.

"Doesn't that feel so nice?" Aspen asked.

Rem stared up at the sky. "It's sticky."

"My turn," Aspen said as if Remington hadn't even answered. She lay down beside her and waited for Remington to sit up and start painting her. "Make sure the lines are even. And criss-*crossed*," she sang.

Remington mumbled something about being drunk, not stupid. She sat up, grudgingly, Aspen thought, to apply Aspen's body art.

When they were all painted to Aspen's approval, Denna insisted that they howl at the moon, and even Raleigh, in her drunken state, complied.

It wasn't long until Aspen and Raleigh were on their knees, throwing up. They emptied out toxins and nutrients alike while Remington and Denna pretty much sat and stared. Denna would have helped, but things were a little too fuzzy.

A strong wind started to pick up and a flame caught the very edge of their pile of clothes, spreading fast. Remington shrieked like a little girl and commenced throwing wet sand on the fire, screaming at Denna to help her. Once Denna got into the mix they were able to put out the flames, but most of their clothes were now useless.

"Shit!" Denna cursed as she held up her jeans. They would barely cover her ass with the holes burned into the seat of them, and the outside of one leg was charred.

Aspen and Raleigh, once done purging their stomachs of everything they'd contained, crawled over to see what the shrieking was about, and when she told them, they both burst into laughter. Hysterical laughter.

❖

After sunset, Denna made everyone get in the car. She turned the heat on, locked the doors, and went to sleep. None of them were in any condition to drive. Remington only just remembered to set an alarm so they'd wake up and could get home at a reasonable hour.

Except to have the heat on meant to have the SUV on, and when the alarm went off at midnight and she woke up and oriented herself, the engine was off. And why was her face—? "Why are we painted with… what is this, clay?" she asked, her face stiff with the dried substance. She swiped a hand over it to try to rub it off, but it was stuck pretty good. Her head throbbed with the aftereffects of drinking. That was the main reason she usually avoided it. "And why are we all naked?" she asked after looking around.

Denna groaned. "You don't remember the shrieking and putting-outing of fire? We took off our clothes to paint ourselves with the clay, and the pile caught on fire. Your jacket's fine, though, don't worry. You kept it on all night."

"That doesn't explain the clay." She paused, realizing the more important aspect of the statement, and she had to keep herself from shouting. "Those were my favorite jeans. Did anything survive?"

Denna shook her head.

"M'sorry, baby," Aspen said groggily, taking the longest to become coherent. "I'll buy you a new pair, just the same, I promise." She rubbed at her eyes and blinked. "Why is the heat off? It's freezing." She snuggled against Remington's side, putting her arms around her.

Raleigh sat up straighter in the front seat, head snapping toward Denna. "I am going to die if I don't get some Advil. Why is the car off? I can't." She held her head in her hands.

Denna's eyes widened, and she faced forward and turned the key in the ignition. The engine spluttered but wouldn't turn over. "Oh my God," she said, slapping the steering wheel. "We left the heat on while we sobered up and ran out of gas."

"You didn't have a full tank to start with?! This is why I don't drink!" Remington said in a panic. "Because things like this always end up happening. Fuck!"

"It's okay," Aspen tried to soothe her, stroking the side of her face. "We'll figure something out. We'll call someone."

"Not my mom," Rem said, allowing the touch. "She'll kill us."

"And then revive us so she can kill us again," Aspen said. "And we know my sperm donor and incubating vessel are out of the question."

"My mother would hang up on me," Raleigh said, face still in her hands, fingertips rubbing her temples in circles.

All eyes turned to Denna.

"I hate that you're all suddenly looking at me, but I guess we knew all along it was gonna be my dad," Denna said with a slight cringe. He was pretty understanding, but this was above and beyond the call of duty—it was midnight and they were an hour out of town.

"We're naked!" Raleigh shrieked. "Him seeing me in my underwear was bad enough!"

"He saw you in your underwear?" Remington asked.

"I have a blanket in the back," Denna said, ignoring Remington's question. "We'll all have to share it."

Aspen visibly perked up at the mention of a blanket and pushed onto her knees, reaching over the back of the seat and dragging the blanket toward her. She spread it out over her and Remington, then scooted even closer to Rem to make room for Denna and Raleigh.

Grudgingly, Denna and Raleigh climbed into the back and squished together to fit on the seat, which was only meant for three people, and huddled under the blanket.

"Damnit," she cursed, throwing the blanket off and leaning forward between the seats to grab her cell phone from the glove compartment. It was a stretch, but she managed, and wriggled back under the blanket, taking a calming breath before she dialed her home number. Her dad didn't answer until the fifth ring, so she knew he'd been asleep. Sometimes he stayed up late on the weekends, but sometimes he didn't.

"Hello?"

"Dad?"

"Denna, what's wrong?" Even half asleep, he somehow always knew when she was in distress. It must be a dad thing. "Are you okay?"

"I'm fine, I'm just out of gas."

"Where are you?"

She hesitated, biting her lip. "At Hastings Beach."

"Aw, Denna," he said. "Well, there's nothing else to do; I'll come out there with a can of gas. Are you sure you're okay? You're with Raleigh, aren't you? You're not alone?"

"No, Dad, not alone. I'm with Raleigh and Aspen and Remington, actually."

"Remington Stone?"

"Mm-hmm."

"I didn't know she was a friend of yours."

"She's Aspen's girlfriend."

Remington raised an eyebrow and Denna waved her off.

"Ah, I see. Well, anyway, give me a little time to get dressed and I'll be there as soon as I can. Keep the doors locked and don't open them for anybody, okay?"

"Okay, I promise. Thanks, Dad."

Luckily, the beach had a designated parking area, and she had chosen to park in it, so it was easy for her dad to find them. When he saw them huddled under a blanket in the back seat, he frowned. "Are you girls okay?" he asked after Denna had unlocked the door for him.

"We're okay, we're just—we're okay," Denna said, offering a smile.

"All right. Want to give me a hand here, Den?"

"Uh, I kind of can't."

He paused in his retreat toward the gas cap and stuck his head back in the door. "What?"

"We're naked."

"Oh dear Lord," he said, shaking his head. "Somehow I think I'm better off not knowing."

Aspen and Remington both hid their heads under the blanket.

"How do you plan to pump gas when you get to a station?"

Denna squeaked. "I hadn't thought that far ahead."

Awkward didn't even begin to cover the situation, but her dad handled it with grace, giving a terse nod. "I'll drive you; you girls stay in the back under the blanket. Then we'll come back here, I'll take my car, give you my T-shirt so you're not driving naked, and we'll pretend this never happened. Deal?"

"Deal."

❖

When they got back to Denna's, getting inside was a little tricky, but they managed it, and once they were safely in her bedroom with the door closed and locked, Denna and Raleigh got into the shower to wash off the clay while Remington and Aspen waited under the blanket, not wanting to get the bed dirty.

Remington texted Mama to say that she and Aspen were crashing at Denna's. She wouldn't get it until the morning, but whenever she did wake up she'd know where they were and not worry.

Once they were all showered and dressed in various items of sleepwear that Denna had rooted out for them, Denna said that they could all share the bed, just this once. Due to bonding and shit.

Remington draped an arm over Aspen and pulled her close, nuzzling her neck and placing a soft kiss there. "Good night," she whispered.

Aspen pressed into her and sighed. "G'night."

"I…I just want to say thank you, to all of you," Raleigh said quietly after a minute or so. "I won't admit this again after tonight, but you're all exceptionally good friends and I consider myself lucky to have you." She paused and then continued. "I mean it, though, don't ever bring it up again; I'll deny having said it."

Rem grinned, Denna chuckled, and Aspen spoke for all three of them. "We have no idea what you're talking about, Ral."

Raleigh picked her head up to look over. "Exactly."

❖

Denna was the last to come out of her room in the morning, and when she saw everyone at the table already eating, her stomach growled. "French toast?" she asked, hurrying to sit down. "Thanks, Dad!"

"Mm-hmm," he said, flipping a couple of pieces onto her plate. "It already has butter, and the syrup and powdered sugar are on the table."

Nearly drooling, Denna picked up the bottle of syrup and poured it over her French toast, then stopped to look up at her dad. "I really appreciate you coming to g—"

"LALALALALA," he interrupted her, fingers in his ears. "I meant it when I said we were going to pretend the whole thing never happened."

Denna stared at him when he sang and plugged his ears. Aspen was the first to start laughing. Denna followed, and Remington and Raleigh just chuckled a little.

"What are your plans for the day, Den?" her dad asked, moving the subject along. "There's a baseball game at the junior college at one if you want to join me."

"Can Raleigh come?"

"I abhor baseball. You go."

Denna frowned at Raleigh, but then smiled toward her dad. "Okay. Just me and you, then. If it wouldn't be too *horribly* boring hanging out with me by yourself."

He snickered, pointing the spatula at her. "Very funny."

CHAPTER TWENTY-THREE

Finally, the next Friday night, Denna was having her birthday party come hell or high water. The one for the friends who had been out of town for the first party. Aspen was impatiently waiting for Remington to get ready so they could meet up with the birthday girl at the Farm.

"Are you ready?"

"Almost."

"How about now?"

"Aspen."

"What?" Aspen asked, swaying her hips in what she hoped was an innocent-looking manner, her hands clasped over the front of her skirt.

"I'll be ready when I'm ready. Stop asking."

"I don't want to miss cake!"

"Aspen! Stop it! Go without me if you don't want to wait," Remington said, grabbing her boots from the closet and stamping her feet into them.

"No," Aspen said, shaking her head. "I'll wait."

Remington zipped up her boots and pulled her jeans down over them, then pulled on a white tank and shrugged into her jacket. She dragged a brush quickly through her hair and tossed it on the bed. If Aspen ever brushed her hair like that, she would lose chunks of it. "Okay, I'm ready."

"Took you long enough."

"It took me five minutes!"

Aspen snickered and moved to her, pressing their bodies together, and their lips. "Just kidding," she said, nuzzling her nose against Remington's. "Can we have sex in the hayloft?"

"*Wow*, Aspen, please, don't buy me flowers or chocolates, just fuck me in the hayloft," Remington said, staring at her.

Aspen stared back. "So is that a yes?"

Remington rolled her eyes and spun to the door, smacking Aspen's ass on the way out.

❖

The party was well underway when they got there. Denna had a microphone and was dancing on a table while Raleigh watched from an old tattered couch, a grimace on her face.

Before Rem could catch her, Aspen squealed and ran for the table, jumping up beside Denna and joining in.

Remington sank down beside Raleigh on the couch. "Isn't this something girls are only supposed to do when they're drunk?"

Raleigh ran her hands over her cheeks and flopped her head back, staring at the ceiling. "This is my punishment for refusing to dance with her."

"I wouldn't put my head on this sofa. Why would you refuse to dance with her?"

Raleigh's head snapped up. The look she gave Remington could have cut glass. Whether it was for the sofa comment or the question, she wasn't sure. "I don't dance."

"It's her birthday," she said, unaffected by the look either way.

"It's her birthday party," Raleigh said. "Her birthday was weeks ago."

"And did you dance with her on her birthday?"

Raleigh looked a little bit like a kid with a cookie. "If that's what you want to call it."

Remington leaned back and folded her arms across her chest, keeping her head away from the decaying velvet. "Your girlfriend is stripping."

Raleigh's head spun toward the table and she lunged off the couch, catching Denna's wrists before she could pull her shirt over her head and forcing them back down. "Don't you dare."

Denna pouted. "Pay attention to me, it's my birthday."

"It's your birthday *party*, and I am paying attention to you. What are you talking about?"

"You weren't watching me. I was dancing for you, you know." She handed the microphone to Aspen and put her arms around Raleigh's neck, hopping down off the table.

Raleigh's expression softened and she smoothed her hands up and down Denna's back. "I'm sorry, baby. I'll pay more attention to you."

Aspen grinned and turned to Rem, bringing the microphone to her lips. She waited for the beginning of the next eight count and joined in with Kid Rock. She dropped into a crouch and slowly rolled her way back up, dragging the microphone up her body as she went, then joined in the song again in time for the chorus.

Oh, the singing. It was making Rem shiver.

Aspen was straddling her lap by the end of the song and whispered the last line against her lips.

Remington cut her off with a kiss, one hand fisted in her long, dark hair.

Aspen whimpered into the kiss, dropping the microphone, which made a loud thud over the music. She moaned when Rem squeezed her waist. "Remington," she said, nuzzling her lips over Rem's cheek and to her ear. "I'm so wet for you."

Remington's nostrils flared with the effort to control herself and she clenched her thighs against the discomfort between them. "I want to fuck you," she said with a growl, squeezing Aspen's waist tighter.

"Yes, please," Aspen said, one hand reaching down to grope for Remington's, guiding it under her skirt.

"Not here." Remington frowned. "The hayloft." No, she did not miss the irony in that.

Aspen laughed and kept hold of her hand, dragging her out the front door and toward the stable. They barely made it up the ladder to the loft before Remington's hands were back under Aspen's skirt, stroking up and down her thighs and rubbing across the seams of her panties.

Aspen gasped, hands fisting in Rem's hair. Her back hit the pile of hay and she leaned her head against it.

"You *are* wet for me," Remington said when she finally moved her hand between Aspen's legs.

"I always am," Aspen whimpered, wrapping her legs around Remington's waist.

Remington grunted at the sudden shift in weight and leaned

forward, bracing her free hand in the hay next to Aspen's head. "Always?"

"Fucking always," Aspen panted, pulling her hair and scraping her scalp lightly with blunt fingernails. "Please."

"I will," Remington promised, dropping her mouth to Aspen's neck and sucking softly on the pale flesh as she crawled her fingers over damp fabric.

Aspen mewled, rocking her hips. "Please," she said again.

"Sorry," Remington breathed, capturing her lips in a kiss, shifting her weight again so she could use both hands to tug Aspen's panties down her thighs, over her knees, and off. She dropped them and leaned over Aspen again, one hand back on the hay and the other back under her skirt.

Her heart was pounding, hearing blocked by the pulse in her ears, and she trailed one finger slowly against Aspen's bare skin, a noise escaping her throat at the wet heat. "I…" She started to talk but didn't know what she wanted to say, and her hand was shaking even though she'd done this with Layla so many times. With Aspen it was just different.

She realized the difference with a gasp, staring into Aspen's eyes as she choked on the words, getting lost in that tumultuous sea of green. "Aspen, I—"

"It's okay," Aspen breathed. "You're not ready?"

"That's not it," Remington said in a rush. She was still stroking one finger back and forth, barely touching Aspen, but she wasn't trying to tease.

"What's wrong?" Aspen asked, her gaze flicking between Rem's eyes and her mouth.

"I love you," Remington said in a whisper.

Aspen gasped and her hips jerked, and Rem realized she had slid her finger in a little, and that was not the timing she was going for, but it seemed to work for Aspen, so she slid in a little farther and said it again.

"I love you."

Aspen's eyes closed and her head tilted back, and when her eyes opened again they were shining with tears. "I can't believe you said that right at this moment, but I love you too, Remington. A whole lot of a lot."

Rem kind of liked that Aspen could take time out of their physical connection to share the moment without begging her to keep going. That meant almost as much as the I love you, and she knew she was probably grinning like an idiot, but she ducked her head and kissed Aspen, starting to move her hand.

Aspen's hips lifted to meet her and Remington held back a groan, not wanting to overpower the tiny noises Aspen was making because she wanted to remember them forever. "You feel really good," she said, moving a little faster, watching Aspen's face closely. Every little nuance, little twitch was like a thunderbolt, loud and powerful, and she dropped her mouth to Aspen's neck, adding a second finger.

"Rem," Aspen said, throwing her head to the side. "Please."

"I'm right here," Remington said, stroking gently until Aspen got used to the rhythm, and then she pushed a little harder and swiped her thumb across Aspen's clit. "Go ahead, baby."

Aspen groaned, clenching her thighs around Rem's hand and digging her fingertips into Rem's shoulders as she fell into bliss.

Remington rode her through it and swallowed some of the noise with a kiss, and then her attention was pulled by someone bursting into the stable and yelling, "CAKE!"

She couldn't help laughing, even though Aspen was still coming down and breathing hard, and she nuzzled their cheeks together. "Let's have some fucking cake."

CHAPTER TWENTY-FOUR

Raleigh was surprised when her phone rang in the middle of the night. She was more surprised when it was her father. "Hello?" she asked quickly. "Are the boys okay?"

"They're fine," her father said, and it sounded to Raleigh as if he'd had a few drinks.

"Are you drunk?" That would be new.

"Getting there," her father said.

"Dad, what's going on?"

Denna mumbled and rolled over in her sleep so Raleigh quietly got out of bed and shut herself in the bathroom.

"I'm divorcing your mother. I want you kids to live with me. I know I'm no father, but you've raised the boys and you can keep raising them. Okay?"

"What?" Her eyebrows nearly hit the ceiling and she sat down on the closed toilet to avoid falling.

"I'm sorry I was never there. I didn't know, I swear that to you, Raleigh. I didn't know. Not until after. And what Danny said, that your mother knew? We argued and it's true. She knew. I can't be with her anymore. It's over; the papers are already drafted. I just want you kids to live with me. I won't interfere in your lives, I promise. Please consider it."

"If it's a choice between you and Darlene, you have nothing to worry about," Raleigh said. She was a bit shell-shocked, but she knew that much was true without even having to think about it. "We'll live with you if we're allowed to choose."

"Thank you." Her father sighed with obvious relief. "Sorry to bother you, I just wanted to tell you. Good night."

"Good night." She hung up before it could get more awkward. When she left the bathroom, Denna was sitting up in bed waiting for her.

"Is everything okay?"

"Yes, actually," Raleigh said, still shocked as she climbed back into bed. "That was my dad. He's divorcing Darlene and wants me and the boys to live with him."

Denna's jaw dropped. "Fuck me, are you serious?"

"He apologized for not being there and swore he didn't know until after the fact. And when he found out that Darlene knew all along, he couldn't be with her anymore. He said I can raise the boys and he won't interfere."

"Wow. I think this is like the second-best news of your life."

Raleigh finally let herself smile. "Yes, I believe you're right."

"The judge will let you choose, right?"

"That part I don't know."

❖

Denna was helping Joey pack since Jackson was working and Raleigh and Danny had their own rooms to pack. It turned out the judge hadn't given anyone a choice after she listened to the recording of Jason's parole hearing, and granted Jackson full custody of the boys, with Darlene having visitation every other weekend. Raleigh said she doubted Darlene would even follow through with visitation, that she didn't care about seeing them, really, she just didn't want to be seen as a bad mother. Denna figured she was probably right. That was a good thing, though, she thought, because who wanted to be around that fucking coiffed disaster?

"What about this poop emoji pillow? Does that have to come with you?" she asked, holding up the offending item by the tag, refusing to actually touch it.

Joey burst into laughter, rolling around on the floor. "*Yes*, that's my poop pillow," he roared. "Put it in the *box!*"

Denna gagged at him and dropped it in the box under duress. "And this thing?" She picked up a weird-looking plastic toy.

"That's Optimus Prime!" he squealed. "You don't know Optimus Prime?"

Denna shook her head and dropped the toy into the box. "And this?" She picked up another toy from his floor.

"EVERYTHING IS GOING!" Joey said, still in hysterics on the floor. "I'm keeping all my stuff! Quit trying to get rid of stuff!"

"Okay, squirt, okay," Denna said, raising her hands in surrender.

"I'm *not* a *squirt*!" he yelled, getting up off the floor and rushing her like a linebacker. He took her down easily since she wasn't expecting it.

"Aah!" Denna shrieked, pretending he was some kind of monster. "Help, somebody, it's got me!"

"Oh my God, it's just me," Joey said, pushing his bangs out of his eyes so she could see his face.

"Oh, wow, thank goodness," she said, putting a hand to her heart. "I thought you'd turned into a monster."

"You need to stop watching scary movies. That can't happen in real life," Joey said, shaking his head.

"Are you sure?" she asked, and then when he was about to answer she launched into a tickle attack.

"Aah, *no*, *stop*," he said, batting at her hands and giggling.

"I hear entirely too much fun in here when you're supposed to be packing," Raleigh said, appearing in the doorway.

Denna and Joey both stopped and turned to look at her. "Um," Denna began, then watched in utter shock as Raleigh advanced on Joey and took over the tickle attack. It was the first time she had ever seen Raleigh touch him at all. The implied progress made her giddy.

Raleigh smiled over one shoulder at her. "What are you waiting for? Double team!"

Denna didn't need to be asked twice. She dove back in.

Joey squealed and squirmed and screamed and laughed, and finally managed to wriggle away from them. "Oh my GOD," he said, panting. "I'm just trying to pack!"

❖

"So," Aspen said, flopping onto the grass and, as usual, putting her feet in Denna's lap during cheerleading practice. "Shower sex. Yes/no?"

"Yes," Denna said, just as Raleigh's eyes widened and her jaw tightened to indicate she'd rather choke to death than answer the question. "You?"

"Way."

"Way is not an actual answer," Raleigh said. "At least not one that doesn't make you look like you have the vocabulary of a two-year-old."

"Don't be jealous because I can talk about anything and you can't," Aspen said, sticking her tongue out at Raleigh.

"I can talk about whatever I like," Raleigh said. "I simply have class."

"And Denna and I don't?"

Denna's eyes snapped to Raleigh. "Be careful how you answer that question."

Raleigh's lips formed a tiny smirk and she leaned over to steal a kiss from Denna, at the same time roughly shoving Aspen's feet off Denna's lap. "Do not touch my girlfriend," was her answer.

"Ha ha," Denna said to Aspen, kicking her ankle lightly.

"I hate you both," Aspen said, sticking her tongue out again, then turning around as a shadow fell over her.

"What are you doing with that tongue?" Remington asked, hands on her hips, leather jacket hanging open over a white beater.

"Nothing good," Raleigh said, shielding her eyes from the sun with her hand as she looked up at Remington.

"Fuck off." Aspen flipped Raleigh the bird and got to her feet to kiss Remington in greeting. "Practice is almost over."

"Are you sure it's not already over? You're not doing anything."

"We're seniors. We can take breaks."

Remington laughed. "See you in the locker room." Aspen watched her head off to wait.

"Why is she in such a good mood?" Denna asked.

"We have the house to ourselves for the weekend," Aspen said with a coy smile.

"PARTY!" Denna shouted, fist pumping the air.

"No fist pumps, please," Raleigh said, shaking her head.

"And no party," Aspen said. "I said to *ourselves*, not to the whole school. We're gonna fuck all weekend, so don't come over."

"Wouldn't dream of it," Raleigh said before Denna could pout and throw a fit.

Denna scowled. "That's very un-senior of you, you know. An empty house and no party."

"Do you want to deal with Catherine when she finds out?"

Denna scrunched up her face.

"Didn't think so. No party."

"It's not even just un-senior, it's un-American," Denna said.

"Shut the fuck up," Aspen said, rolling her eyes and jogging over to the rest of the squad to join in the run-through in progress.

❖

Remington lay on her back on the bench by Aspen's locker and sat up when Aspen finally came into the locker room. "I thought you said it was almost over. I've been waiting for twenty minutes," she said, stalking purposefully toward Aspen and pressing her into the wall by the door. Some of the other cheerleaders skittered by, but Rem didn't care anymore.

"I thought it was, but the coach wanted one more run-through," Aspen said with a little wheeze.

"Hmm." Remington's hands went to Aspen's hips and lightly squeezed. "Twenty minutes seems like an eternity today," she whispered.

"I know what you mean," Aspen said. "Denna wanted to have a party, but obviously I told her no."

"Good choice." Remington stepped back to let Aspen go get changed.

❖

"Hey," Denna said, flopping on Raleigh's new bed.

"Hey," Raleigh said, taking a two-second break from folding clothes to lean down and kiss her.

Denna had just come from therapy. "So, I have good news."

Raleigh abandoned the clothes altogether.

"I don't have schizophrenia. They don't even know if my mom has it. My therapist thinks it's just mild depression mixed with a regular teenage temper, and we're gonna try doing two sessions a week over the summer to see if it helps before she thinks about an antidepressant."

Before she even registered that Raleigh had moved, she was being squeezed to within an inch of her life, and she didn't think she had ever grinned any bigger. "Air, baby."

Raleigh threw her down on the bed and went to the door, poking her head into the hall. "BOYS!"

Both boys came skidding into the room at the same time, and when they saw her, Joey jumped on top of her and Danny laughed.

"Hey, Denna," Danny said with a wave that she barely saw before she had a face full of Joey.

"Hey, Danny," she said while fending Joey off, throwing him in the air and then rolling out of the way so he didn't land on her.

Joey bounced around for a minute and then stood up on the bed. "Do you like our new house?!"

"I love it!" She could see Raleigh out of the corner of her eye trying to sneak up on Joey, so she kept his attention. "Do you guys like it?"

"*Yes*," Joey said, and then shrieked when Raleigh grabbed him from behind and started swinging him around in circles.

"Do you like it, Danny?"

"It's cool," Danny said. "I like not having Mom here."

"Who wouldn't?" She snorted, loving the way he went from looking a bit nervous at his confession to completely at ease. She mouthed the words "fucking bitch" at him, and he cracked up.

Raleigh threw Joey on the bed and grabbed Denna instead. "You are a very good partner in crime."

"Thank you, I agree," Denna said, leaning her head back on Ral's shoulder. "Come to think of it, I am a good partner in everything."

"Yes. And so modest."

"You know it."

"Are you spending the night?"

"Yep. I have a date with Dad tomorrow afternoon, and then I'll be back tomorrow night too, and maybe we can do a sleepover with these tiny people and make blanket forts in the living room?"

Before this year, Raleigh would have tensed at the idea and disregarded it. Actually, Denna would probably never have suggested it. Seeing Raleigh's eyes sparkle as she gave an enthusiastic yes was the best feeling in the world.

❖

The weekend was amazing. When Catherine got home on Sunday afternoon, she and Rem went with Aspen to her parents' house so she could safely get everything she'd had to leave behind.

Catherine and Rem were just standing there staring at her while she decided what she wanted. A lot of it she didn't want anymore, but some of her more expensive makeup and clothes had to make the trip. And she wanted all of her stuffed animals. Then there was her TV. It was a sixty-two-inch plasma. She looked at Catherine. "Can we bring my TV?"

Catherine glanced at the item in question, and Aspen could see her trying to calculate space in her head. "It should fit in the back. Don't you think, Rem?"

Rem eyed the TV. "Probably."

"If not, it's okay," Aspen said in a rush. "It's not as important as getting out of here." She shifted nervously. "And speaking of that, are you s—"

"Aspen Wellington," Catherine said, pinning her with a very parental-type glare.

Remington leaned up and whispered something in her mom's ear and Aspen's jaw dropped at the ganging up.

Catherine laughed and walked over to give her a hug, and Aspen desperately wanted to know what Rem had said. "What did she say?" She was definitely not whining.

"She said maybe if we started calling you Aspen Stone, you would stop asking if we're sure."

"Mama!" Remington said, eyes wide. "You betrayed me!"

Aspen did a last cursory sweep and grabbed her Bliss shampoo, wagging her eyebrows at Rem as she tossed it in one of the bags they were using for transport. And then she was ready.

Luckily, the TV fit in the car, and Aspen looked back at the estate as Catherine drove away, a weight lifting from her shoulders at being able to close that chapter of her life and never have to open it again.

Between having so many of her own things in the house and Rem and Catherine's constant reassurance, Aspen felt more home than she ever had.

About the Author

Lexus Grey lives in Pennsylvania with her two dogs, ten cats, two horses, and guinea pig. She's been writing since age six. She enjoys reading, writing (obviously), and *Killing Eve*. She does not enjoy being outdoors, unless she is on horseback. As a self-proclaimed computer geek, her social skills rival the Borg. She currently has a girlfriend over in England and hopes they will both be on the same continent someday soon.

Books Available From Bold Strokes Books

All That Remains by Sheri Lewis Wohl. Johnnie and Shantel might have to risk their lives—and their love—to stop a werewolf intent on killing. (978-1-63555-949-1)

Beginner's Bet by Fiona Riley. Phenom luxury Realtor Ellison Gamble has everything, except a family to share it with, so when a mix-up brings youthful Katie Crawford into her life, she bets the house on love. (978-1-63555-733-6)

Dangerous Without You by Lexus Grey. Throughout their senior year in high school, Aspen, Remington, Denna, and Raleigh face challenges in life and romance that they never expect. (978-1-63555-947-7)

Desiring More by Raven Sky. In this collection of steamy stories, a rich variety of lovers find themselves desiring more: more from a lover, more from themselves, and more from life. (978-1-63679-037-4)

Jordan's Kiss by Nanisi Barrett D'Arnuck. After losing everything in a fire, Jordan Phelps joins a small lounge band and meets pianist Morgan Sparks, who lights another blaze—this time in Jordan's heart. (978-1-63555-980-4)

Late City Summer by Jeanette Bears. Forced together for her wedding, Emily Stanton and Kate Alessi navigate their lingering passion for one another against the backdrop of New York City and World War II, and a summer romance they left behind. (978-1-63555-968-2)

Love and Lotus Blossoms by Anne Shade. On her path to self-acceptance and true passion, Janesse will risk everything—and possibly everyone—she loves. (978-1-63555-985-9)

Love in the Limelight by Ashley Moore. Marion Hargreaves, the finest actress of her generation, and Jessica Carmichael, the world's biggest pop star, rediscover each other twenty years after an ill-fated affair. (978-1-63679-051-0)

Suspecting Her by Mary P. Burns. Complications ensue when Erin O'Connor falls for top real estate saleswoman Catherine Williams while investigating racism in the real estate industry; the fallout could end their chance at happiness. (978-1-63555-960-6)

Two Winters by Lauren Emily Whalen. A modern YA retelling of Shakespeare's *The Winter's Tale* about birth, death, Catholic school, improv comedy, and the healing nature of time. (978-1-63679-019-0)

Calumet by Ali Vali. Jaxon Lavigne and Iris Long had a forbidden small-town romance that didn't last, and the consequences of that love will be uncovered fifteen years later at their high school reunion. (978-1-63555-900-2)

Her Countess to Cherish by Jane Walsh. London Society's material girl realizes there is more to life than diamonds when she falls in love with a non-binary bluestocking. (978-1-63555-902-6)

Hot Days, Heated Nights by Renee Roman. When Cole and Lee meet, instant attraction quickly flares into uncontrollable passion, but their connection might be short-lived as Lee's identity is tied to her life in the city. (978-1-63555-888-3)

Never Be the Same by MA Binfield. Casey meets Olivia, and sparks fly in this opposites attract romance that proves love can be found in the unlikeliest places. (978-1-63555-938-5)

Quiet Village by Eden Darry. Something not quite human is stalking Collie and her niece, and she'll be forced to work with undercover reporter Emily Lassiter if they want to get out of Hyam alive. (978-1-63555-898-2)

Shaken or Stirred by Georgia Beers. Bar owner Julia Martini and home health aide Savannah McNally attempt to weather the storms brought on by a mysterious blogger trashing the bar, family feuds they knew nothing about, and way too much advice from way too many relatives. (978-1-63555-928-6)

The Fiend in the Fog by Jess Faraday. Can four people on different trajectories work together to save the vulnerable residents of East London from the terrifying fiend in the fog before it's too late? (978-1-63555-514-1)

The Marriage Masquerade by Toni Logan. A no-strings-attached marriage scheme to inherit a Maui B&B uncovers unexpected attractions and a dark family secret. (978-1-63555-914-9)

Flight SQA016 by Amanda Radley. Fastidious airline passenger Olivia Lewis is used to things being a certain way. When her routine is changed by a new, attractive member of the staff, sparks fly. (978-1-63679-045-9)

Home Is Where The Heart Is by Jenny Frame. Can Archie make the countryside her home and give Ash the fairytale romance she desires? Or will the countryside and small village life all be too much for her? (978-1-63555-922-4)

Moving Forward by PJ Trebelhorn. The last person Shelby Ryan expects to be attracted to is Iris Calhoun, the sister of the man who killed her wife four years and three thousand miles ago. (978-1-63555-953-8)

Poison Pen by Jean Copeland. Debut author Kendra Blake is finally living her best life until a nasty book review and exposed secrets threaten her promising new romance with aspiring journalist Alison Chatterley. (978-1-63555-849-4)

Seasons for Change by KC Richardson. Love, laughter, and trust develop for Shawn and Morgan throughout the changing seasons of Lake Tahoe. (978-1-63555-882-1)

Summer Lovin' by Julie Cannon. Three different women, three exotic locations, one unforgettable summer. What do you think will happen? (978-1-63555-920-0)

Unbridled by D. Jackson Leigh. A visit to a local stable turns into more than riding lessons between a novel writer and an equestrian with a taste for power play. (978-1-63555-847-0)

VIP by Jackie D. In a town where relationships are forged and shattered by perception, sometimes even love can't change who you really are. (978-1-63555-908-8)

Yearning by Gun Brooke. The sleepy town of Dennamore has an irresistible pull on those who've moved away. The mystery Darian Benson and Samantha Pike uncover will change them forever, but the love they find along the way just might be the key to saving themselves. (978-1-63555-757-2)

A Turn of Fate by Ronica Black. Will Nev and Kinsley finally face their painful past and relent to their powerful, forbidden attraction? Or will facing their past be too much to fight through? (978-1-63555-930-9)

Desires After Dark by MJ Williamz. When her human lover falls deathly ill, Alex, a vampire, must decide which is worse, letting her go or condemning her to everlasting life. (978-1-63555-940-8)

Her Consigliere by Carsen Taite. FBI agent Royal Scott swore an oath to uphold the law, and criminal defense attorney Siobhan Collins pledged her loyalty to the only family she's ever known, but will their love be stronger than the bonds they've vowed to others, or will their competing allegiances tear them apart? (978-1-63555-924-8)

In Our Words: Queer Stories from Black, Indigenous, and People of Color Writers. Stories Selected by Anne Shade and Edited by Victoria Villaseñor. Comprising both the renowned and emerging voices of Black, Indigenous, and People of Color authors, this thoughtfully curated collection of short stories explores the intersection of racial and queer identity. (978-1-63555-936-1)

Measure of Devotion by CF Frizzell. Disguised as her late twin brother, Catherine Samson enters the Civil War to defend the Constitution as a Union soldier, never expecting her life to be altered by a Gettysburg farmer's daughter. (978-1-63555-951-4)

Not Guilty by Brit Ryder. Claire Weaver and Emery Pearson's day jobs clash, even as their desire for each other burns, and a discreet sex-only arrangement is the only option. (978-1-63555-896-8)

Opposites Attract: Butch/Femme Romances by Meghan O'Brien, Aurora Rey & Angie Williams. Sometimes opposites really do attract. Fall in love with these butch/femme romance novellas. (978-1-63555-784-8)

Under Her Influence by Amanda Radley. On their path to #truelove, will Beth and Jemma discover that reality is even better than illusion? (978-1-63555-963-7)